CARNIVALE
DARKE

Stephen H. Provost
Sharon Marie Provost

STEPHEN H. and SHARON MARIE PROVOST

Cover design: Stephen H. Provost and Sharon Marie Provost
Interior design: Stephen H. Provost and Sharon Marie Provost
Cover images: Stock images from Deposit Photos
Interior images: Public domain from Library of Congress and Wikimedia Commons

All stories are collaborations between Sharon Marie Provost and Stephen H. Provost

ISBN: 978-1-949971-79-8

"Welcome to the Carnival of Life, where dreams are reality and reality is dreams gone mad."

L. Scott Ward

"A carnival in daylight is an unfinished beast, anyway. Rain makes it a ghost."

Katherine Dunn, Geek Love

"Be careful of success; it has a dark side."

Robert Redford

"If you don't like my dark side, then don't take it out of its cage and feed it."

Jury Nel

AUTHORS' NOTES

This is a work of fiction that takes place in an alternate universe but includes some figures from history, for whom we have retained their actual names. Other characters, such as Rob-Bert, have been given fictional names, but are based on real people. Among these are sideshow performers with extraordinary physiques and characteristics, historically known as "Freaks," but preferring to be known in modern parlance as human oddities and prodigies. Photos of both actual historical figures and those upon whom we have based fictional characters have been included to illustrate this work.

This book is not meant to diminish or degrade sideshow workers in any fashion. On the contrary, it is intended to portray a realistic picture of carnival life, language, and norms during the times covered (albeit with a little magic and speculative science thrown in). Within that context, we wish to emphasize that we view "oddities" not as freaks, but as real people no different than anyone else and, in fact, worth celebrating for their courage, determination, and authenticity.

We strongly believe that our differences make us stronger and more beautiful. Having been bullied in the past for not fitting in with "normal" society, we seek to celebrate the qualities that make each of us unique. In this spirit, we proudly declare ourselves to be in support of those who have been misunderstood and mistreated. And we encourage all our readers to... get your freak on!

CONTENTS

STEPHEN H. and SHARON MARIE PROVOST

INTRODUCTION

The Show to End All Shows needs no introduction, and this book chronicling its history needs but a brief one. Welcome to the world of Carnivale Darke, the most famous carnival ever conceived of and executed on the soil of Mother Earth. These stories, spanning multiple generations reflect a mere sampling of the astounding, scarcely believable events that occurred on the midway, under the big top, and in the carnival sideshow tent.

Ten tales have been chosen here to reflect the Ten-in-One, a popular staple of carnivals and a particularly noteworthy attraction at Carnivale Darke. But the curtain has already risen on our Darke Universe. The curious reader can find a story about Dr. Zim's Carnival of Oddities in *Shades of Love, Vol. 2* by Sharon Marie Provost, and an origin story for Artemus Darke himself in Stephen H. Provost's *A Twisted Carol*. And now, let the show begin!

ROLL UP!

Roll on up, let's go!
See the Show to End All Shows
It will captivate your soul
Come with me!
Come and see!

Overcome your fear
And be ye of good cheer
All is just as it appears
Guaranteed!
Guaranteed!

Everything before your eyes
Will amaze and hypnotize
You'll never want to leave

Just believe!
Just believe!

Come on in
And find yourself a seat
It's no sin
You're in for quite a treat

Come and join the fun
It's a Ten-in-One
Open up your mind
And see what you'll find

Now gather young and old
That your fortunes may be told
Revelations bought and sold
Just a dime!
Just a dime!

See feats of derring-do
And a boxing kangaroo
It's the finest of the fine
Just in time
Just in time

Balloo the dancing bear
Juggles three balls in the air
It's a feat beyond compare
Holy cow!
See it now!

CARNIVALE DARKE

Step up to the mark
I can be your guide
Into the House of Darke
Aboard the endless ride

Win your gal a prize
Step right up and don't be shy
You can have a thousand tries
If you stay...
And you pay!

If you're feeling down
Laugh it up with Kelsey Clown
He will chase you round and round
Run away!
Run away!

Travel down the golden road
There are marvels to behold
Wondrous stories to be told
Lend an ear!
Lend an ear!

Heed the call!
Come see the curtain rise
Welcome all!
You won't believe your eyes

Roll the dice!
Surrender to your fate
Don't think twice
The hour's getting late

STEPHEN H. and SHARON MARIE PROVOST

Now it's time to go
Time to end the show
But never fear
We'll be back next year!

THE LEGEND

Greetings and felicitations! Gather 'round the bally stage for The Show to End All Shows. Every one of our acts and exhibits is one hundred percent authentic, guaranteed, or your money back!

Step right up for a thrilling, chilling, fantastical journey beyond your wildest imagination! Discover

Carnivale Darke, the show that set the standard, broke the mold, and silenced the competition.

Allow me to introduce myself: Artemus K. Darke, at your service. I'll be your host, ringmaster, and tour guide on the adventure of a lifetime.

Welcome one and all to Carnivale Darke, home to the finest performers, the most amazing exhibits, and the wildest rides ever assembled in a single location. Witness a traveling extravaganza I created in the image of my own imagination, a portal from this world of disease and deception to the true world which lurks in the shadows of our own. This is what I have to offer my patrons, those with discriminating tastes who will settle for nothing but the pure, unfettered truth.

I have no use for the "suckers who are born every minute," the ignorant masses my competitors rely upon to keep the carousel turning and the popcorn popping. They all envy and revile me—if they stay in business long enough to raise a stink. Most of them don't. I rake in more profits than they do. I draw bigger crowds. And I make bigger promises, which, unlike those charlatans, I always keep.

Barnum was so jealous of my success, he tried to besmirch my name. He accused me of cooking the books to cheat the taxman and selling alcohol to the kiddies. Put me on the wrong side of the Temperance League and the IRS. Did it surprise me? Hardly. He told so many lies about his own feigned magnificence, it was only natural that he should use deceit as a weapon against those he despised. Nothing ever came of it, though. The truth was on my side—along with the highest-paid legal team on the Eastern Seaboard.

Money was no object when it came to protecting what I'd built, just as it had never been an obstacle in building it to begin with. Unlike many of my peers, I did not "start at the bottom" and work my way up. I never wore clown makeup, worked a ticket booth, or cleaned an elephant cage. I descend from a long line of English, and now American, aristocracy. My father, Alexander "the Great" Darke, built on the wealth of my grandfather, Avernus, by investing heavily in the railroad, oil, and steel. I inherited their substantial wealth and immediately set about building upon it.

Why, you may ask, did I choose to invest in a carnival? The answer lies buried in the human subconscious. The rich might paper it over in greenbacks, stocks, and bank statements, but beneath this thin façade, they are the same as the hobos who ride the rails. Insatiably curious, human beings set the standard for self-contradiction. They are equal parts zealots and skeptics, fawning after heroes and demigods only to seek their downfall a moment later.

I put a stop to this vain and duplicitous cycle by giving them something to believe in—something they can neither disprove nor discredit. I transform them from doubters into acolytes, thereby guaranteeing their continued patronage. And their effusive recommendations. It's really no different than any other business: If you serve the best cup of coffee in the county, word gets around, and loyal customers keep coming back for more.

It's as simple as that.

But that's not to say it was easy. It was the product of hard work, a clear vision, and more than anything, diligence. When I set my sights on an objective, I always make it happen, because I never quit. I just adjust my course to ensure it leads to the end of that proverbial rainbow. I operate under no illusion that the road will be smooth or direct. I expect nothing—and aspire to everything. There will be setbacks along the way, and I sear them all into my mind's eye. A failure recalled is a chance to get better; a failure forgotten is an opportunity lost.

I've built Carnivale Darke into America's favorite pastime (with apologies to baseball), and I've made my share of wrong turns along the way.

Perhaps the worst came at the outset, when I formed a partnership with a childhood friend named Harold Zimmerman. We shared one thing in common: ambition. But it wasn't long before I discovered that this alone was not enough to build a successful business. In fact, it can set men against each other when they have different ideas about how to do things.

Harold didn't share my core belief that every act had to be authentic. His ambition, or should I say greed, outweighed his integrity and any sense of duty he had toward the way we'd *agreed* to run our carnival. I should have known better than to go into business with him. His bloated sense of self-worth had been a problem from the very beginning. He always *thought* he knew best, so he tried to take control of every project we were assigned back in school. Now, he was trying that again, but, this time, I had the money and *all* the power behind this venture.

I thought I could make it work if I ran the business side of things and hired all the big acts. He'd always been interested in the dark and twisted side of nature, so the sideshow acts and the curiosities seemed the perfect fit for him. He had made a point of showing me his most fantastic oddity scores: the pickled mermaid baby with fused legs, the two-headed snake and so on. But when I walked by one day during the pitch and heard about a "real" shrunken head and a six-legged calf, I wondered why I hadn't seen them.

After a quick inspection later that evening, I found out why. He'd either manufactured or purchased a fake shrunken head. That taxidermied calf had legs sewn on from another, larger calf. Harold had not made those purchases by accident. He'd done so with the express

intent of pulling the wool over our customers' eyes—and mine.

Harold's treachery shouldn't have surprised me. Sometime before, I had hired a young boy whose well-to-do family had abandoned him because his face was covered with hair. Harold tried to bill him as the Wolf Boy, half-man and half-beast, raised by a pack of wolves in Montana. I insisted he be called the Wolf-*Faced* Boy. Children cowered and women were titillated at the mere sight of him but laughed uproariously when he read from the works of Shakespeare.

No fraud needed.

We had several heated arguments during those first few years, and we nearly came to blows over those fake exhibits. Zimmerman swore that he'd changed his ways. I couldn't have imagined how far he'd go until one day in late summer of 1898.

I ended our partnership that day and bought his share out. But that's a story for another time...

From the point that Zimmerman and I parted ways, I never again took on a partner—friend or otherwise. I built my executive staff around members of my own family, headed by my sister Adoline Darke, whom I named vice president of operations. I trust Adoline implicitly. We are always brutally honest with each other, and she never fails to carry out my directives. Such loyalty is hard to come by, but I demand nothing less from my employees.

Considering what I paid them, it wasn't too much to ask. I put a premium on attracting the best of the best. My strongman had to be the strongest. My magician had to do real magic. My fortune teller could never be wrong. But I never did employ a mind-reader, because I never found one who was on the level. I put many of them to the test— completely without their knowledge. I hired spies known for their powers of observation, and I paid for their admission to a mentalist's show. Without much difficulty, they were always able to discover the fraud behind the bravado. Suggestive phrasing and sleight of hand were commonplace. In many cases, their hoax relied upon the use of sophisticated ciphers of key words or tapping sequences similar to morse code.

The most famous mentalists at the turn of the century were the Zancigs, a husband-and-wife team who approached me about joining the carnival. I was offering

$1,000 a week to any bona fide telepaths who were willing to work the circuit for one season. I was initially hopeful that an act of such renown would draw huge crowds, but first I had to put them to the test. As with all the others, my agents were able to debunk their "mentalism" as a fraud relying on an intricate series of codes they passed between them. When they returned to my office following the crucial performance, fully expecting to be hired on the spot, I refused to even see them, leaving a note with Adoline that informed them I would not be requiring their services. I did not tell them why; I was not obligated to do so.

Some years later, in 1924, Julian Zancig published a book revealing the secrets of his method—the very same method my own operatives had described to me!

Tesla's Magic

The Zancigs were far from the only celebrities I attracted. When it came to the attention of Mark Twain that I only hired authentic acts, he became interested in testing *me*. Now the tables had turned! But I was more than up to the challenge. I invited him to attend the show when we stopped in Yonkers, just outside the Big Apple (where he was living there on Fifth Avenue at the time). He turned up before the gates even opened and was in a sour mood because the dust was settling on his white coat and slacks. He kept brushing at them as though he were being assaulted by mosquitoes.

I remember greeting him with a proffered handshake inside the gate, but he refused to accept my welcome and grumbled something like, "This had better be good." Twain had long been acquainted with Barnum, whose fraudulent "Cardiff Giant" he had famously—and quite humorously—debunked. "Phileas Fogg is full of hot air," he declared, purposely confusing *Phineas* T. Barnum with the similarly named character from Jules Verne. "Not unlike one of your helium balloons."

Twain had every reason to be a skeptic. By the time I was finished showing him around, though, I had converted him. His departing handshake was firm and enthusiastic—but it only came after I had persuaded him to give one of his famous lectures from a podium on the midway the next time we were in town. Not only that, but he promised to spread the word around, most especially to his friend Nik, a fellow New Yorker who was known for scientific innovation and inclined toward big ideas.

He was almost as famous as Twain, having been given the impressive nickname "The Man Who Invented the Twentieth Century." And Twain was right. I had never thought about inviting Nikola Tesla to go on the road with me, but now here he was approaching me. He suggested traveling with Carnivale Darke on the eastern swing of our circuit and showcasing his work at a semi-permanent exhibit. I enthusiastically accepted, suggesting that he showcase the Tesla coil and a remote-control device he had invented.

Tesla seemed even more eager than I to inaugurate our alliance. This puzzled me at the time, but I later discovered that the man had fallen on hard times financially and was relying on the $15,000 I had promised him to seal the deal.

He also hoped to use the exposure to jump-start interest in his latest inventions. The man told me flat out that he was hoping to recruit investors, and he even proposed that I provide him with explicit financial backing. I told him, however, that I had long ago resolved to pour my entire fortune into the carnival. He said he understood, but looked crestfallen at my rejection.

I therefore made him a further offer: If he would show me his latest invention, I would consider buying the patent from him... if it was good enough.

It was far better than I ever imagined.

Tesla had created a talking box with moving pictures that could be viewed through what he called a MasterView Audiomation Device. He demurred that he had yet to perfect it, but I saw its potential that very moment. Moving pictures were all the rage at so-called Nickelodeons across the country, but these projected shorts were missing something: sound. Edison had invented a contraption called a kinetophone, but he never succeeded in keeping the "aural element" in sync with the pictures—which were themselves of inferior quality. An actor's voice would come before his mouth movements, which audiences found less satisfactory than a fully silent experience.

Tesla had solved the problem, but he had been unable to market his MasterView device because Edison had sued to prevent it. Tesla, lacking the funds to contest the lawsuit, had dropped the project. But I was amazed to discover, when he demonstrated it, that the MasterView was light years ahead of anything Edison had developed. I told him I would pay him $20,000, cash on the barrelhead, for the MasterView and its schematics, as long as I would hold exclusive rights to it for twenty years.

"What about Edison?" he asked.

I told him to leave that to me: Every man had his price, and I had the wherewithal to pay Edison's. What I didn't tell him was that I planned to direct my magician, Magnus the Magnificent, to make a few strategic improvements in Tesla's design. Foremost among these was a function that made everything seen on the MasterView appear in three dimensions. And there were other, shall we say proprietary, improvements that I will not discuss here.

I set up MasterView stations at various points on the grounds at every stop, inviting attendees to marvel at "another dimension" unfolding before their eyes. The most popular of these was, naturally, the peep show. It was so popular, in fact, that men swore they couldn't tell the difference between my MasterView shows and the real thing.

I did not need to patent this conjured element of the

MasterView, since it relied on Magnus' unique skill set and was protected by a gypsy curse cast by my Romani medium, Cassandra. I had approached her early on about a protective charm over every scientific exhibit at Carnivale Darke—a charm that would bring all manner of calamity down upon any miscreant who might seek to sabotage or make off with them. Or, for that matter, to use them for anything other than their intended purpose.

I eventually sold the rights to Tesla's basic MasterView system—minus Magnus' adjustments—to a nascent company called MovieTone, which had been working to develop its own system. But instead of adapting Tesla's technology to meet their goals, they killed it to protect their own investment.

It was a bad call. Five years later, the MovieTone technology was eclipsed by another system developed by General Electric. But even that couldn't hold a candle to Tesla's invention.

Other than the MasterView, however, my association with Tesla fell short of what either of us had envisioned. His exhibit failed to draw any new investment in his work—or a significantly larger gate. We only worked together that one season, but neither of us bore the other any ill will. Like me, he knew that a failure duly considered was the path to future success.

Trial and Terror

But each failure also comes at a cost, and sometimes the cost is more than just financial.

When I first set out to recruit talent, I placed a "help wanted" ad in newspapers across the country: "CARNIVALE DARKE is seeking unique acts and performers to join The Show to End All Shows. ONLY THE BEST need apply. We will exceed any competitor's offer, with payment guaranteed even in the event of cancellations. Any fraudulent applicants will be DISQUALIFIED. Can you raise the bar? Can you defy expectations? If you are confident you can exceed the high standards we have set, please send your proposal via first-class post to Box 349, Stamford, Connecticut, USA. Include telephone exchange and return address."

That brought the termites out of the woodwork, many of them determined to bite off more than they could chew. I chose the most ambitious proposals that came my way, but that also meant they were the most likely to fail. I challenged a pole-sitter to stay aloft while two men shook his pole at the bottom. He fell to the earth after just five minutes. Two brothers claimed they could fence with each other on unicycles, but they drifted onto the trolley tracks without realizing it, fell over simultaneously, and were crushed to death beneath the weight of a speeding streetcar.

I granted an interview with a gentleman named Sebastian Ward, who threatened he could break the record for the longest sword ever swallowed. He certainly looked capable of such a feat, thanks to an extremely long neck and an extended torso that was out of proportion to his spindly legs.

I told him no official record existed, but that I'd seen claims of men capable of swallowing a 3-foot-long blade. He blanched a little at that, but he forced himself to regain his composure and laughed loudly... a little too loudly. "You need to understand," I told him, as sympathetically as I could, "I can only hire someone whose *true* achievements surpass the claims others make—however spurious they may be."

I thought that might discourage him, but instead he leaned forward and told me, without blinking, "I can do three. And. One. Half."

I admired his bravado, but I thought less of his judgment. Still, I had no desire to talk him out of it. The only way to discover whether he was a man of his word was to test him. I would either have a huge drawing card... or proof that he was *lying to me*. That, of course, could not be tolerated. If he were lying, there would be consequences. But they would be consequences of his own making, not of my design. It was a test, and he would either pass or fail. It was as simple as that.

"You understand that I will need a demonstration," I told him.

He nodded, though he seemed a little bit less certain.

"Unfortunately," I continued, "I have only brought with me a 4-foot-sword. But you will only need to swallow 3½ to support your claim. Is that acceptable?"

He nodded again.

I leaned forward. "You do understand that you will need to prove yourself in a private place. No one else can see you perform this miracle, because if you do, you will only do so at my carnival. Nowhere else. Your talent will belong to me. If you have any doubts about this, now is the time to walk away. Let me be clear, though: If you do, you will be walking away from $1,000 a week, and... I will let it be known that you are a fraud, just like all the rest."

He gulped, and I wondered what would happen if he did so while swallowing a sword.

I led him to the docks, a space that I had set aside for

just such an occasion. He moved a little more slowly with each step, and I thought he might dart away into the shadows at any moment. But a man's pride will drive him to great heights—or depths—especially if accompanied by an element of fear. I could see both of these things on Sebastian Ward's face: the determination and the mortification concerning what he was about to undertake. He looked every bit of the 19-year-old man-child bumpkin that he was. This, I realized, was his coming-of-age ritual.

I opened the door and ushered him in. Then I led him to the center of a vacant warehouse and pointed to the place I wanted him to stand. And wait.

I never took my eyes off him as I retreated to the entrance. His knees were shaking now, almost knocking together. I flicked the switch, and I thought that he might faint. Instead, he jumped a little and squinted as the spotlight shone full on his face from above. It wasn't enough that he be skilled; he needed to stay composed as well. Eventually, he would have to evolve into a showman. But there would be time for that... *if* he passed the test.

I dropped the sword on the floor and kicked it over to him, nodding for him to pick it up.

Ward bent down and took it, then raised it high above him, craning his head back to align it with his neck and esophagus, down to his stomach.

The point disappeared into his mouth. So far, so good.

He had obviously practiced this technique. No gag reflex. Pure concentration.

Within a few moments, 18 inches of sword had disappeared. Then 2 feet. Half the blade was inside him, and he seemed frozen in time, not moving a single muscle except those within his hands and fingers, lowering the blade ever so slowly toward his stomach.

Then, all of a sudden, it stuck. In the bright spotlight, I could see panic dueling with determination, and I saw determination win. *Bravo*! I thought. Perhaps he was really going to do it.

He took hold of the hilt and began to wiggle it, as if searching for a way forward. Downward. Then he began to twist it like a screw, forcing it deeper inside him.

He'd made six more inches. Only a foot to go.

But then, something on his face changed. He tried to hold himself steady, but he was starting to gag. Then he did it, the very thing that I had been hoping and dreading to see: He gulped, and the sword plunged a full foot deeper inside him.

There it was! The record!

I shouted at him to pull the thing out, but he could not. He had gone too far. I saw something protrude from his stomach, and when he convulsed, the point broke through his skin. He looked like a skewered pig roasting on a spit. He had the same dead look in his eyes as he collapsed onto the floor and the sword rent a huge gash in him from the inside out. Blood came pouring out, and as the gash grew broader, bits of intestine slopped out onto the floor.

I walked back to the door and flipped the switch, cutting the spotlight. My hired men emerged from the shadows and gave me the cue that the coast was clear outside; they would clean up everything in here while I made my retreat. It had been a failure, but I had learned from it. Carnivale Darke would never employ a sword swallower.

If I couldn't do it right, I wouldn't do it at all.

Doctor Who?

Adoline came to me one day in the late spring of 1906 about a telegram she had received. We were about to do a show in New York state. A gentleman named Dr. Martin Couney had a proposal for me. Not being familiar with his name, I was intrigued. He arrived soon after we began to set up the show.

He told me he had trained under a doctor in Germany who had set up a display of premature babies in incubators at the 1896 Berlin World's Fair. Incubators had been used for animals in zoos but had never been considered for humans. Dr. Couney had begun exhibiting babies, first across Europe, and then in America. He'd had one of his so-called "Infantoriums" set up at Coney Island since 1903. He explained that, for a mere 25-cent entrance fee, people could come in and watch the babies being cared for, with all proceeds going toward the cost of their care.

Dr. Couney expected me to take on his exhibition, at no profit to myself, but at great personal expense. Caring for these babies and ensuring their safekeeping while we traveled the circuit was a massive undertaking. But if it could draw more customers, I couldn't dismiss the proposition out of hand.

First, however, I had to do some research of my own. I told Dr. Couney I would consider his proposal and get back to him, but not before warning him that I didn't take kindly to fraudsters. He assured me that I had no worries. However, the detectives I hired to investigate him soon found a deception of untold proportions.

Dr. Couney, they informed me, was not a doctor at all. They could find no proof that he had ever attended any medical school in Europe or the United States. He had trained under the man in Berlin who had created this spectacle, but that certainly didn't qualify him to tend to these poor, helpless souls. Why did all these people think they could fool me?

While Mr. Couney's selfless deeds might have benefited as many as 6,500 premature infants at no cost to the parents and no personal gain to himself, I could *not* tolerate a liar.

Time would bear out the wisdom of my decision. Mr. Couney's large Infantorium exposition at Coney Island nearly ended in tragedy. Dreamland wasn't held to the same fire regulations as the rest of Coney Island, so it was extremely vulnerable to fire. An accident during renovations led to a double nine-alarm fire early on the morning of May 27, 1911. The Infantorium went up in flames, and thanks to the heroics of a New York Police sergeant who made repeated trips into the burning building, all the babies were miraculously saved. Incubators in parks were subsequently banned in New York state and frowned upon throughout the country.

Carnivale Darke, however, continued to thrive, in no small part because we knew which acts to spotlight and which ones to send packing. We continued to enhance our reputation and build on our success through the second decade of the 20th century. The adversity of the war years forced us to improvise, but that's what we've always done best. We emerged from the 1910s safely in the black and poised for our greatest success yet.

A TWIST OF INSPIRATION

Stories all have a beginning, and inspired beginnings can lead to... uncomfortable ends. Witness the principal character in the story you are about to read. The gentleman in question stepped onto the fairground at Emporia, Kansas, on his birthday in May of 1896. This birthday was his fortieth, one of those important milestones men set for themselves to gauge their progress on the road of life. Yet our friend arrived on the threshold of middle age with little to show for his efforts, having performed on the stage before undertaking various ill-fated attempts at raising poultry, working as a shopkeeper, and later, as a newspaper publisher. He could not have conceived of the ways in which that fateful day in Emporia would change the course of his future... at Carnivale Dark.

—*Artemus Darke*

1896

The wind ran her fingers through the wheat stalks, kicking up dust as she dashed across the old dirt road. That dust whirled and danced skyward, embracing the roiling gray thunderheads. The golden sun dipped her feet in the brown-gray morass and, finding it to her liking, disappeared beneath the surface of the airborne sea.

No one at the carnival expected a big turnout in this weather.

Adoline Darke sat in the ticket booth, waiting for paying customers. On a normal day, she would be roaming the grounds, looking for problems to address. That was her job. The ruffians handled the dirty work, but she was paid to point them in the right direction. Today, with so few people on the carnival grounds, she'd instructed many of the workers to take the day off, which was why she found herself working the gate, her hands tucked between her legs, and her shoulders wrapped tightly in a woolen blanket.

She shook her head, shivering. What had gotten into Artemus?

She knew the answer perfectly well. That Romani fortune-teller had *advised* him to add a stop here, and he was determined to follow her instructions to the letter. It seemed, at times, that she was the one calling the shots at

Carnivale Darke, regardless of his reassurances. Cassandra Vine had never steered him wrong, he told her. If there ever came a time that she did, he'd sign her walking papers. Adoline would need to deliver them, though, which made it seem like he was scared of the woman. But even Adoline had to admit that she'd never known Cassandra to be wrong.

Then there was her brother's grandiose ego. Nothing was ever enough for him. He had conquered New York, Pennsylvania, and the entire Midwest circuit, so he had cast his gaze westward, to the open prairie. It didn't get more open than this. Everything was flat, flat, flat: wheatfields spread out as far as the eye could see in every direction, except where they were interrupted by corn. The streets of nearby Emporia seemed all but shut down; scarecrows stood propped up on every acre, bundles of dried-up grass with eyeless faces that stared out over their own silent kingdom.

Silent except for the howling wind. These crucified straw men of the plains outnumbered the population of human beings, at least when it came to those passing through the front gates of Carnivale Darke.

A solitary figure appeared on the horizon, leaning in against the wind as he came toward her. He was not your typical country bumpkin in a straw hat and overalls. He was dressed like a city slicker in a dress shirt and jacket, with a bowler atop his head and spectacles across his nose. New York? Chicago? Adoline would have to hear his accent to be sure. Of all the "types" she might have encountered here, she had expected to see one of his kind the least.

His left arm hung at his side. Was it paralyzed? No, it

looked more like he was holding a child's hand or a dog's leash... yet neither child nor dog was in evidence.

"One, please," he said before he even reached the booth.

"Two bits." Adoline reached out from under her blanket and extended a hand. "Attractions inside are extra."

"Of course," the man said.

She wished he'd say something more so she could pinpoint his accent. She wasn't sure why, but she always felt safer knowing a ticket-buyer's point of origin. It wasn't as though she could track them down if they passed a fake note—which happened more often than she liked—but she still wanted to know. Artemus had asked her to be aware of everything that went on inside the gates, and this was part of it.

"No refunds," Adoline said sternly. "Rain or shine."

"Or wind," the man chuckled, his teeth chattering as he held his bowler in place with his right hand. "What do you charge for a child's ticket?"

She still couldn't nail down the accent. The biggest part of it was "New Yawk," but there was more than a little of the upper Midwest there too. She couldn't decide if it was Chicago, Minneapolis, Sioux Falls, or a hodgepodge.

Adoline craned her neck to look behind him, but she still saw no evidence of a child. "A dime," she said.

"I'll take one of those too, just in case."

She wanted to ask him what he meant by that, but if he wanted to buy a child's ticket for an apparition, that was his business. On a slow day like this, she wasn't about to turn down an extra dime.

She handed him the ticket, and he tipped his hat. "Much obliged, ma'am."

He walked through the gate and quickened his stride, his left arm still hanging rigid at his side, the wind nipping at his heels and churning up dust as he turned the corner onto the midway.

Lyman looked up past the Ferris wheel that loomed above him, watching the restless clouds crashing into each other like silent, slow-motion waves. A pair of teenagers passed him, but they were headed toward the exit, having no more tolerance for the blustery weather. The midway games were deserted, and the bally talker shouted at the nearly empty promenade, urging the few people lingering there to "step inside for a cup of hot cider and ten acts you'll never forget! Ten for one! Just a dime!"

The "mythic marvels," as Artemus had dubbed them, were depicted on canvas posters that billowed like sails in the wind. "Ten for one!" Lyman's eyes scanned the canvases, set side by side atop the temporary sideshow building. The Pretzel Family of contortionists; the Solar Armor exhibit; the Acrobatic Apes of the Simian Circus; the Lion-Headed Man; King Poseidon, who could hold his breath underwater for fifteen minutes with no ill effects... On any other day, the marvels would have been paraded before the crowd in the Carousel Plaza. But there was no crowd today, and the few patrons who heard the talker's pitch were more interested in the hot cider and shelter from the wind than they were in the acts themselves.

Lyman started to walk past: He had come here with a clear purpose, and he hesitated to waste time, especially with the weather being what it was, but some of the marvels piqued his interest, and he couldn't deny the appeal of the cider. He felt a tug on his left hand, pulling him in the opposite direction, toward his right, and had a sudden inclination to turn in that direction. He was greeted by a high-pitched bark and a ball of fur crashing into his leg.

He thought he heard joyous laughter, and realized that, unless he found the pup's owner, he would be obligated to keep it. "He's all I've ever wanted, Uncle Lyman!" a silent voice squealed in his ears.

"All I've ever wanted..." Lyman said, sounding out the words he had heard from nowhere. "All I've ever... All I've... Ollie! That's it. I shall call him Ollie."

He wasn't sure about the name, hearing no confirmation in his head, but it would do for now. It would do.

If he's still here when I come out, I will take it as a sign, he told himself.

That other silent voice raised an objection, though. "But you've already named him! Even if it isn't the right name."

There was no help for it. He would have to forgo the Ten-in-One and find a leash for Ollie—although the pup didn't appear interested in wandering off. He sat obediently at Lyman's side, as though he'd been trained to do so. "All right, boy. All right," Lyman said, chuckling as he pulled a small notebook from his inside coat pocket. If he couldn't go inside, at least he could make sketches of the mythic marvels as a keepsake.

Ollie waited patiently, but Lyman felt a tug on his coat that might have been a gust of wind, though he couldn't shake the idea that there was something—or someone—

else behind it: the owner of the silent voice that he'd heard for the first time a week earlier. That voice was the reason he was here today. He had to determine the source of it, and he couldn't confide in anyone he knew. They'd think he was out of his mind. But carnies were a different breed. They saw the incredible every day; they *were* incredible themselves, and Lyman had heard about the reputation of Carnivale Darke: no shams, no frauds, no hoaxes. And, in particular, he had heard about the fortune teller Cassandra D. Vine, whose readings were reputedly never wrong.

This was the person he'd come to see, and he set off directly to find her. Even the wind couldn't overwhelm the expectation he felt rising in his breast. Something was about to go right for him, and it was about damned time. Ollie nipped at his heels and snapped at the wind as they set off down the midway, which was still just dust but felt like it was paved in something far more precious: the hope that he would find the answers he sought.

When Lyman got to the fortune-teller's tent, he was disappointed to find that the curtain had been pulled and a signboard had been placed out front declaring that Cassandra had retired for the day. It was only noon, though, and Lyman heard the sound of movement inside the tent.

"Hello?" he ventured.

"Go away!" a woman's voice called from inside. "I'm closed for today. There's bad weather coming. Very bad. You'll go home too, if you know what's good for you."

Lyman persisted: "Just a moment of your time. What do you charge?"

"A dime for ten minutes," the woman said, "but not

today."

"Four bits," Lyman countered, and the woman again said no, but she'd hesitated just a moment before answering, and he knew he had her attention.

"Two dollars," Lyman said, determination in his voice.

The woman pulled back the curtain and poked her head out. "Fool," she said, and Lyman had to agree with her. Despite his spiffy outfit, he could not afford to be throwing money around. But he had to have answers, and he knew of no other way to obtain them. The woman's hand beckoned him urgently inside. "Ten minutes," she said. "No more."

"Of course," Lyman said as he hastily entered the tent, though he was determined to stay as long as was necessary to discover the truth.

"Sit," she said, her eyes looking him up and down. The woman's expression, a mixture of surprise and recognition, took him by surprise. But before he could figure out the meaning behind it, she started speaking.

"You have brought a friend," Cassandra stated matter-of-factly as she sat down behind a small, round table draped with a purple cloth adorned in golden stars and silvery moons.

"A ghost," Lyman said, confidently. He had figured that much out.

Except he was wrong.

"Not... exactly," Cassandra said.

Lyman sat up straight. "You don't mean to say...?"

She chuckled ruefully, having read his thoughts. "No. An evil spirit has not attached itself to you," she said.

The woman's talent was impressive.

"This spirit is benign," she continued. "More than benign. Loving. I should like to introduce you properly to Dot, your niece." Her words were polite but her tone bore a chill that was colder than the wind outside.

Perhaps, he thought, she wasn't so impressive after all. He'd been fairly certain the spirit was female, a young girl not yet in her teens. "But I don't have a niece," he protested.

"Not yet," Cassandra said. "But you will."

Lyman shook his head vigorously from side to side, trying to make sense of what she was saying. But instead of an explanation from the seer, he heard that silent voice inside his head: "I haven't been born yet," it said. "But my name is Dot. I wish she hadn't told you." She tittered playfully. "I wanted to make you guess!"

"I'm sorry, Dot," Cassandra said soothingly, looking

down beside Lyman's knee. "I didn't mean to spoil your fun."

"It's okay," Dot said. "I like you."

"I like you too."

Ollie barked and spun in a circle.

Lyman returned his attention to the seer. "How can I be conversing with someone who has yet to be born?"

Cassandra raised an eyebrow, as though the answer should have been obvious. "In the same way that people converse with ghosts."

"But you said..."

"I said *she* was not a ghost, correct. But in the worlds beyond this realm, those who have passed on live side-by-side with those who have yet to be born. The unborn know their mortal fates while they reside there, though they forget them the moment they pass through the birth canal."

Lyman's breathing quickened. "And what will her fate be?" he asked in a whisper, already dreading the answer.

Cassandra pursed her lips. Was she smiling? "Tell him," she demanded.

Dot responded obediently. "I will live but a few months," she said, her voice filled with sorrow. "That is why I came to you now. We will be together on this earth but a short time. But I knew you and Auntie Maud would never have a daughter, and I wanted to spend more time with you. I wanted to be the daughter you never had. I took this form to make it easier for us to communicate. You don't want to listen to a baby crying all day, do you?" She chuckled.

"All right," Cassandra said harshly, not to Dot but to Lyman. "Your ten minutes are up." She handed the two dollars back to him, and he raised an eyebrow.

"Take it," she said. "You won't need it, and I don't want it from the likes of you."

Lyman was taken aback, but he took the two dollars. He most certainly *did* need it, and a lot more if he was going to support Maud and their four sons. None of his bright ideas had come to fruition so far, but he couldn't afford to be bitter. He needed to lift his spirits so he could lift theirs. He needed them to believe in him, like he now believed in Dot. Her presence was like a tonic for him, her childlike innocence a balm.

He squeezed her invisible hand as they exited the tent with a perfunctory "thank you" for Cassandra, who met his gratitude with silence.

Even in the rising storm, Dot seemed carefree, dancing in place beside him as the pup tugged insistently on his sleeve. "I think Ollie wants us to start moving," Lyman said.

"His name's not Ollie," Dot protested. "It's..."

But Ollie, or whatever his name was, was growling now, jumping at him repeatedly and barking.

Something was wrong.

Lyman looked around and saw the midway was fully deserted. Even the talker had left his station, and it was clear to him why: The sky looked like it was falling down on top of him, snatching the bowler from his head and sending it flying willy-nilly out in front of him. Ollie barked, as though offering to fetch it, but the hat was already too far away, and the wind was so strong that Lyman feared it might carry the pup away too. He reached out and scooped Ollie up into his arms, but in doing so, he let loose of Dot's hand.

He flailed around with his arm, trying to find her, but to no avail.

"Dot!" he called, but his voice was carried away upon the wind. "Dot! Where are you?!"

The carnival magician poked his head out from behind the curtain on his tent. Not everyone had left. Did this wizard have some enchanted means of weathering the storm? That was patently absurd. Even if he believed in magic, which he certainly did not, whatever the magician had at his disposal could certainly never withstand... this.

The magician pulled the curtain shut again and disappeared inside the tent.

Don't be distracted, Lyman told himself. *You have to find Dot.*

Lyman fought against the strong winds that buffeted him back and forth across the midway. He screamed for Dot to grab his hand, but his voice disappeared into the vacuum. Ollie wriggled loose from his grasp and stood barking at the fortune-teller's tent.

Apparently, he didn't like her any more than I did, Lyman thought. *No matter!*

He had to find Dot before this whirlwind dropped upon their heads. He ran toward the midway tent, dodging debris that had taken to the air. Maybe Dot had wandered over there to see some of the oddities on display.

The wailing of the wind crescendoed while the falling sky coalesced into a dark, swirling mass—the tornado was about to touch down. "Dot! Dot, where are you?" Lyman wailed in terror. "We have to seek cover now."

He spun in a circle, searching the entire midway. He saw movement out of the corner of his eye. Thinking it was Dot, he turned just in time to see a wooden plank fly toward him—and hit him squarely in the forehead. Lyman dropped to the dirt, unconscious, a trickle of blood running down his face.

"Wa-wake up, mister. Come on n-now," Bert the Lion-Headed Man coaxed the unconscious Lyman, shaking him. The funnel cloud was coming their way quickly. Desperate, Bert slapped the man's cheek, "Wake up!"

Lyman woke up in a daze. His vision was blurry, and he didn't recognize his surroundings at first.

Dot, where's Dot? he thought in a panic.

He ignored the man trying to help him. Although, he was still disoriented, all his thoughts were centered on finding his precious niece. He looked up to see one of the many scarecrows from the nearby fields drifting down the gold-colored dirt path of the midway, almost as if he were skipping. A beautiful little girl with dark brown hair in two long, braided pigtails tied with blue ribbons held the scarecrow's hand.

Dot? That's Dot! Lyman thought. *I can see her. But how?*

"We n-need to find c-cover. The tw-twister's coming our way," the Lion-Headed Man said, tugging on Lyman's arm.

"I can't. My niece. I have to save her," Lyman cried, watching as she and the scarecrow were joined by a man in some kind of suit. It covered his whole body like armor.

"That's j-just the solar armor display blowing away... and one of th-those scarecrows," Bert replied, his panic mounting. The tornado would soon be upon them. Both men were clutching at the tent stakes in the ground.

Lyman ignored Bert.

"Forget y-you. I'm going over th-there to hide under the r-railc-c-cars." Bert began to army-crawl along the ground a couple hundred feet over to where the train had been left, clutching at anything staked to the ground along the way.

The side of the midway tent nearest the cyclone ripped free from the ground, exposing all the terrified freaks and other midway performance acts hiding within. The chimpanzees from the Simian Circus, many of them dressed in little black suits with red zigzag trim along the edges, began to screech and jump up and down. It appeared as if they were in the middle of rehearsing their acrobatic feats. The twister veered toward them, and when the apes jumped again, they took flight, whirling through the air, diving and swooping as if they had wings, until they disappeared from sight.

A man in the back holding a trident jumped up and ran, determined to escape. In desperation, he wrestled a bicycle away from one of the clowns and mounted it. He pedaled as fast as his legs would allow him, but the whirling dervish picked him too. His eyes, though big as saucers, could not adequately reflect the gravity—or lack thereof—of his situation, as he flew through the air. He kept pedaling as if he could ride right out of that storm, but he vanished from sight a short time later.

In the blur of activity, Lyman had lost sight of Dot and her companions. Hopefully, they'd found cover. He wouldn't be able to help her if he lost his own life or became too injured to move.

He began to crawl along the ground and joined the group of sideshow acts fleeing from the far side of the tent toward one of the railcars.

Lyman saw a small form run and hide under the caboose. "Dot!" he exclaimed, running to join her. He slipped under the car to find a whole troop of small people—the "Munchkin Menagerie"—none of them Dot. Nobody had seen a young girl in pigtails. All he could do was wait.

Bert, the Lion-Headed Man, was hiding there as well. He was whimpering and cowering, his face buried in his hands. He might've had the long mane and face of a lion, but he sure didn't have the courage. "I wanna go home. I wanna go home," he chanted over and over, in a mind-numbing mantra.

After an interminable amount of time, the air became still and the silence was oppressive. They could have heard a pin drop across the expansive fairgrounds. Gilda, the fat lady, who had wedged herself between two train cars, began to wail and moan in pain. "I've got to get out of here. I can't take it any longer." She wiggled and kicked to free herself.

"No, Gilda. We're in the eye. It's not safe," Willem the Strongman called out from one of the other train cars.

"It passed over us. I'm leaving," she replied, adamant.

"No," a chorus of voices yelled out.

A few moments later, just after wrenching herself free, Gilda struggled to rise—just as the howling storm itself began to rise to deafening levels. The swirling winds picked Gilda up and slammed her head against one of the cast-iron wheels of a boxcar. Lyman and the others heard a sickening crunch as her body fell to the ground with a thud, rolling to a stop just under the edge of the car. Blood pooled under her head, and rivulets ran downhill toward the Munchkin troop. Lyman could see the deep concavity in her head, exposing bits of bone and brain.

Finally, the howling winds began to slow, and

everyone at the circus watched as the cyclone drifted away and then receded back into the sky. Lyman climbed out from under the train and looked around at the field of ruins. Signs of devastation were apparent everywhere, except for the pristine, undisturbed tents of the magician and the fortune-teller, the small ticket booth, and the larger, imposing tent labeled Artemus K. Darke. How had they survived without a scratch?

The pain in Lyman's head had lessened, and his vision was clearer now. He saw no sign of Dot anywhere. He began to call her name, but there was no response. He headed over to the magician's tent to see if she had taken refuge there. He entered the darkened tent and found the curtain to the stage area closed.

A deep booming voice issued from the dark depths behind the curtain, "May I help you? Carnival is closed, in case you hadn't noticed."

"Yes, I was just looking for..."

"She's in the corner, by the oil lamp."

"Uhh... excuse me. Who?"

"Your niece."

Lyman turned, flustered, and reached out his hand. He couldn't see Dot in front of him, but if only...

"Here, I am, Uncle," said a sweet voice from the darkness. Lyman felt Dot take his hand and then wrap him in a bear hug.

"Thank God, sweet girl. I was so worried about you. Come out of the darkness so I can see you."

"Oh, I'm fine, Uncle, but you can't see me, silly. I was playing with my new friends."

"Oh... umm... I can't? Well, yes, of course not. You'll have to tell me all about your friends on the way home, darling. For now, I think we should get going." Lyman walked out of the tent, gripping her small hand firmly. They walked toward the ticket booth and heard yapping approaching from behind, rapidly. Lyman turned around to see Ollie bouncing at his heels. "There you are, chap. S'pose you'll be going with us, Ollie." The trio exited the fairgrounds and walked toward town.

Adoline watched them from the ticket booth, wondering at the man with the strange accent who left holding a conversation with no one in sight and somehow had gained a dog along the way. He had a head wound, but otherwise didn't seem any worse for wear or any less strange than he had when he arrived.

It was time to surveil the damage the unexpected tornado had caused.

Adoline hadn't taken two steps when she was accosted, and nearly knocked down by Bert the Lion-Headed Man, who came hurtling at her. "I'm... I'm leaving. It's not safe here. G-G-Gilda's d-dead. Her brain's all over the place. Poseidon was impaled on his trident. There's bl-blood everywhere. I am s-scared" Bert ran off and out of sight before Adoline could even respond.

Adoline's determined strides took her quickly over to the midway tent, or at least to where it had once stood, to see what had caused Bert such distress. She found a group of people, including the Menagerie Munchkins, standing a couple of hundred feet away by the train cars, surrounding Gilda's body. It was just as Bert had said.

Wallace, one of the animal trainers, was sniffling near the ruins of the tent. "What's wrong, Wallace?" Adoline asked, afraid to hear that another act had been lost in the storm.

"They're gone... all gone."

"Who?"

"The monkeys. They just flew away."

"Flew away? You're not making sense, Wallace."

"They were nervous and jumping about when the cyclone tore the tent open. The winds ripped them off the ground, and they just flew away. I've looked everywhere, but I can't find them."

"Relax, Wallace. I'll get a group together, and we'll go looking here in a bit. I have to check on everyone else first. I heard that something happened to King Poseidon. Do you know where he is?"

Wallace began to cry harder. He was too choked up to speak, but she started out in the direction he was pointing.

Adoline walked to the far recesses of the fairgrounds, taking note of all the damaged tents, bally cloth, and props along the way, before she finally found another crowd. A bicycle lay next to King Poseidon's body, tangled in the limbs of a tree and impaled by his trident.

"What happened to him?" Adoline asked in horror.

Tiny, one of the clowns, turned to Adoline, "He was scared when the tornado hit our tent on the midway. We had all been practicing for the evening show, in hopes that the weather would turn and allow us to hold it. He took my bicycle and rode off; he must've thought he could outrun the storm. But it picked him up and took him away. We didn't know what happened until we came across him when we were all out searching for the chimps."

Once all the injured had been seen to, Artemus and Adoline assigned people to clean up and sent a search party to look for the chimps.

But they were never found or heard of again.

This was the first time that Carnivale Darke had not continued on the circuit immediately. In the past, every week, or nearly every one, the whole troop would pick up stakes and move to the next destination. Even with all the money at Artemus' disposal, it took several weeks to repair or replace the tents and the acts that had been lost. The emotional damage took longer to pass, not that Artemus tolerated anybody languishing in their fears. And for those like Bert, it never did. He didn't return to Carnivale Darke, and neither did some of the hired help.

1900

Cassandra and Adoline looked through the window of the Rosenberg General Store. A wax mannequin was showing off a tan woolen coat and matching hat next to a hardware display. Sprigs of freshly cut pine lined the bottom of the casing, resting on cotton snow, and figures of elves danced in place gaily around a tiny barber pole. A small noble fir decorated in bulbs and popcorn looked down over the scene.

"Christmas tree already?" Adoline said.

Cassandra shrugged. "It's the thirteenth. Twelve days of Christmas."

"That's supposed to *start* on Christmas Day and end on Epiphany."

"They want customers. A tree in the window makes the place seem..."

"Homey."

"Sacred." Cassandra's eyes roved to the right, scanning the display case again before stopping on a small wooden shelf of dime-store novels. "Look there," she said, pointing to a children's book with a bespectacled lion on the cover. "What does that remind you of?"

Adoline laughed. "It looks a lot like Bert. Too bad he quit after that tornado spooked him in Emporia. Except he was just the Lion-*Headed* Man. That's a whole lion wearing eyeglasses!" She chuckled some more.

"It doesn't just *look* like Bert," Cassandra said. "It *is* Bert. That's a drawing of him."

Adoline leaned forward and squinted, examining the book more closely. "Well, so it is! And quite the likeness too."

"That's no accident."

Adoline gave her a quizzical look. "You know the author?"

Cassandra nodded. "I met him some years ago, at the carnival in Emporia, but I knew about him before then. Cocky fuck."

Adoline recoiled. She'd never approved of Cassandra's coarse language.

"You might remember him," Cassandra went on. "The overdressed jerk who didn't have sense enough to stay home during tornado weather. He came to me that day, wanting to have his fortune told. Didn't realize I knew who he was."

"You don't like the man?"

Cassandra's voice lowered to something like a growl. "I despise him. Before I joined the carnival, I was living in Aberdeen."

"Yes, South Dakota. I remember. You responded to one of my brother's ads..."

"I needed to get out of there. Around Christmas of 1890, there was an Army operation on the Great Sioux Reservation near the Nebraska line. Word spread just before New Year that the United States forces had slaughtered three hundred Lakota Sioux. It was horrific, and it was big news in Aberdeen. One of the newspapers there, *The Saturday Pioneer*, ran an editorial."

She reached into her pocket and pulled out a torn and faded newspaper clipping, handing it to Adoline, who carefully unfolded it. The first part of it had been torn off, but parts of the rest were legible—if with difficulty.

Adoline read aloud:

"The Pioneer *has before declared that our safety depends on the total extirmination of the Indians. Having wronged them for centuries, we had better, in order to protect our civilization, follow it up by one more wrong and wipe these untamed creatures from the face of the earth... An eastern contemporary, with a grain of wisdom in his wit, says that 'when the whites win the fight, it is a victory, and when the Indians win it, it is a massacre.'"*

Cassandra was shaking now. "I moved away from there but never found anything permanent for the next few years, until I contacted your brother."

Adoline barely heard her. She was troubled by something else. "I don't understand," she said. "That looks like a *children's* book in the window. It could not have possibly come from the same pen, the same mind, that advocated wiping people from the face of the earth."

"Yes, it could have," Cassandra seethed. "And it did. Lyman." She spat the name. "That's not the name on the book. He doesn't like anyone to call him that—which is why I do. He wrote other things as well. The Lakota in his mind were miserable wretches who were better off dead. Despicable beings destined to be forgotten by history. Some of these people were my friends. And then there's me."

"What?"

"Look at me!" Adoline had never heard the seer raise her voice. Until now. "I *look* like them. Dark hair. Dark skin. That editorial roused the people of Aberdeen to shun and threaten to 'extirminate' anyone who looked like the Lakota who perished at Wounded Knee. I went into hiding, but I could never escape those angry looks. When I couldn't take it anymore, I sent my letter to your brother. He probably saved my life by hiring me."

Adoline frowned, trying to take it all in. "Why do you keep that news clipping with you?"

A curious smile spread across Cassandra's face as she took the paper back, and Adoline could see a glint of something in her eye. Mischief... or perhaps worse. No, not perhaps.

"He made it, so I kept it. I own a piece of him now." Her tone was rooted in rage. Controlled rage, but rage nonetheless. It was unmistakable. "I used this scrap of paper to cast a Romani curse upon him," she hissed. "By possessing this piece of paper..." She shook it in front of her. "...I made sure that this disgusting rag would fail. And that he would never possess the thing he wanted most in the world: a daughter. Not even a surrogate daughter. When he arrived at the carnival, I knew the longing of his heart, and I used his longing to torment him. I taunted him with the knowledge that his niece, whose spirit had come to him before her birth, would die while still an infant."

Adoline stared at the elves in the window. They had been set in place, staged by the human hands that controlled them. The window designers had placed them in poses of their choosing, forcing them to do their will like puppet masters pulling the strings of their wooden prisoners. She cast a sidelong glance at Cassandra, wondering what might happen if she ran afoul of the seer. She shivered involuntarily. She didn't want to think about it.

"Dorothy's death was not by my hand, though I did foresee it, and Lyman sensed my enmity in Emporia once the truth had been revealed. He must have thought me a witch!" She laughed. "Do you know he offered me two dollars to tell his fortune? I took it, then I gave it back... but not before I had laced his foul money with another curse—one that transferred itself to him the moment he accepted it."

"What was this curse?"

Cassandra stood up straighter, looking quite pleased with herself. "He will not live to see his greatest success, his fondest wish fulfilled. He will squander his money in repeated attempts to adapt that book in the window..." She nodded toward the display. "...into a moving picture. He will even start a company with the intent of doing so, producing several films based upon his fantasies—each of which will fail because of my curse. Every venture he undertakes will be carried away upon the wind. All except his books."

Adoline's eyes narrowed, and Cassandra answered her unspoken question: "I foresaw how he would steal the ideas for this book from Carnivale Darke, and I thought it fitting that your brother should profit from it. Once the public sees that picture of Bert on the cover, reads about the flying monkeys, and recognizes the tin woodsman's resemblance to our Solar Armor, they will know the source of Lyman's inspiration. The carnival's gate will only increase, mark my word."

Adoline seemed at once pleased and unsettled.

Cassandra raised a finger and wagged it slowly back and forth in front of her face. "But many years from now, a motion picture based upon his work will finally be produced. It will become his greatest success, its fame eclipsing that of his books. Yet he will profit nothing from it, and his own name will be all but forgotten. He will have spent twenty years moldering in the grave by the year of the moving picture's release, and his spirit..." She followed this with a lengthy pause that had Adoline squirming right there on the sidewalk.

"His spirit will never be reunited with his precious Dot. He will be in a place, I can assure you, where no trumpets sound, no choirs sing, and no streets are paved in precious gold. He will have left his vision of heaven behind in the fantasies he concocted from his time at Carnivale Darke."

STEPHEN H. and SHARON MARIE PROVOST

DARKE HOUSE

Carnies have spent decades trying to build the most unsettling, even horrifying funhouse attraction in the land. They've constructed elaborate set pieces, installed mirrors, and dressed their clowns up as vampires, werewolves, savages, ghouls... you name it. Yet they all failed spectacularly for one simple reason: They refused to recognize that horrifying sights are never nearly as frightening as that which remains unseen. Imaginations can conjure far more terrifying what-ifs than any carny can manufacture. This principle lies at the heart of the Darke House of Horrors, which gave birth to more terrors than it could possibly contain... on the midway at Carnivale Darke.

—Artemus Darke

1898

"**B**e afraid of the Darke."

Adoline watched alongside Artemus as the sign-painter added gold lettering to the maroon background.

"What do you think, Addy?"

"Ummm..." Adoline pursed her lips. "Do you really want people being afraid of *you*?"

"Hmmph. Of course not. It's not finished yet."

"Then perhaps you should wait until it *is* finished to ask me what I think of it." Why did Artemus always have to be so impatient? He didn't just put the proverbial cart before the horse; he put an entire train of boxcars before the engine.

"Well, uh, yes, of course," he said as the painter added the last word. "*Now* what do you think?"

"Be afraid of the Darke House," Adoline read. "So *that's* what you're calling our new funhouse?"

"Catchy, isn't it? But it's not really a 'fun' house. It's a house of horrors."

"What kind of horrors?"

Artemus spread his arms wide. "*Authentic* ones, of course. Remember those murders back in '93, around the time of the World's Fair?"

"Of course I do. It was all over the newspapers. That dreadful man... what was his name?"

"Holmes," Artemus said nonchalantly. "The Torture Doctor."

"Yes, he killed how many people?"

"No one's sure. He *confessed* to twenty-seven, but some say it was in the hundreds. Did his dirty work in a place they call his Chicago 'Murder Castle.' Claimed to be possessed by Satan. Gassed some of his victims, chloroformed others, and burned some of them alive. Then he got in a local doctor to wire some of the skeletons together for him. That's where they caught him: at the doctor's home."

"You know *far* too much about this monster," Adoline said. "And you talk as if this holds some great amusement for you."

"Well... not really. But it will for our visitors."

"I don't like the sound of this," Adoline said. "What are you up to?"

Artemus raised a finger. "Now, Addy, don't judge."

"Artemus. Tell me now."

"I *bought* the Murder Castle."

"You *what*?"

"I bought it. For a pittance, really. No one wants anything to do with a murder house."

"Except you."

"Think of it, Addy! We could even hold a special event there."

Addy slapped Artemus' finger aside and stood on her tiptoes as she pulled within a few inches of him, wagging her own finger in his face. "We will do no such thing!"

Artemus took half a step backward. "All right, all right. Addy, get a hold of yourself. In any event, that wasn't my primary purpose in purchasing the Murder Castle. From what the press said about the place, with all its trapdoors and secret passages, I knew there had to be something there of value the police had missed. And I was right. Remember that trip to Chicago I took in November?"

Adoline frowned. "All right, Artemus... what... did you find?"

"I went over the place with a fine-tooth comb until I found a passageway that had been sealed off from one of the smaller first-floor rooms. So I took a crowbar to the wood and pried the hidden door loose. It was pitch dark—which gave me another idea, but I'll get to that—so I lit a lantern and found myself at the head of a stairway that led me down below ground level. Human skulls lined the stairs in small recesses to either side, some of them with remnants of skin still attached.

"I must have gone down a hundred steps before the stairway ended at another sealed door. Fortunately, moisture had weakened the wood, and I battered it with the crowbar until it gave way and I gained access. The doorway opened out onto a large room with a dirt floor, and I realized I was in the basement—actually a *second* basement, unconnected to the first, which the police had discovered. This one was entirely untouched!"

Adoline shivered.

"My god, Artemus..."

Artemus went on, almost gleefully, ignoring her. "Addy, I hit the jackpot. I found two of the articulated skeletons the doctor had wired together for Holmes, sitting opposite one another in dusty old easy chairs with a table between them, as though they were enjoying a spot of tea. They were situated next to what looked like a fireplace, but on closer inspection, I noticed the opening was guarded by steel doors. It was a crematory, Addy! Can you believe it?"

"I don't think I want to hear..."

"Torture devices were scattered around the room: thumbscrews, surgical tools, even an iron maiden and a torture rack. And that's not all: There was an empty ceramic tub cemented into the floor and coated with a green residue. I didn't touch it, because I knew what it was: a vat of acid. I even found an antique mirror with an ornate gold frame stained with dried blood."

"Good heavens, Artemus. I've heard enough. What does any of this have to do with our new attraction?"

"I hired men to haul out everything they could carry and bring it here and use it to furnish the Darke House. They couldn't move the vat, but I did manage to remove the rack, the iron maiden, and the smaller items. I'm having our workers set them all up in the Darke House. It will be glorious!"

Adoline looked at him, incredulous. "And the authorities did nothing to stop you?"

"Why would they?" Artemus said. "They're as scared to go in there as anyone else. Even if they weren't, they'd have no use for any of my new treasures: They don't need any 'evidence' against Holmes; he was hanged two years ago. Besides...” He rubbed his thumb and forefinger together. “...money can make any problem disappear.”

“You’re sick, Artemus.”

“Not sick. Ambitious.”

“Really? Is that what you call it? No one will actually want to go through a real house of horrors like this!”

“That’s where you’re wrong,” Artemus said. “Kids these days are always daring each other to visit the scariest haunted house in town, and what could be scarier than a house containing skeletons of a serial killer’s *actual* victims and the torture devices he used to kill them?

“But here’s the proverbial kicker, dear sister, Darke House will be just that: *dark*! When our visitors enter, they won’t be able to see a thing. I’ve had our new attraction insulated so that no light can enter from the outside. The floors are undulating, and the passageways are full of curves and spirals. Our guests will be funneled into rooms where the doors close abruptly behind them. Then, when they step inside, one of our workers hidden in a crawl space above the ceiling will use flash powder to illuminate one of my trophies from the Murder Castle. Tell me it’s not brilliant.”

“It’s... something,” Adoline said, shaking her head. “But I don’t want any part of it. How do I know you haven’t brought any spooks with you: the ghosts of those skeletons?”

“Come now, Adoline. You don’t really believe...”

“Not normally, but when it comes to murder victims, I’m not taking any chances. You won’t catch me within ten feet of Darke House. This is *your* project, Artemus. If anything goes wrong, it’s your mess to clean up, not mine.”

Artemus chuckled. "Have a little faith, my dear. I promise you, nothing can go wrong."

"I hope you're right. This structure seems awfully cumbersome to move. Don't we have enough to worry about?"

"I've hired a few more men to help out with that. Besides, this was all designed with the help of J.T. Meyers." Artemus beamed as if she should be impressed.

"So?" Adoline held her hands out in mock supplication.

"Sometimes I forget you're a woman and don't know these things. J.T. Meyers is only the greatest architect of his time. He designed this whole attraction to fit together like one big jigsaw puzzle. The whole is made up of smaller, manageable pieces that can be moved on and off the train easily and assembled in less than an hour. All the artifacts are attached to the pieces."

Adoline sighed loudly and glared at Artemus. "Sometimes I forget that *you're* regarded as gentleman. So when does this nightmare open?"

"Officially? Friday night at the opening of the carnival in St. Louis. But our first victim shall enter tonight after the paint dries."

"Victim?"

"That's how I'm going to advertise it. Don't you think it's brilliant?"

Adoline put her head in her hands. "And who's going to be the first victim? Never mind... forget I asked. I mean it, Artemus. Count me out." Adoline walked off without a backward glance.

As darkness descended, Artemus walked down to the

cooch tent. He couldn't wait to see what Rose thought of the Darke House. When he arrived, she wasn't there. Artemus continued down to the Darke House, in case there had been some miscommunication as to where to meet. There she was peeking inside the darkened doorway. "Ah ah ah, Miss Daniels."

Rose jumped with a little squeal. "Hello, Mr. Darke. I'm afraid you caught me red-handed. I was just so excited I couldn't wait. Thank you so much for choosing me. It's such an honor to test out your latest attraction."

"Take a breath, my dear, for I'm sure your heart will soon be pounding. Are you certain you're ready for this?"

Rose covered her mouth and giggled like a schoolgirl. "I'm ready, Mr. Darke. I heard some talk around the carnival that this house of horrors is based on H.H. Holmes' Murder Castle. Is that right?"

"Yes, my dear. Are you scared?"

"I must admit I am a little. I followed that story in the papers. It was just terrible. Acid vats and trapdoors!" Rose shivered and held the back of her hand up to her forehead.

"I sure hope you're not prone to the vapors. Can't have you falling in a vat of acid now, can we?"

Rose giggled nervously. "No, sir. But there's not really acid in there, right?"

Artemus shook his head.

"Is it time then?" Rose put on a brave smile.

"Give me one moment to make sure the crew is ready." Artemus walked around the back of the attraction and returned a few moments later. He took Rose's hand and led her up the short flight of stairs to the attraction. When he opened the door, inky blackness poured out into the moonlit night.

"It's awful dark in there, Mr. Darke. Do I get a candle to see by?"

"No, my dear." He pointed up the at the sign, just visible from the moonbeams shining down. "That's why it's called Darke House. You'll be walking through pitch-black, narrow passageways by feel. Do not run, because you could hurt yourself."

"How?"

"The corridor is tortuous, and the floors are uneven." He used the word to tease her, hoping she might mistake it for "torturous" and become unnerved.

Annoyed when she didn't react, he added, "It means 'curving'."

"I know what it means, Mr. Darke," she said, her annoyance momentarily matching his. She hated being talked down to because she was a woman—and a cooch dancer—but she forced a smiled; he *was* her boss, and she *was* eager to experience this new attraction.

Artemus continued: "At times, you will enter larger rooms, and you will find your way by feeling the ropes that delineate your path."

"Well, how will I see anything scary?"

"You will, Miss Daniels, trust me."

Rose took a deep breath and a few tentative steps into the corridor before turning back to see Artemus close the door, erasing any trace of light. She placed her hands on the walls and began to move forward. A few more steps, and she startled when her foot dropped lower than expected. On her next step, her foot scuffed the floor as it rose higher again.

Oh! That's what he meant. This is kinda fun.

As Rose's courage grew, she began walking down the hall faster and ran into the wall suddenly. She returned her right hand to the wall and walked with her fingertips just brushing it. She soon found herself walking in what felt like circles. Just as she began to question whether she had missed a passage that led off to the left, she no longer felt a wall. She leaned forward and flailed with both hands, finally finding a rope. She took two small steps forward. She jumped, stumbling over her own feet, and screamed at the sound of a door slamming shut behind her.

Rose heard a rustle in the room, seemingly from above her. She looked up and then around her, trying desperately to discern a shape in the darkness. Suddenly, there was a loud crack and a blinding flash of light. For a split second, Rose saw a skeleton standing right in front of her, behind the rope line. It was reaching out to grab her and pull her into the murky green depths of a vat behind it—a smaller-scale duplicate of the one at the Murder Castle. The skeleton's mouth was open in a scream matching her own. Rose's glass-shattering shriek echoed through the house of horrors.

There was blood! Blood dripping from its chest. He's going to get me!

"Stay away from me! Don't touch me!" Rose screamed into the void. "I want out!"

There was no response. When nothing grabbed her from the darkness, Rose tried to slow her breathing.

This is just a funhouse... just a funhouse. But this isn't fun!

Rose felt around, trying to find a knob on the door that had shut behind her, but there was no way to open it.

There was only one way out... forward. She took a few cautious steps, using the rope to guide her until she returned to a narrow hallway again.

After a few sharp turns, she realized she had reached another room.

What horror awaits me now?

Rose took a few deep breaths before setting foot in the room, holding onto the rope for dear life. Nothing happened this time. After a few moments, she proceeded forward, confident that she'd endured the most jarring display. But the worst was yet to come.

As she neared the exit, she told herself not to turn around when she heard a noise. But her fear overwhelmed her resolve. The loud crack announced another flash of light that exposed a tableau of horror, arranged right next to her hand: skull after skull peeking out from ledges cut out in the wall. As she turned to escape, another flash of light appeared in front of her, exposing a figure standing over a body with most of its flesh removed.

As Rose waited for her pupils to adjust, she heard another noise nearby. She strained to penetrate the jet-black gloom and thought she saw movement coming toward her from the vacuity. Her heart began to pound, her breath catching in her throat. All rational thought fled from her racing mind.

Losing her sense of direction in the chaos, she hurtled headlong into the shadows. Off balance from the return of the undulating floors, she skidded through an unexpected curve into another room. She only made it two small steps before the boundary rope—rising from its low connection on the wall up to the first post—clotheslined her at the knees. She stumble-stepped over it in a panic, bouncing off an object to her right.

Blinding light from the flash powder lit up the room again, allowing Rose only a split-second view of the open iron maiden before she landed face-first, splayed against the inside. Her scream of terror was cut off when a spike punctured her chest. She emitted one wheezing gasp before weakly trying to push herself off of the innumerable spikes piercing her body.

"Are you hurt?" A voice called down from above.

Rose, too afraid to answer, held still, hoping he—or *it*—would go away. She pushed back against the unyielding metal surface, and her hand slid on the slick blood, impaling itself on one of the razor-sharp blades. "Uhhhh!" Rose's cry came out muffled, accompanied by a sucking sound as she gasped for breath. With one last desperate push, she flung herself loose from the iron maiden, landing on the long, sharp saw that Holmes had used to dismember his victims. The blade cut deep into her thigh, just a few inches above the knee.

Rose's eyes fluttered. Starbursts of light flashed in front of her eyes.

Where is that light coming from?

She heard screams of "Help" but couldn't figure out whether it came from her or someone else. Her thoughts were disjointed, and it felt as if she was floating, just before she blacked out.

"Artemus, I need help now! She's hurt real bad. Get the doctor." Artemus didn't recognize the voice, but he jumped up from the hay bale he'd been perched on and ran over to Darke House.

The area around the attraction was in chaos as the

men who'd been hiding in the crawlspace above came out and ran around to enter it from the front.

"I need light. Where's a lantern?" Albert screamed.

Adoline was out walking when she heard the flurry of activity. She came running up, carrying a lantern. "What's wrong? How can I help?"

"Rose Daniels is hurt very bad. Do you know where Doc is?"

"I'll go find him." Adoline ran off in a panic and searched all the usual places, finally finding him in the freaks tent, playing cards with Harold Zimmerman.

"Doc, we need you. One of the cooch girls got hurt," Adoline said breathlessly.

"I'll go grab my bag. Where is she?" he asked as he rose unsteadily from the table, grabbing onto it to regain his balance. The bottle of whiskey in the center of the table fell, spewing its contents across the cards before rolling off and shattering.

"Down by Artemus' creepy new attraction. Are you.,. uh... feeling well enough to care for her?" Adoline asked, concern in her voice.

"He's all we got. I'll help him get down there." Harold grabbed his elbow and led him at a teetering trot over to the man's tent.

Adoline returned to Darke House and turned her ire on Artemus. "What happened? How'd she get hurt?" Her tone made it clear she wouldn't tolerate any subterfuge.

"It was a simple accident... really, she hurt herself. She got scared and..." Artemus' voice cut off as the men carried an unconscious Rose outside, bleeding from countless wounds all over her body. A belt had been cinched tight on her upper thigh to stanch the flow of blood from a deep wound just above her knee. Her lower leg had nearly been severed.

"Simple accident? You bastard!" Adoline shouted. "It's supposed to be a house of horrors, not a torture chamber."

"If you can't stay calm, maybe you should leave! She's the one who needs attention now."

Adoline turned and stomped off toward where Rose had been laid. She crouched beside her and softly stroked the stricken girl's forehead.

Doc appeared a few seconds later, Harold at his side. "What happened to this girl?"

Artemus nodded at Albert.

"She was testing the new Darke House attraction. Bob and I were setting off flash powder above her as she went through. She must'a gotten spooked and went plain cuckoo. All I can think is she started running and tripped. When I found her, she was lying on the saw blade, but she's got all these holes in her and blood was dripping from the iron maiden, so she must'a hit it first."

"Help me carry her back to my tent. I don't know what I can do to save her, but I certainly can't do it out here."

Harold, Bob, and Albert rolled her onto a blanket and carried her up. Adoline followed them, wringing her hands, silently whispering a prayer.

"God doesn't answer prayers of unbelievers." Artemus shrugged, "Or anyone for that matter."

"Well, if there's a God—or a devil—there's a special place in hell for you." Adoline retorted.

"That may be."

Doc Adams turned to the two men who'd helped him carry the injured girl and the others who'd assembled as word spread. "I need you all to leave so I can take care of her."

Artemus, Adoline, and Harold stayed behind to see what needed to be done.

Rose's pallid complexion was turning ghostly.

Doc Adams turned to Adoline. "I need you to help me bandage the less serious wounds while I assess that sucking chest wound. Her chest cavity's been punctured; her lung might collapse."

Rose's chest rose and fell unevenly. The skin around the wound caved in with each halting breath.

"I'll need to do surgery immediately, but I'm not sure she's going to survive." Doc cinched the belt on her leg even tighter. "Not sure that I'll be able to save that leg, though, once I'm done."

Adoline put a hand to her head and grabbed Artemus' arm to steady herself.

"Get her out of here, Artemus. I can't be helping two people right now," Doc Adams grumbled.

Artemus helped Adoline out of the tent and set her down on a nearby hay bale. "I'll be right back."

He returned to Doc's tent. "Put her out of her misery, Doc. She'll never work the cooch show again in that condition... or any other, for that matter. We can't afford the liability either. The carnival's barely been in operation for four years."

"But..." Doc Adams stammered.

"You heard me. Harold, see that it's taken care of. We'll give her a proper burial and take care of her family. I know she sent money home to support her ailing mother." Artemus turned and left before either man could reply.

Artemus helped Adoline to her tent, then proceeded on to his own to see about making arrangements.

Two hours later, Adoline entered the tent and asked about Rose's condition.

Just as Artemus was about to tell her, Harold entered the tent. "I need to speak to you in private, Artemus."

"What about, Harold? You know Adoline's integral in helping us with all the carnival's operations. Anything you have to say, you can say in front of her."

With a sigh, Harold continued, "Fine. Follow me. I have something to show you."

Artemus rose, annoyed, and followed Adoline and Harold out of the tent. "And where are we going for this little adventure?"

"Doc Adams' tent."

"Rose! Did she make it? Was he able to save her leg?" Adoline cried out.

"Not exactly. I'll explain when we get there."

Artemus shot a glare at Harold. "I was under the impression..." Artemus stopped abruptly as they entered the tent and he saw the horror before him.

Rose Daniels was nearly unrecognizable. Both arms had been removed at the elbow, along with the lower half of the leg that had been nearly severed in the accident. Her body was covered in over a hundred wounds that had been stitched together in a sloppy puckered manner with thick, black suture. Her eyelids had been removed, leaving her orbs exposed to the elements. They were already drying and bloodshot. Large patches of skin were covered with deep cavities filled with red, blistered skin, peeling away in places. Her lips appeared to have been burned off—the skin was blackened and charred—and they would now form a ghastly, unnaturally large grin when she smiled because they'd been slit open at each corner.

If she ever had any *reason* to smile after this.

Adoline screamed and broke down into sobs as she collapsed into the chair at Rose's bedside.

The weak girl—once a beauty, but now a nightmare to behold—awakened at the disturbance. "Aadoliffth, waa happnth?" The girl struggled to speak with her bleeding, swollen tongue, which had been cut into a deep fork.

Adoline hugged the girl, at a loss for words and crying hysterically. She pulled back and fought to retain eye contact with Rose before finally responding, "It'll all be okay."

Rose reached over to the table near the bed and picked up one of Doc's empty booze bottles, catching a glimpse of her terrifying visage through the blurred vision of her always-open eyes. Her ear-piercing shrieks rang throughout the entire encampment before she finally passed out.

"What in the holy hell have the two of you done?" Artemus bellowed, his face glowing red. Adoline could feel the waves of heat emanating from his body as his blood boiled.

Doc Adams was tucked in the corner, lost in a bottle of bourbon. His already red-rimmed eyes were swollen with tears. "I didn't. I wouldn't. I just..."

Artemus could see he wouldn't be getting an answer from Doc. Clearly, he hadn't been the ringleader in perpetrating this macabre act. Someone else was the instigator, and it was clear who that someone else was. Artemus turned the full depth of his rage onto Harold, who stood next to him, chest puffed out in pride. "What did you have him do? Explain yourself before I kill you."

"I couldn't see letting this whole farcical experience end in failure. Now Miss Daniels can live and continue to earn money for her family, while remaining a productive member of Carnivale Darke. It's a win-win situation."

"You bastard! I told you I would take care of her family. The only humane thing to do was to put the girl out of her misery."

"You were going to have them kill her?" Adoline screamed.

Artemus ignored her outburst. Adoline laid her head, sobbing, on Rose's hand as she clutched it.

"This is an abomination! Where would you have her work in this state?" Artemus' thundering voice filled the room.

"You're such a stickler about everything being authentic. This girl will be covered in scars anyhow from all those wounds. We just *enhanced* them."

"By 'enhanced' you mean you disfigured her further? She's got burn marks now and at least two dozen incisions on top of the puncture wounds she had when she arrived. And what happened there?" Artemus pointed to the blistered areas."

"That's just from some..." Harold mumbled the last word.

"*What* was that?" Artemus' eyes were bulging from the sockets.

"Acid. They're acid burns."

Adoline squealed and hugged Rose even tighter.

"And just *how* exactly is acid used in the treatment of wounds? And what happened to her arms? Her leg needed to be amputated, but other than a few deep cuts, her arms are *perfectly* functional... or they were."

"Uh... umm."

"It ISN'T used that way! Only a sick bastard would apply acid. And don't even bother trying to come up with some pathetic excuse. I already know you're a sadistic monster! But are you brain damaged as well? Why can't you understand that adding wounds to her already scarred and maimed body takes away every trace of authenticity?"

"I thought we could use her in the freak show as 'The Human Scar.' Maybe even bill her as the only survivor of H.H. Holmes' atrocities, you know, to help support your house of horrors."

"Don't even try to push the blame off on me. I should call the authorities and have you arrested right now."

"Don't do that, Artemus. We can come to some kind of arrangement."

"You're absolutely right! But first, I need to deal with Doc Adams here. Doc, are you still with us over there?"

Doc Adams looked up bleary-eyed and nodded.

"Leave Carnivale Darke immediately and never return." Artemus reached into his pocket and fished out some bills from his billfold, throwing them at the doctor's feet. I will have Adoline pack your belongings, when she gets herself together, and send them over to you at the local rooming house. Mention one word about what you've done here, and it will be your last."

"Please don't, Artemus. I won't do it again. Harold is your partner: He told me to do it."

"Never fear, *doctor*," he spat out the last word derisively. "Harold shall be right behind you." Artemus turned to Harold with a wicked smile on his face. "I'm officially ending our partnership as of this moment. Same rules apply to you..."

"You can't do that. I'll sue."

"Oh yes, I can. I'm the brains, the money, and shockingly enough, the morality behind this operation."

Adoline's face flew up and burned a hole through Artemus at those last words.

"Don't start, sister. We'll talk shortly." He turned his attention back to Harold, "I will buy you out. You'll be paid handsomely for whatever contributions you *might* have made in the creation of Carnivale Darke—more than you would have ever earned in your lifetime, especially with your paltry skill set. All association ceases now. Or if you prefer, I'll just call the sheriff and have him sort this matter out?" Artemus cocked his eyebrow, waiting for Harold's answer.

Harold came at Artemus, fist raised. Artemus stood up straight and tall, towering over his one-time friend and longtime nemesis. He'd always thought it was wise to keep your friends close and your enemies closer. Now he'd learned the hard way that *burying* the sonofabitch would have been better.

"I... you..." Harold blustered.

"Yes?"

"You haven't heard the last of me, Artemus Darke. I will make you pay. I'll take this whole place down with me, so help me."

"Good luck with that, Harold. Now if both of you will kindly leave." Artemus pulled back the curtain and called out to Billy, a local tough guy he'd hired a few weeks earlier. "Please see Doc Adams and Mr. Zimmerman out the front gate, and make sure they never again 'darken' Carnivale Darke with their presence."

Billy escorted the two men out, and Artemus turned back to Adoline, who was ready for a fight. "I'm going to burn down that house of death."

Artemus turned away, too tired to deal with her histrionics. "You'll do no such thing. That attraction will open in St. Louis. I'll be making some adjustments to increase safety, including using lanterns to light the way."

He turned around, ready for her next volley, to see Adoline holding a pillow over Rose's face, suffocating her. "I won't let you suffer this way," she leaned over the girl and whispered.

Artemus looked at her with a smirk. "Guess I'll be seeing you in hell, sis. Stay away from Darke House."

STEPHEN H. and SHARON MARIE PROVOST

OUT OF ALIGNMENT

The human animal yearns to be at the center of things, the star attraction made in the image of God himself. For millennia, we imagined ourselves at the center of everything, with even the sun orbiting our magnificent Mother Earth. Then, at last the truth became known: that we were but passengers on a speck of celestial dust in thrall to a mediocre star. But we, in our hubris were having none of it. Deprived of our galactic throne, it became our manifest destiny to go forth and conquer other strange new worlds. The moon, seductive Venus, and Mars, the bringer of war, lay tantalizingly close. Our imaginations ran amok with visions of what we might find there, even as we lacked the means to confirm them. I was not immune to these fever dreams, and when one of my trusted employees offered me a pathway to the planets, who was I to say no? But I was about to learn what happens when dreams become nightmares-come-true... at Carnivale Darke.

—Artemus Darke

1907

Tripoli Zayn Amira drew the thick red curtain closed, covering the only window of the small booth and stood up, intending to exit through the black exit door on the opposite side. A boy of about 12 years and an older man with a beer belly had already stepped into the "peep box" that separated the window from the midway.

"Hey!" shouted the man, who Tripoli assumed was the boy's father. "I already paid, bitch. Open them curtains NOW!" He started banging his fist against the glass.

"You break that, you pay for it," Tripoli said with a sigh.

"I'll break *you* if you don't open that curtain. I paid..."

"Yeah, I know. Y'already told me. Put your kid on the merry-go-round and come back by yourself, old man. Then I'll show ya somethin' that'll make ya rub one out. I'm takin' five." She didn't wait for an answer. She had no time for dirty old men wanting to "initiate" their sons at a peep show. Most of them expected some personal attention afterward. She drew the curtain across the window and stepped out the back door, pushing her way past the gawkers that had assembled in the corridor. They weren't supposed to be allowed back there, but people were always sneaking under the burlap tarp that acted as the flimsy outer wall, and men who'd gotten all hot and bothered over the show were always eager for a more hands-on experience.

Especially with Tripoli. That wasn't her real name, of course. She'd been born plain old Julie Paulson, but women had to have exotic names to work in the carnival business, so she'd adopted a stage name after her handler, Ronnie—really her pimp—sold her to the circus. People weren't supposed to be bought and sold like chattel in the 20th century, but the reality for runaway girls was different than the "supposed to be." It was when she joined the Rayburn-Freeman Circus that she was forced to change her name—legally.

Zayn meant "beauty," and Amira meant "princess" in Arabic. The Tripoli part was obvious, and not because she had any connection to Libya. Her three perfectly formed breasts made her a star attraction, and exotic names were all the rage. At least they hadn't called her "Little Egypt," a name already taken by three different belly dancers on the circuit. Carnival Darke had hired her when Rayburn-Freeman folded.

She managed to make it through the crowded corridor without being grabbed at and groped, which was par for the course most days. But her luck ran out when she rounded the corner onto the midway and ran smack-dab into that beer-bellied heel who'd been harassing her. Before she could turn away, he grabbed her roughly by the arm, nearly jerking it out of its socket.

"Davey Junior wants to see the goods," Mister Obnoxious demanded, tightening his grip on her arm as she tried to wrestle it free. From the look of things, though, it wasn't altogether Junior's idea. The 12-year-old was standing part of the way behind him. It looked like he'd been hiding behind his father most of his life but had recently grown too big to remain fully hidden. Odds were, Tripoli thought, he was afraid of his dad, not her.

"I already told you," Tripoli growled, "I don't do shows for kids, an' I don't put out for anyone but my boyfriend." She didn't have a boyfriend, but she hoped bringing a man into it, even an imaginary one, might force him to think twice. The gambit failed, though, and he only grabbed her arm tighter and forced it behind her back as he started pushing her toward the front gate. "If you won't give us a show here, then we'll go to my place. More private there anyway."

He twisted her arm so far behind her she thought he might break it and she staggered forward a few steps, unable to resist. Then, all of a sudden, he let her go.

Tripoli whirled around to see the man lying on the ground, unconscious, blood flowing freely from a large gash in his head. Linus, one of the roustabouts, was standing over him, a 2-by-4 in hand that had splintered from the impact on the heel's skull.

The boy didn't cry out or kneel down beside his father. He just stared at the man with a blank expression on his face, then ran around behind Tripoli the way he had with his father earlier. She felt him clutching her skirt, trying to pull it protectively around him, so she took his hand gently to make sure he wouldn't accidentally rip it off.

None of the passers-by gave the fallen man more than a quick glance before hurrying on, not wishing to be involved. Such indifference was typical among the rubes and lot lice. None of them had looked twice when Tripoli had been assaulted, either, but that was the way of things: Most of them didn't give a damn about each other and had better places to be. Linus shooed away the few gawkers that hung back with a sneer and a short "nothing to see; move along."

"You all right?" Linus said in a clipped tone. She knew he didn't care about her, either. He was just doing a job. He'd made it clear in the past that he was as gung-ho to get her in the sack as Mr. Obnoxious had been. The only thing that held him back from treating her with the same contempt was Artemus' rule against quarrels among the staff. As an unskilled laborer, Linus knew he'd be out the door if the owner found out—and that Tripoli was sure to tell him.

"Fine," she said through pursed lips.

"Take care of that kid," he added. "See that he don't get into no trouble." He turned without waiting for an answer and stomped off, dragging the heel's lifeless body behind him.

It wasn't until he was gone that the boy ventured out from behind Tripoli. She expected him to be traumatized by or broken up over what had just happened, but he just stood there, shaking slightly, staring up at her.

"What's your name?" she said softly.

The boy didn't answer. She could see tears welling up in his eyes.

"You're Davey, aren't you? That's what your father called you."

The boy nodded once, then shook his head fiercely from side to side and bent down to pick up a discarded fairy floss stick and wrote something on the ground. Tripoli came around behind him and looked over his shoulder to read it.

"HAT HIM."

"Hat... oh, you mean hate. You can't speak, can you, sweetie?"

Davey shook his head and opened his mouth, and Tripoli was shocked to see that he had no tongue. He hadn't been born that way, either. It had been cut out right at the base, probably with a paring knife, and scooped out like a peach seed.

"My god," Tripoli said, pulling him to her. "Who did that to you?" She knew the answer, though.

He pulled away long enough to point at his writing in the dirt, then stomped his feet on it hard.

"I'm sorry," Tripoli said, and he thrust himself back into her arms, clinging to her tightly. "I'll take you back to my tent and get you cleaned up. You're part of our family now."

Magnus the Magician walked into Artemus' tent, trying

82

his best to look at ease.

"Sit," said Artemus, not bothering to look up. "What do you have for me?"

Artemus had tasked him with coming up with a new attraction to confound his competitors and "knock the socks off" his patrons. Magnus had raised the bar when Artemus had hired him on the condition that he perform actual magic without resorting to sleight-of-hand or trickery; with that established, Artemus had come to expect the moon and the stars from him. But those raised expectations had led Magnus to suggest several new acts, none of which had met with Artemus' approval.

"Already been done," he said to one idea.

"Not grand enough," he said to another. "I don't just want something that isn't fake; I need a showstopper that *can't* be faked. I need the people to believe they're experiencing something so incredible that they can't help but accept it. I need it to be immersive. I need them to walk out of that tent convinced that they've taken a journey where no man has gone before!"

Artemus had slammed his fist on the desk in front of him and all but thrown Magnus out of the tent. He hadn't wanted to hear any more ideas. "Just do it!" he'd demanded.

And the magician had taken him at his word. He had hit upon an idea so vast in scope that it involved creating a special Ten-in-One sideshow stage on which to execute it. There was no way he or anyone else could possibly fake what he had planned this time. The only question was whether even he could pull it off. That's where the doubt crept in: He worried that this attraction might be beyond even his abilities.

But he was determined not to show it now that he was ready to present his proposal to Artemus.

He cleared his throat, and Artemus finally looked up at him.

"Well?" he said.

"If I may," Magnus said, "I think it would be better to show you what I've come up with, because it truly defies description. If you will, sir, be so kind as to follow me to our new sideshow tent."

Artemus rose and pulled down on the front of his vest. "This had better be good," he grumbled. "I've already put a pretty penny into whatever it is you've cooked up, and I'm not paying another dime if it doesn't work."

"Oh, I assure you, it will work," Magnus said, his confident tone masking the lie in his words, as he himself was not sure at all. He'd chosen to put his project to the test for the first time with Artemus observing, as a sign of his faith in it. And now, the moment of truth had arrived.

"Let's see the bannerline!" Magnus shouted to his assistant, Nipsey Day, a nimble yet well-muscled man dressed in suspenders and a backward ball cap. The man was standing on a ladder in front of a long canvas tarp that concealed the bannerline behind it, with another carny at the other end. Nipsey signaled the other man with a tip of his cap, and unfastened the tarp simultaneously, letting it fall to the ground. There behind it were majestic artists' conceptions of the earth, the moon, and the eight planets with their mythical rulers:

The moon was a reproduction of the moon with a rocket in its eye, taken from the silent film *A Trip to the Moon*. A man with a winged helm rode the red disk of

Mercury, and a finely dressed woman who looked suspiciously like Lillian Russell straddled the green orb of Venus. Mars was surmounted by a man who looked like Hercules; Jupiter had a man throwing a thunderbolt; a man juggling twelve rings stood atop Saturn; a smiling cloud encircled Uranus, its feathery arms outstretched; and Poseidon held his trident on Neptune.

"Behold the Darke Skies Planetorium!" Magnus announced, beaming.

"Nice name," Artemus quipped. "What does it do?"

"To find out, you'll need to step inside," Magnus said. "After you, boss."

The two men stepped through an entrance at one end of the long tent and stared up at the canvas above them, which was adorned with images of galaxies, stars, and constellations, all faithfully reproduced to match their positions in the summer sky. Bleachers lined either side of a central corridor, upon which were painted circles to match the planets on the bannerline, though not quite in their proper order: Earth came first, then the moon, followed by Mercury, Venus, Mars, Jupiter, Saturn, Uranus, and Neptune.

"What is this?" Artemus asked.

"You've heard of the Sawau firewalkers from Fiji."

Artemus scowled. "A group of them tried to get a job here a few years ago," he said. "Their act is child's play. All they do is put themselves in a trance and walk fast. If that's what you've got to show me..."

"No, no, no," Magnus interrupted, waving his hands in front of his face. "This is much more impressive. But the principle is somewhat the same. It's like a gantlet; it starts out easy, but it gets more challenging near the end."

"The end of what?"

"Volunteers get to actually visit each of the planets in our solar system."

Artemus broke out laughing. "That's impossible!"

"Oh, is it?" Magnus replied. "Tell me someplace on Earth you've always wanted to go, and step into the first circle."

Artemus looked incredulous.

"Humor me."

Artemus thought for a moment, then finally said, "the pyramids of Giza" as he stepped into the Earth circle. In the same instant, he vanished... only to reappear a few seconds later, rubbing his eyes.

"How did you do that?" he gasped. It was nearly impossible to surprise Artemus, who often remarked he'd seen it all. But from the look of him, he wasn't just surprised, he was astounded. "I... I... was standing there... looking up at the Sphinx!"

Magnus smiled, pleased that he had passed the first test. "Before you hired me, I showed you a very simple example of my magic: I made your pen disappear from your desk and deposited it in the wastebasket."

Artemus nodded. "I remember."

"What I just did works the same way. It's simple teleportation, but on a much grander scale. I've learned to enhance and magnify my ability and transfer it to these circles, so that anyone who steps into one of them will reappear on the corresponding planet. As you directed, they will literally be taken on a journey where no man has gone before."

Artemus drew in a deep breath. "You've tested this, I presume."

"I just did," Magnus replied. "With you."

"I'm not sure whether you've given me a great honor or used me as a guinea pig."

Magnus chuckled. "A little of both. But I guarantee you, it's perfectly safe. The trickier part will be sending our volunteers—who'll be paying a premium for the privilege—to other planets. I'm not worried about getting them there; what concerns me is that, since no one's actually *been* there before, we don't know what they'll be facing. Are there really Martians or men in the moon? Will they be hostile? I don't know. That's why I've set things up so our volunteers will return, automatically, within a few seconds. There won't be time for anything to happen to them."

Artemus took a long look at the rings, then back at the magician. "I can't agree to this without more testing," he said finally. "I can't take a chance of someone getting hurt or killed on another planet and having it pinned on me: Here's what you are going to do, Magnus. You will test the other rings yourself before we open this Planetorium of yours to paying customers. And you'll need to bring back a souvenir for me to prove you were actually there. If you end up drowning in some Martian canal, I won't shed a tear for you. I do not tolerate incompetence. And mark my word: If you fail and come crawling back to me, I'll make you wish you'd been captured by the men in the moon!"

Tripoli had taken Davey back to her tent that night and fed him a good meal. He'd clearly been through a recent growth spurt, but his thin frame betrayed his malnourished state. When he was finally satiated, she'd taken him to bathe and found some old clothes that fit him—although loosely. He'd fallen into a deep slumber the moment his body hit the straw mattress she'd brought in for him.

What did she know about raising a kid? Although she couldn't do any worse than that good-for-nothing man who'd brought him there.

When they reached the next stop, Tripoli slipped into town and bought him a slate and some books. She was determined that she'd teach him how to read and communicate, even if it couldn't be verbally. Each night, she curled up next to him, his head against her chest, as she read to him from the books, pointing out each word as she went along.

Davey was eager to learn. When he didn't understand something, he'd point to the word and draw a question mark in the air with his finger. One night a few weeks later, that progressed to him jumping out of bed to grab his slate, where he wrote out a slew of questions for her. She'd never seen anyone learn so fast, especially one who'd been so badly treated. Eventually, she found a book on American Sign Language, and they began to learn together.

Every morning, Davey rose with a smile on his face and gave her a hug. With time, his trust grew to the point that he opened up to her about his home life with his father. He'd grown up without his mother. She'd run away, leaving him behind when he was only a year old, to escape the vicious clutches of her abusive husband. He'd broken down in tears, thinking his mother didn't care about him.

Tripoli wrapped him in a bear hug, comforting him, while she explained that his mother couldn't care for an infant alone. She'd probably hoped he'd have a better life with his father than on the street with her. It broke Tripoli's heart to find out that Davey's father had instead treated him like an indentured servant, making him work around the house and on the farm to earn his meager meals and his ragged clothing.

Tripoli soon discovered that Davey loved science. She always found him engrossed in the science-based attractions that were beginning to gain favor at the time. He loved to study the primitive robotics demonstrations, the "Palace of Electricity," that sought to replicate Nikola Tesla's laboratory, and, of course, Tesla's MasterView stations. Tripoli stoked his interest, buying him books on science whenever she had time to go into town on one of their stops.

After a time, she convinced some of the other performers to let him help them out, but it always galled Davey that they used him as a gofer instead of letting him assist. Most of them couldn't be bothered to have an actual discussion with him; they were too impatient to wait for him to use his slate. Tripoli tried to make him understand that some of them probably couldn't read themselves.

Recently, Davey had finally developed a burgeoning friendship with Magnus. While magic was not science, it still fascinated Davey. Since Tripoli spent a fair amount of time with Magnus working as his part-time assistant when she wasn't in the peep show, Davey had started accompanying her to Magnus' tent. He was especially excited to experience Magnus' new attraction, which would be opening soon. What could be better than magic mixed with science?

Well, isn't this a pickle? Magnus thought as he stared at the rings in front of him, trying to maintain an air of confidence under Artemus' watchful eye. He'd arranged to borrow the Solar Armor, one of the carnival's oldest exhibits, for protection against extreme heat, though he didn't think he'd need it for his first stop, on the moon. And he didn't know about what kind of atmosphere each planet had, but he wasn't worried about that: He knew he could hold his breath for the duration of each brief journey. The rest he would have to leave to God, or the fates, or the four-leaf clover he'd kept in his pocket since childhood. His only precautions were a pair of eye-protectors that had been designed for ironworkers and a pair of Goodyear rubber gloves.

"Here's to the luck of the Irish. All I need is a shot of whiskey and a mug of Guinness to steady the old nerves."

"What are you waiting for?" Artemus demanded. "Off with you."

Magnus nodded and stepped into the lunar circle; a moment later, he was on the surface of the moon. It had worked! He immediately felt lighter than he had on Earth, which didn't surprise him—scientists had already reached that conclusion—but he hadn't been prepared for how much lighter. He felt that if a stiff breeze came along it might just carry him off to Mars. But there was no breeze, not even the hint of one. He was not surprised, though slightly disappointed, to find the moon was not, in fact, made of cheese; some new variety of Swiss would have been the perfect souvenir to give Artemus. All he saw were rocks, so he snatched one up, and a second later found himself back in the Planetorium tent, a little dizzy but otherwise none the worse for wear.

"What's that?" Artemus asked, nodding toward what he was holding in his hand.

"For you," Magnus said with a grin. "A rock direct from the moon."

Artemus took it and raised it to his eyes, examining it closely. "Unremarkable," he said. "The least you might have done was bring me back a lunar diamond. You could have picked this up anywhere."

Magnus' smile dissolved into a frown. "But I didn't. And I didn't see any diamonds. I did, nevertheless, set foot on the surface of the moon. If you don't believe me, though, I'll move on to Mercury next." The magician discarded his goggles and stepped over to where the Solar Armor was hanging. "I took the liberty of borrowing this from your display of scientific marvels," he said. "It's said it worked so well that the inventor froze to death in the middle of Death Valley."

"I'm well aware of that," Artemus said, scowling. "I'm the one who procured it."

Magnus nodded. "Quite true."

"And I do not appreciate you 'borrowing' it, as you put it, without asking my permission."

Magnus nodded. "Noted," he said through pursed lips. "But I believe you will be pleased with the results."

"Protocols," Artemus muttered, then raised his voice: "Proceed."

Magnus stepped forward into the circle, held his breath, and Artemus waited...

Ten seconds later, Magnus reappeared, lying prone on his back. The solar armor, which had been saturated with water before his departure, wasn't just dry, it lacked even the slightest hint of moisture.

"Take it off! Take it off!" Magnus wailed weakly.

Artemus rushed to his side, bending over and tentatively extending a hand to touch the armor. He immediately withdrew it when it scalded his fingertips, leaving painful blisters. "What the...?! Hold tight." The absurdity of that request rang in his own ears. The man was in sheer misery; possibly dying. But there was no other option. "I'll be right back."

Artemus returned a moment later with a medical kit and, donning a pair of gloves, began using a pair of forceps to gingerly pull at the armor's thick material. But the material had adhered to the magician's skin, and each gentle tug produced a scream of agony. Finally, unable to make any progress, he decided to use an old trick his father had taught him as what he called an "object lesson." He'd slapped a section of adhesive tape on Artemus' short-cropped hair and ordered him to remove it. Artemus remembered that the effect of trying to peel it off carefully was only to prolong and amplify the pain.

"Tear it off in a single motion," his father had told him. "Then you'll be done with the pain."

The resulting pain had been exquisite but temporary. Artemus was no doctor, but perhaps, he thought, the same principle would apply here.

The material had cooled enough for him to take hold of an edge with his gloved hand, which he did... and yanked. Hard.

Magnus screamed an unholy scream, the likes of which Artemus had never heard, and began convulsing on the floor before passing out.

Artemus jumped back instinctively. A strip of Magnus' skin still clung to the material, torn away to reveal a bloody soup underneath. It looked like every bit of his body had started to boil from the inside, his organs charred and partially liquified. The rubber sack inside the suit, which had been placed there to hold a reserve of icy water, was not only empty but fused to his ribs.

Artemus had visited Death Valley explicitly to test the solar armor and ensure its authenticity. Only a moment after donning it, he had begun to feel numb from the cold and had hastily removed it. The temperature that day had registered 114 degrees; the solar armor, perfectly insulated and equipped with a series of tubes, reservoirs, and sponges to hold more than a gallon of ice-cold water, had seemed a rousing success.

Had it malfunctioned? If not, the surface of Mercury must have been ten times as hot as the hottest place on Earth to produce such a gruesome result. The tubes were all melted and the sponge bone dry.

Artemus recoiled in horror as he noticed the magician had stopped breathing.

Davey was bored. Tripoli had left him behind to do her show, and none of the workers had either the time or inclination to entertain his active mind. He hadn't seen Magnus—the one person beside Tripoli who ever gave him a second thought—in the past two days. The magician had promised he'd let Davey help him work on his knife-throwing performance, The Twisted Blade. The

first part of the performance was the standard act: His assistant would stand with her back against a board and he'd throw the knives so they formed an outline pattern around her, coming within inches of her body. The "twisted" part came when she stepped out away from the board and he used magic to throw the knives at her. They would pass directly through her body and embed themselves in the board behind her.

Tripoli had volunteered to serve as his target, but had been called upon to do an extra stint at the peep show when one of the other girls had quit abruptly.

So Davey had gone by himself, but Magnus hadn't been there. He started asking around, only to be met several times with the usual "scram" or "don't bother me, kid." This was odd: He hadn't seen the magician in a couple of days, and it wasn't like him to just not show up. He knew Magnus had been hard at work on a new attraction called the Darke Skies Planetorium—the banner fluttered in the slight breeze over a newly erected tent. Maybe that's where he was.

Davey made his way over to the tent, which had been roped off and affixed with signs that read. "Danger. No admission. Attraction off limits."

As with any curious boy, such a prohibition only fed his curiosity. What hidden wonders might lie beyond those ropes? The exhibit had probably been roped off because it wasn't ready yet, which meant Magnus was almost certainly inside applying the finishing touches.

Davey's feet stirred up dust as he ran over toward the tent, eager to see what was inside. Tripoli had just finished her shift and was making her way back up the midway when she saw him moving toward the entrance of the tent.

"Davey!" she called, but he didn't hear her, and she quickened her pace. "Davey!"

He heard her and stopped just long enough to sign to her, "I'm just going in here to find Magnus, Mom."

Her breath caught in her throat. He'd never called her that before.

He seemed so carefree... but her chest tightened and her throat constricted, warning her that something was wrong. She had no idea what, but it was a feeling: the same feeling she'd had when Davey's father had tried to attack her. Her trot became a full-out run, propelling her forward until she reached the cordon and, ducking under it, rushed to the tent.

Tripoli threw back the tent flap and entered.

But Davey wasn't there.

It had only been a matter of seconds since he'd disappeared inside—not time enough for him to reach the exit at the other end.

Could he be hiding?

No. The tent was empty except for wooden bleachers and some circles painted in a line down the center of the floor. She scanned the bleachers quickly; the open slats between the levels affording no place to hide. She started across the floor when she saw a blur of something, or someone, materializing on the largest circle.

It was Davey... or what was left of him. His body looked like it had been crushed in a giant vise, bones crumpled in as though they'd imploded. What was left of his blue-gray skin gave off a faint glow where it wasn't covered with blisters, and his eyeballs had been forced out of his skull before bursting as they hung from his optic nerves.

He was not breathing—could not breathe; his crushed lungs would not allow for it. Blood had pooled at the center of his shirt, having collected there when his heart burst.

Tripoli thought her own heart would burst when she saw him. What, or who, could have possibly done this to him?

"Davey! Oh my Davey!"

She sprinted toward him and finally reached him, throwing herself to the floor beside him.

In the circle.

Tripoli gasped as the suffocating weight of Jupiter's atmosphere took hold of her and squeezed, pushing her down and forcing radioactive hydrogen, helium, and ammonia deep into her lungs even as it closed them up. The planet invaded her, trying to force its entire gigantic mass down her throat, then crushed her from the outside. She wanted to vomit but was thwarted; tried to scream but couldn't. The single glimpse she caught of her new surroundings, with their colorful, swirling gases, reminded her of what hell must be like.

Then she passed out, never to awaken.

Artemus found her broken body, shattered and motionless, slumped across Davey's.

"A lot of good those signs did," he snorted. "When are people going to learn to read?"

STEPHEN H. and SHARON MARIE PROVOST

Three-Ring Pandemonium

Human beings, it's been said, are but civilized
animals. We've learned to set aside our baser instincts
and rise above the constraints that bound our Ice Age
ancestors to their barbarous ways. But does that mean we
are fit to rule the "lesser" beasts of Planet Earth? Did God
really give us dominion over all the animals, that we could
serve as their masters? Or was that story just an excuse
for us to make them beasts of burden to do our bidding—
or quadrupedal jesters to entertain us in a three-ring
circus? I considered them the latter, and became

determined, as was my wont, to exploit their talents as a means of boosting my profits. Yet far from being soulless puppets, these animals are creatures with minds of their own... and a tendency to become recalcitrant when pushed beyond their limits. This is a lesson I was to learn the hard way on a particularly bloody Saturday at... Carnivale Darke.

—Artemus Darke

1910

Artemus was a quiet, stoic man by nature, unless provoked to anger. But for the past week, Adoline had noticed an unusual pep to his step. He clearly had something in the works.

But what?

Artemus was getting ready to depart for a "meeting" as the train neared its stop in Pennsylvania in the early morning hours Thursday. As vice president of operations, Adoline was certainly qualified to oversee the carnival set-up, but Artemus, as per his custom, felt compelled to be on hand.

As the train squealed to a stop, Artemus jumped up and grabbed his satchel. "Make sure the carnival is up and running no later than 2 p.m. We're already getting a late start with the train running late."

"Of course. Where are you going in such a hurry, Artemus?" Adoline asked, falling into step behind him.

"I have some important business to attend to."

"Oh. What's that?"

"You'll find out in due course. I have big plans for the future of Carnivale Darke. If all goes to plan, we'll be here all week or at least through the weekend. I'll be back late tonight so let everyone know."

Artemus rushed across the platform and met a man waiting for him by a wagon.

Adoline's curiosity fell by the wayside in the rush to unload the trains and erect the tents. Once the set-up was completed, everyone lined up and began the parade through town. To the strains of the calliope riding on a wagon pulled by two gigantic black Belgian horses, Jean the Giant carried Tom Thumb and led the procession back to the gates, where Adoline waited to sell tickets. Blippo the Clown and "Sheriff" Cal, the trainer of the Poodle Posse, waited at the gates to stop the excited, giggling children from following the performers in without purchasing tickets.

The crowd streamed into the carnival nonstop until just after 6. Adoline had Mary take over the booth while she checked on the rest of the operations and sent one of the roustabouts to chase off a geek show that had tried to set up a short distance away. Adoline went to the cookhouse and sat down to eat, pleased with how well the show was running.

When the carnival finally shut down at 10, Adoline did a final walkthrough to make sure there were no stragglers trying to hide out. As she headed back to her tent to settle in for the night, she was surprised to hear Artemus' animated voice calling out to her.

"Adoline! Adoline! You must come to my tent, dear sister. I have so much to tell you." With Artemus' long strides, he had nearly reached his tent by the time she turned. He was carrying something covered in cloth.

"I'm tired, Artemus. Can't this wait until the morning?" she called out.

"Afraid not. There's much to do tomorrow."

"Fine." Adoline sighed and trudged over to his tent.

When her hand touched the canvas flap, his booming voice called out, "The Show to End All Shows is even grander."

Adoline entered to find a small organ-grinder monkey sitting on his lap, eating a banana. She pressed her hand to her mouth to stifle her giggle, not wanting to scare the poor little guy any more than Artemus had with his yelling. With a tiny screech, the little monkey jumped onto her shoulder and started running his little fingers through her hair.

"Sorry, little one, no bugs here." Adoline looked up at Artemus. "Kinda skinny little guy. Is this what all the excitement was about?"

"Not nearly. He's just the beginning. The rest will arrive tomorrow, so I'll need you ready before sunup. You'll be running the carnival while I make arrangements for our new menagerie."

"So why are you keeping me up now? Don't I need some sleep at some point?"

"There's no time for sleep. Sleep is for the shiftless. Our family didn't rise to our position through indolence."

"Wait... go back a moment. Did you use the word menagerie?"

Artemus clapped his hands together and broke out into a wide grin. "Why yes! I think that's what you'd call a *circus*, with all the attendant animals and performers." Artemus paced, stroking his chin and appearing deep in thought. "Am I right?"

"Nooo! Really? Please don't be teasing me. You know I've been dying for us to have more animals than just the poodles and the small petting zoo. I've missed the chimpanzees we lost back in '96. I feared you'd never bring in any more animal acts."

"I just had to wait for the right time."

Adoline danced in place, giggling wildly. She spun around to face him, "A real circus with a big top and three rings?"

"That's customary for a circus. Is it not?"

"But how? Where?"

"I've been searching for some time. You know I'm always seeking ways to expand Carnivale Darke. Onward and upward, as they say. I heard that the Flamel Circus was on the skids and seeking a buyer before the bank took over."

"So you bought it all?"

"Of course. Now understand, they've been through some hard times as of late, so it's a bit rough around the edges."

"Oh yes, I'm sure, but we can fix it. If anyone can make it successful, it's you, Artemus."

"Now go get some rest, Adoline. See you at 5 when the first wagons arrive. Tomorrow a carnival, on Saturday, a circus!"

Adoline couldn't sleep that night. She rose early and found Artemus already outside with some of the roustabouts preparing for the animals' arrival. They had already roped off an area in the back of the lot to set up the big top and house the animals and new performers.

A short time later, the wagons began pulling up and unloading. Adoline was delighted to see six elephants, a team of eight beautiful roan Percheron horses; a large Russian brown bear; a male and two female lions; four tigers; and other animals. She wasn't as thrilled to see a handler carrying large snakes around his neck. She hadn't expected that, but as long as she didn't have to deal with them, it was no concern of hers.

As the time to open the carnival drew near, she was pulled away from her duties inventorying their new acquisitions. She knew she'd become familiar with all the new faces in the coming days as she added them to the payroll—a contortionist; an acrobatic and aerialist troupe eight strong; fourteen clowns; trick riders; a tightrope walker; fire jugglers; and the animal handlers. Her main concern was the appearance of the animals—many were emaciated, seemed weak, and had a poor disposition.

As the day progressed, Adoline noticed a wooden platform, probably 40 feet tall, was being built next to the pool on the far side of the fairgrounds. She didn't remember hearing about divers joining them. She made a note to ask Artemus about it later.

Late that afternoon, Artemus came to find her at the ticket booth. "I have a surprise for you. We'll have our first new act debuting this evening near sunset. Spread the word for people to come to the pool at 7. We'll have seating set up by then."

"Do we have a high diver?"

"Not exactly. You'll see."

Adoline shaded her eyes to look up at the tall white platform. "I was going to ask you about that. I have another concern, though. The animals look pretty thin and stressed. I know you said they'd been through a lot. I'm not sure we're ready to put on the circus tomorrow, or at least not with the animal acts."

"Poppycock! I didn't invest all that money just to watch it go to waste. These animals were performing for Flamel, and they shall continue to do so for me. You're anthropomorphizing them, Adoline. I'll not tolerate that. We have enough temperamental humans to worry about without adding to it."

Adoline scowled at him. "I'm not trying to be difficult, Artemus. It's a matter of safety for the handlers, us, our audience, and the animals themselves. Some animals are very sensitive to stress and could become ill or die. What about your investment then? Have you asked the handlers... they'd know best?"

"I shall not ask my employees now or *ever* about how to run my carnival. Am I not the owner and president of Carnivale Darke? This conversation is finished." Artemus harrumphed as he pulled down his long velvet, deep burgundy tailcoat and stalked off toward his new circus.

Just after 6 p.m., Artemus led Adoline back to the pool, where a large, red-and-yellow banner had been hung from the 40-foot platform that read "Doc Carver's Diving Horse Act" in large letters over another line of slightly smaller type: "Featuring Luna Red and the equine marvel, Pussyfoot."

"What do you think?" Artemus asked, beaming with pride.

Adoline fixed him with a skeptical gaze. "How deep is that pool?"

Artemus shrugged. "I think Doc said it needed to be 12 feet, so I guess that's what it is."

"Twelve feet!?" Adoline burst out. "You mean to say you are asking a thousand-pound animal to dive 40 feet into... that?" She pointed accusingly at the pool. "You'll kill the poor animal. And... and... where do you get off making Luna Red perform this ludicrous stunt of yours. She's our second-biggest draw in the coochie tent. She doesn't know a thing about... whatever *this* is."

"Horse diving. And she'll learn by doing it."

Adoline's face grew red as she crossed her arms tightly in front of her, but Artemus just burst out laughing.

"Do you really think I'd ask someone with zero experience to perform a stunt like this?" he crowed. "Luna *grew up* with horses in Wyoming. She even worked in Doc Carver's show before she joined us. You of all people should be aware of how thorough my background checks are."

Adoline relaxed her arms but kept them crossed. "I still don't like it," she said. "Did you even ask if this Doc Carver character is a real doctor? And where is he? I'd like to speak with him."

"He's a dentist. Or was. Like Doc Holliday. But no one's saying his experience as a dentist has anything to do with this act. He runs a Wild West Show. It's all on the up-and-up. But he's not here. I bought the rights to use his name on that sign." Artemus pointed to the ballycloth. "He's signed off on it, and Pussyfoot is one of his trained horses."

"So she's not from Flamel?"

"No, I made a separate agreement with Doc. I thought one of his diving horses would fit in perfectly with the other new animal acts."

"Just how long have you been planning this?"

Artemus looked away, then back at her. "It was *meant* to be a surprise."

Adoline just grunted. She still didn't like being kept in the dark, and she hadn't been convinced by Artemus' reassurances, but she knew there was no stopping him once he'd set his mind to something.

Adoline was standing at the foot of the diving tower when Luna Red ran up and threw her arms around her neck.

"Isn't it exciting?" she enthused. "Look at my new outfit!"

She wore a skin-tight wetsuit colored red and blue, with white stripes on each side and a painted leather helmet on her head with a strap under the neck.

"That won't protect you if you hit your head on the bottom." Adoline pointed to the helmet. "Or if the horse rolls on top of you, or..."

"Please, stop worrying, Addy." Adoline only let a few of the staff call her that, she'd taken a liking to Luna the first time she'd stepped through the gates—a connection that made her even more worried than she already would have been.

Luna, a petite girl a few inches shorter than Adoline, reached up and put both hands on the older woman's shoulders. "I've done it before, and it's perfectly safe. Besides, nothing can be worse than working the coochie booths."

Adoline couldn't argue with that, and felt a pang of guilt. Luna had been willing to do whatever job she was assigned ever since she joined the carnival. She'd never had any outstanding talent, so she'd started out taking tickets, picking up trash, and washing dishes. But she was attractive enough, so Adoline had assigned her to the coochie booths, knowing she'd make more money there. She hadn't known she was a skilled equestrian, but they hadn't *had* any horses until now, except for draft horses.

Before she could say anything, Artemus walked up and patted Luna on the back. "So, are we ready for a grand adventure?" he said.

Adoline glared at him. She hated when he used the word "we" when he really meant "you." Artemus wouldn't be riding a horse off a 40-foot-high platform into a pool of water.

"Yes, sir!" Luna beamed, saluting.

Just then, there was a drumroll, and everyone in the stands fell still. Then a talker bellowed his introduction through a megaphone: "Ladies and gentlemen, boys and girls, for the first time ever in Wilkes-Barre, P.A., Carnivale Darke is proud to present Doc Carver's fabulous horse-diving extravaganza!"

Loud whoops and applause rose from the temporary stands, which were packed to overflowing.

"That's my cue!" Luna said. "Wish me luck!"

"Bon voyage, fair maiden!" Artemus said, and Adoline just shook her head before giving Luna a brief hug and wishing her well.

"Must you be so *dramatic* in everything?" Adoline asked.

Artemus chuckled. "That's why I'm the face of Carnivale Darke, and you aren't," he said, then added hastily when she bristled at his words: "although your fair face is *almost* as pretty as mine."

Luna hurried up the steps to the platform, where she smiled and waved upon appearing and took a bow for the audience.

"See?" Artemus needled Adoline. "She's a natural. She's got this down to an art form."

A moment later, the door to a portable livestock stall at the foot of the scaffolding opened and Pussyfoot emerged. A handler led her to the tilt chute, and she walked up on her own without any prodding. When she reached the top, Luna waved again to more applause and mounted the filly cleanly.

The horse stepped to the edge of the platform and balked.

Luna shouted. "Onward ho!" But Pussyfoot just pawed at the air with one hoof, then took a step backward.

The audience gasped as the scaffolding beneath the platform seemed to shudder for a moment, then settled.

Luna reached around and gently stroked the side of Pussyfoot's face, eliciting a soft nicker. "It's OK, girl," she said. "We've both done this before. There's nothing to be scared of."

The filly gave a gentle toss of her head, as if she understood, and stepped once more to the edge of the platform. A moment later, she rocked back on her haunches and leaped forward into the empty air, extending her legs forward as Luna leaned over her neck like a jockey.

The crowd shot to its feet as the horse hit the water and disappeared, along with Luna, beneath the surface. The spectators didn't even have time to hold their collective breath, though, before Pussyfoot emerged at the other end of the pool and ambled nonchalantly up a ramp that had been positioned there. Luna turned to face the crowd and waved excitedly, then dismounted and took a bow.

Pussyfoot bowed her head alongside her, as she'd been trained to do, and the audience erupted in cheers and applause.

Artemus and Adoline hurried around the pool to greet them, with Artemus grabbing the megaphone from the talker and shouting, "Ladies and gentlemen, Pussyfoot and Luna!"

Adoline clapped him on the shoulder. "I have to admit, that was one hell of a show," she said. "And they both look just fine."

Artemus turned to her with a self-satisfied I-told-you-so grin. "See?" he said. "You had nothing to worry about.

When the rest of the acts debut tomorrow, you'll see: Artemus Darke has thought of everything."

The next morning dawned bright and early. The roustabouts had worked overnight setting up the big top. A crew had gone through the town, plastering posters on every inch of free space touting the circus was in town, with the big show at 8.

Artemus had mounted an expansive line of ballycloth advertising the new animal acts along the long dirt road leading to the fairgrounds. Lines of red-and-white-striped pennant banners stretched from the sideshow tent over to the big top.

The bally stage for the sideshow was positioned at the end of the path to the big top, far from the carnival exit. After the circus performance ended, the bally stage would be pulled out to narrow the path of exodus—which would be further tightened by sending out a few of the freaks to put on a teaser show to attract the lot lice. They could always be counted on to block the path of those trying to leave. With any luck, those that hadn't already seen the sideshow would be funneled right in.

Artemus had thought of everything to maximize his profits that day. Or at least he thought he had.

Artemus decided to hold the parade through town once more—this time with the line of elephants leading the way, single file, with each elephant's trunk holding the tail of the one ahead of it. It all started normally enough... until the children streamed into the street, screaming and jumping at the giant bull elephant in front.

The bull trumpeted and pulled his ears back, stopping all the other elephants in their tracks.

The blond toddler in curly pigtails squealed in delight

—and then terror when the bull picked her up with his trunk and slung her into the dirt 5 feet away. Her terrified mother ran to pick up her daughter, but that was just the beginning. Spooked by the lead elephant, the others began stampeding down the road, trampling a pair of wagons along the way.

Splinters of wood from the wreckage stabbed upward into the bull's foot, and it rose up on its hind legs, screaming in pain. The handler rushed forward to calm it, and with some effort managed to get the animal under control. The other elephants, still spooked, finally settled down a little when they saw that the handler had everything in hand. He led them hastily back to the fairgrounds and locked them up.

The carnival's doctor had been riding in a wagon along with Artemus, Adoline, and Ozymandias—the magician who'd replaced Magnus—who was standing up pulling flowers and long strings of colored handkerchiefs from his pockets. Artemus stopped the wagon and sent the doctor to tend to the child's minor wounds: a few bruises and some scraped knees.

The townspeople, initially scared, calmed down quickly and laughed off the mishap. Artemus distracted them by handing out wads of cash, and it was hard to hold a grudge when this was the most activity the town had seen for years.

Adoline, however, was not so easily calmed. "Artemus, I told you something like this might happen. Now, will you listen to me? We could still have the equestrian acts and some of the others."

"We'll have all of them. Discussion over," Artemus snapped, and turned on his heel, walking briskly toward the big top.

Despite the earlier fracas in town, the ticket-takers greeted a never-ending flood of people all day. Even those who had been to the carnival at the start of the engagement returned to see the circus that night.

At 7:30, when the seating began for the circus, the crowds streamed from the rides, sideshow, and other acts and filled the tent to capacity. By the time Big Bertha, the matriarch elephant of the herd, led the procession into the big top with her handler, Susie, atop her head, it was standing-room-only.

Adults and children alike oohed and aahed as the trapeze act, aerial silks, and the tightrope walker performed above their heads. The clowns then skipped and stumbled in for a bit of comic relief after the tension of the high-flying show.

Everyone knew the next act would be thrilling when they saw the fire jugglers enter the big top from the back in both directions, filling the middle ring, before being joined by a contortionist and hand-balancing act in the left ring. While the crowd was captivated, a circle of netting was set up to enclose the third ring, to the right, and platforms were set in place for the big cats. The acts concluded dramatically, with a fire juggler balanced precariously on the backs of two hand balancers, deftly tossing and retrieving both torches and knives until, all at once, the lights went out.

A few cries of alarm echoed through the big top—followed by screams of delight when a spotlight came on, illuminating the enclosed right ring, where two female lions and four tigers were arranged in a pyramid. The king of the jungle stood in front, roaring at the crowd, as crimson-suited handlers stood by, holding whips.

With a crack of his cowhide, the lead handler cued the big cats to jump down and run over to their platforms.

As the big cats settled, the rest of the lights came on, and the Russian bear entered the left ring, riding a unicycle clockwise as a scantily clad beauty on another unicycle rode alongside, whip in hand, along the inner edge of the circle. Their entrance was quickly followed by the eight magnificent Percheron horses prancing counterclockwise around the center wing, each adorned in long white ostrich plumes attached to a golden bridle. Another flaxen-haired beauty rode one of the lead horses,

performing tricks as they rode around the ring in formation.

The male lion, situated closest to the horses, became agitated, swiping at them as they rode past. But the handler cracked his whip on the lion's back to redirect his attention. Everything was under control.

The other handler sent the three male tigers to platforms placed right next to each other near the front of the ring. Then the other man sent the female tiger to a platform set up perpendicular to the others. With a quick cue in French and a crack of the whip, the female stepped onto the back of the first tiger and began to walk across the trio.

At that moment, however, the horses once again distracted the male lion, who struck out at the netting that separated them. One of the horses startled and whinnied, as the other lion handler walked over to reprimand the big cat. But the sudden movement and sounds of distress from the horse alarmed the Russian bear, who was about to come face-to-face with the horses in the adjacent ring that had changed their pace as they rode in the opposite direction. The bear launched off the unicycle and toward the girl as it lunged for the throat of the lead, unmounted horse.

The bear fell short of its target, though, and landed on the girl, long claws slicing deep into her throat and chest. Blood gushed from the gaping edges of the wound. She wrapped a hand around her throat but couldn't stem the flow of blood from her severed carotid, which flew out wildly and sprayed a line of children in the front row. Futile, whistling gasps for air filled the audience's ears as her punctured windpipe flapped uselessly.

The bear, meanwhile, vaulted off the girl and slammed against the shoulder of the horse on its next pass around the ring, sending it hurtling into the side of the other lead horse, carrying the trick rider, before crashing to the ground. The rider was thrown, and her legs quickly trampled by the other horses as they galloped out of the ring and fled the tent en masse.

Blood trickled from her shins where shattered bits of tibia and fibula protruded from jagged tears in her skin.

One of the clowns ran into the fray and dragged her out of the ring.

The injured horse struggled to rise.

The bear reared up, swiping out with one razor-clad paw and ripped the horse's throat out.

Circusgoers in the front rushed forward and tried to flee across the dirt floor, only to slide and fall in large pools of blood. The gory mess only added to their panic, they rose and ran faster toward the exits, trying frantically—and in vain—to brush the bloodstains from their clothes as they went.

The large cats, riled up by the frenzy of activity, began to growl and snarl. The female tiger that had been traversing the backs of the others pounced from her temporary perch atop the second one and onto the chest of the handler waiting for her on the other side. She opened her mouth and latched onto his head, ripping his face off and swallowing it whole.

The male lion who had started it all jumped onto the

netting and ripped it from its tethers. The other handler backed off and fought to control the other big cats, while an assistant backstage retrieved a gun, if needed, to subdue the tiger and the rampaging lion.

The lion began to stalk a crying child, who started to back away slowly. When the little boy turned to run, the big cat rushed forward and caught him between his two powerful paws, slamming him to the ground. The child's father ran up to the lion and began to beat it on the back, trying to chase the animal away. The king of the jungle lived up to his well-earned title by whirling and disemboweling the man with one devastating slash of his paw. With an ear-shattering roar, he turned back to his meal, still pinned under his other paw.

By this time, the big top had been abandoned except for the circus handlers fighting to regain control of the rampaging animals. One of the bear's caretakers managed to lure him away from the fallen horse using honey and safely locked him away again.

The horse trainers had run out of the tent behind the herd but found devastation in their wake. The bottlenecked passageway leading away from the big top had increased the horses' anxiety, and as people rushed out of the tent, the animals thought they were under attack. Caught up in the mad rush, the horses reared up and kicked, breaking ribs and trampling anyone who got in their way.

The carnival doctor ran up to help a woman whose jaw had been broken and hung askew at a horrifying angle. A hoof to the face had split the corner of her mouth open.

As the field cleared, the horses gathered in the back corner, and their handlers finally rounded them up.

Eventually, the lion was subdued and returned to his cage along with the other big cats, but the carnage wasn't over.

The tiger, having grown tired of her first kill, turned on one of the clowns who'd been trying to distract her. She slashed out at him, leaving three deep gashes across his face and blinding him in one eye.

Then, suddenly, heads turned at the sound of hoofbeats approaching and the crowd parted to make way for Brandon Tirico, sheriff of Luzerne County. A tall man with broad shoulders, he wore typical civilian clothes except for a badge and what looked like a modified train conductor's cap. Two deputies rode in on either side of him, their mounts apparently unfazed by the chaos that lay just in front of them.

A boxy paddy wagon chugged up behind them, the driver cutting its engine with a clunk and a wheeze.

The tiger was taking all this in, and was not amused.

Typically a solitary creature, she was already agitated by all the commotion. And now, sensing a challenge to her territory, she turned away from the clown and dashed directly toward the three newcomers.

Still in his saddle, the sheriff drew his pistol and took quick aim, firing three shots at the onrushing whirlwind of orange and black fur. The second shot stopped the tiger in her tracks, and the third one put her down for good as the anxious onlookers milled around in the bottleneck, seeking an avenue of escape.

Tirico dismounted and pushed his way through the crowd, followed by the deputies.

"Who's in charge of this shit show?" he bellowed over the cries of pain and terror reverberating throughout the fairgrounds.

"I am." Artemus pushed his way to the front of the crowd and stood, his back straight, staring the sheriff straight in the eye. Adoline joined him a moment later.

"Sheriff, I..." she began before Artemus cut her off.

"I'll handle this," he said.

"You don't seem to be doing a very good job of 'handling' anything, from the look of it." Tirico directed a steely glare at the carnival owner, but Artemus didn't flinch.

"It's not as bad as it seems," he said dismissively.

"Oh, it isn't, is it?" The sheriff looked around him, then turned to one of his deputies, a man named LaFrance. "Get these people out of here!" he shouted. "I won't have people kept in harm's way. Who knows when one of these animals might break loose again."

"These animals are highly trained and have been returned to their cages, where they are quite secure," Artemus replied haughtily. "We take all the necessary precautions; this was merely a... freak accident, I assure you, *mon capitan*."

"It's sheriff," Tirico growled. "I ain't nobody's cap-i-tan, least of all yours. Now, I expect you to have this all cleaned up and be out of here by midnight."

"Sheriff, that's simply not possible. We made arrangements with the fair board to use the grounds until this coming Saturday. I have a signed contract."

"Show it to me."

Adoline, who'd come prepared, pulled out a piece of paper and handed it to the sheriff.

Without even looking at it, he held it up dramatically and tore it in two down the middle, letting the two halves fall to the ground.

"You don't have a contract with *me*, Mr. Darke, and I'm the law here. Tomorrow's Sunday, but I suppose you were counting on me to look the other way while you peddled your filthy 'amusements' on the Sabbath. We're god-fearing people here in Luzerne County, not depraved heathens like you and your lot. We have blue laws here. Strict ones."

"I assure you," Adoline put in, "we fully intended to go dark on Sunday."

Artemus leaned over and whispered in her ear. "Dark?" he said. "Love the wordplay."

She ignored him. He couldn't help but treat even the most disturbing incidents as trifling inconveniences—even when it wasn't in his best interest. Fortunately, the sheriff hadn't overheard.

"You won't just be 'dark' tomorrow," he said. "I've told you once already, I expect you to be gone by 12 a.m. I won't have you transgressing the Sabbath by conducting *any* activity on these grounds after midnight. Am I clear? In the meantime, I'm placing both of you under arrest for disturbing the peace, creating a public nuisance, and being accessories to assault and homicide. Just how many people have died here tonight?"

"Sheriff," Artemus said, "if I may have a word in private." Before the sheriff knew what was happening, Artemus reached forward with a hearty handshake, placing a $20 bill firmly in the man's palm.

Tirico looked around suspiciously, then nodded once and followed Artemus to his tent just as the coroner pulled up in a horse-drawn wagon.

"So, what happened?" Adoline whispered as Artemus

120

approached her while the sheriff walked over to rejoin his deputies.

"What always happens," he whispered with a smile. "I offered him a little something to look the other way and let us be on about our business. I agreed to pack up our things and leave, and he gave us till Monday to get everything together. 'Keeping the Sabbath holy' isn't so important when money's on the table."

Adoline glowered at him. "And?"

"Most importantly, his report will list all the deaths as accidental, and he won't be filing any charges. We'll have to see to our own injured, and, of course, he doesn't ever want us back here, but that's fine with me. This place is a hellhole. I trust you were in contact with the Lehigh County fair board prior to our arrival here, as I instructed."

Adoline nodded once curtly. "They wanted us in Allentown this year, but when I told them we were already booked here, they asked us to keep them in mind. I'm sure they'll be happy to have us there next year."

"Excellent!" Artemus said, sounding cheerful. "We just won't be able to do the diving horse act; my agreement with Doc runs out at the end of the year."

"Of course," Adoline snarked. "The one thing that actually worked."

Artemus gave her a wounded look but said nothing. He knew good and well that their problems here had been caused by his own impatience—even though, of course, he would never admit it.

"Just leave me alone," Adoline snapped. "I need to get everything in order for our departure, and I don't want you getting in the way."

Once the sheriff and coroner left and the wounded were sent to the hospital, Artemus went in search of Adoline. He knew she'd asked to be left alone, but it was unlike her to avoid him for so long: He hadn't seen her in hours.

Artemus finally found her in the cookhouse tent helping the doctor tend to the minor wounds of the carnies and making sure everyone ate. He took a step back at the look of reproach on her face. Obviously, she wasn't done being angry.

"I told you!" Adoline spat.

He held up his hands in surrender. "I know."

"I tried to prevent this. These are still wild animals. Never forget that."

Artemus' face grew red with barely controlled rage. "I'm aware, Adoline. That is why I pay others to do their job controlling these beasts."

Adoline stomped over to him, her hands balled into fists. "Don't you dare! Don't you dare blame any of these handlers *or* the animals. None of them should have ever been put in this position. You can't uproot them from their normal circumstances and expect them to act normally."

"They're used to the circus life. It's always a different town... a crowd of noisy people... nothing's ever the same."

"But this was different. Besides, I told you they were undernourished, stressed, and some of them were sick. They needed to be rehabilitated and allowed to settle in before we put them to work. We all know about the powerful and rich Artemus Darke. You've told us about it enough times. A few days or a week wouldn't have bankrupted you."

"That's enough. I will not have you speak to me this way!"

"I'll speak to you as I wish, or I'll leave this mess to you. Let you run this whole damn carnival yourself."

"You think you know so much, Adoline. It's yours... all yours. VP of Operations, you're now in charge of the animal acts. Find some new trainers who know how to handle wild animals properly. I expect you to have this issue solved in the next ten days. We pull up stakes tonight, and we'll stop outside Pittsburgh, where you can seek the veterinary care they need. Feed them and get them ready for performances, or so help me, I'll send them all to the glue factory along with that dead horse."

MIDWAY MADNESS

Games of chance and skill lie at the heart of midway madness. The shooting gallery, the Adder, the Claw, and Spill the Milk all await visitors to every county fair and traveling carnival. Hawkers stand ready to lure the uninitiated with pocket knives, straw hats, stuffed elephants, and more. The Show to End All Shows was no different in the early years, contracting with operators who ponied up a share of their take for the privilege of a spot on the midway. The only condition was that their attractions had to be on the level: no funny business. This is the story of what happened when one such operator dared to defy that rule and the madness that ensued... at Carnivale Darke.

—Artemus Darke

1918

"Who's in charge here?" The man with broad shoulders and short but curly black hair had already rolled up his sleeves. He meant business.

"Just hold it there, bucko," Jimmy Swanson said, grabbing the man's two arms from behind.

He shook free from the security chief with little trouble and whirled to face him.

"The penny-pitch joint is rigged!" he snapped. "I seen it. Some guy left the curtain open a little at the back of the thing, and I seen him rubbin' down the plates with sticks of butter. You say you run a clean show, but I ain't buyin' it. You're just like every other place, swindlin' honest folks out of their hard-earned dough."

"Now calm down," Jimmy said. "I'm sure that ain't what you seen, but we'll give you your money back for whatever you spent and your carnival admission too. How's that sound?"

"Sounds like you're tryin' to buy me off, that's what it sounds like. I wanna see someone in charge, not a goon like you."

"Wait right here, and I'll see about getting Adoline for you."

"I don't r'member sayin' I wanted to see no woman."

"Well, if you want to talk to someone in charge, then you best be willing to talk to her." Jimmy didn't wait for the man's response. He honestly didn't care if the man stuck around or not.

He found Adoline working the ticket booth as expected. "I've got a problem I need you to handle. Well, actually a couple'a them. There's a tough guy back there trying to cause trouble because he says the penny-pitch is rigged. I offered to give him his money back, including admission, but he don't wanna let it go."

"I'll take care of it." Adoline called over Ruby the clown, who'd been entertaining children as they entered the gate, to watch the booth. Then she turned back to Jimmy, "You go check out that carny's game. If he's not on the up-and-up, bring him right over to me."

As Adoline approached the midway, there was no doubt which man had been causing all the trouble. He was pacing back and forth, face beet-red, spouting off, "One-hundred percent authentic, my ass! These dirty carnies are just takin' our dough."

"Excuse me, sir. My name's..."

"I don't care what yer name is. I asked for someone in charge."

"Then I suggest that you *do care* that I am Adoline *Darke*, vice president of operations. Jimmy told me about your experience at the penny-pitch. I assure you that we're investigating the matter right now."

"Investigatin'? You mean pretendin' to close the game down until I walk away. Not good enough."

As Adoline opened her mouth to respond, she saw Jimmy approaching with Vinny, the penny-pitch operator, in tow. "Thank you, Jimmy. What did you find?"

Jimmy nodded his head at the seething man. "He was right. The plates were all slicked down. I found a stick of butter underneath the counter."

"See. I told you. Now what are ya...?"

Adoline turned away from the man's blustering and cut him off. "I trust you shut down the booth?"

"Yes, ma'am."

"Please escort Vinny to the gate. He's no longer welcome here at Carnivale Darke."

"Hey, whaddya mean? You can't do that. I wanna to speak to Artemus. And what about my cut?" Heads turned on the midway as Vinny's voice rose.

"Your cut of the swindled money? I hardly think you're entitled to that. If you care to pursue it though, I would be happy to bring in the authorities to discuss your crime and what cut is fair." Adoline pursed her lips and waited for a response. "Hmmmm?"

Vinny looked down at his feet, silent.

"That's what I thought. Thank you, Jimmy, for seeing to this matter. When you return, please take down the penny-pitch booth until we find another *honest* employee." Adoline turned her gaze back on the angry customer, who'd gone silent during that exchange. "So, Mr...?"

"Arnold."

"Mr. Arnold, as Jimmy said previously, we will be refunding you for your admission today and whatever you put out playing that game. I'd also like to offer you lifetime admission to our carnival, here or anywhere else you may encounter us. I trust your satisfied with that resolution."

Mr. Arnold stood there dumbstruck. He wasn't used to such a confident, powerful woman. When he didn't immediately respond, Adoline said, "Okay, then," and spun on her heel, returning to the ticket booth.

Vinny boarded the next train out of Boston and returned to his employer. When he entered the tent, Harold Zimmerman looked up, surprised to see him. A young boy, who couldn't have been more than 5 or 6, was solving math problems on a slate beside Harold. The boy must have been part of the freak show: Large veins throbbed visibly across his oversized and misshapen head.

"What are you doing here, Mr. Aberdeen? I thought I sent you to destroy Artemus Darke's reputation."

"Yeah, about that, there was a bit of a mishap."

"Mishap?"

"A mark caught me slicking down the plates, and he complained."

"What happened? Were the cops brought in to investigate Artemus' carnival for grifting?"

"Not exactly. Artemus' sister shut me down right on the spot, threatened to sic the police on me, in fact. She's such a bitch. That woman doesn't know her place."

"At least *she* was doing her job. That's more than I can say for you. You assured me you were a professional, but you got yourself caught in your first week there. Sloppy work, Vinny. Here's your pay. Now get out of here!"

Vinny grabbed the purse Harold had tossed on the ground and stalked out.

"I had expected more for my trouble. No matter! I know better than to put all my eggs in one basket. I've sent others to infiltrate Carnivale Darke. It's only a matter of time."

A swarming sea of bodies, most of them dressed in coats and fedoras, churned outside Newspaper Row, their necks craned and their eyes fixed on the scoreboard over the entrance to the *Boston Globe*.

A group of teenage boys rushed into the midst of the morass, looking at the same thing all the businessmen were focused on. School had just let out, and this was

Game 5 of the Series. They wanted to catch as much of it as they could.

"Hey, kid, watch it!" A forty-something man in a pinstripe jacket spun around toward the kid who'd nearly knocked him off his feet. But he wasn't just a kid: At 6 feet, 2 inches, the broad-shouldered teen stood half a head above the older man. He was probably the biggest person there.

The businessman's eyes narrowed, but the kid turned up his lip in a sneer. He glared right back through ice-blue eyes and tugged at the brim of his Red Sox cap.

"Who d'you think you are, punk?" the man demanded, balling his fists together.

"Zeb Douglass, that's who," the kid spat.

"That's right, mister." One of the other boys with him, Marcus Dempsey, stepped up. "He's gonna be the next Babe Ruth!"

The man threw back his head and laughed. "Sure, kid. Sure. An' I'll be the next Walter Johnson!"

"Are you even a Sox fan?" The higher-pitched voice came from a dark-haired, 5-foot-tall girl in ponytails who'd appeared as if from nowhere at Zeb's side.

"That ain't none of your affair, Missy."

"And that ain't my name, Mister Smartypants. But since you ain't gonna answer my question, I gotta assume you like the Yankees."

"Yeah," Marcus chimed in. "Look at them pinstripes."

"Now, listen here..."

"Just here to stir up trouble," Zeb said.

"Right," said the girl. "Which is why he weren't familiar that the Bambino ain't just a great pitcher..."

"The best!" Marcus said.

"The best," the girl agreed. "But he also hit more home runs this year than anyone else in baseball... except Tillie Walker had 11 too, but it took 'im a hundred more tries!"

The man started to turn away, but before he could get that far, the girl kicked him in the shin. "Now," she said, "as I was sayin', Zebulon Douglass here is gonna be the next Bambino. I seen him playin' out on the sandlot, and he could clear the Green Monster in Fenway today if the Sox put him at the plate."

The man tried to kick her back, but Zeb hit him with a right cross that laid him out on the pavement.

Nobody noticed. A man wearing red suspenders and holding a megaphone had just stepped up onto a temporary podium and shouted: "UPI reports two runs cross the plate for Chicago on hits by Hollocher and Mann. Ruth's record streak of scoreless innings in the World Series comes to an end just one out shy of 30 innings. Score through 7½ innings of Game 4: Your Boston Red Sox 2, Chicago Nationals 2. Douglas moves to the mound for Chicago."

A collective groan arose from the crowd as a man with

a long pole had just raised the number "2" to the eighth box to the blank spot for the top of the eighth inning above the entrance to the *Boston Globe*. Another "2" was raised to replace the zero in the Chicago TOTAL box.

"So much for your precious Bambino," the man in the pinstripe coat muttered as he got to his feet, rubbing his chin and examining the tear in his slacks.

Zeb spat in his direction and turned away, just as a woman walked up to Mister Smartypants and whispered in his ear. "Don't worry," she said. "Your time will come."

It would not, however, come on that particular day. Just a few minutes later, the red-suspendered man ascended the podium again. The crowd fell silent as he put the megaphone to his lips: "UPI reports: Schang leadoff single, to second on Killefer passed ball." He paused a moment, then his voice began to rise in excitement: "Schang lays down a bunt. Douglas fields the ball in front of the plate. Throws to first. It's wild! Schang around third! Racing home! He beats the throw! Red Sox 3! Cubs 2!"

Hats flew up into the air, including Zeb's cap, which came down near the man he'd cold-cocked a few minutes earlier. The man flung it away in disgust, and Zeb went to retrieve it.

The crowd settled down into a nervous silence, waiting for the final update. The Sox just had to make it through the top of the ninth, and they'd be up 3 games to 1, on the verge of giving Beantown its fifth world championship in seven years.

The man with the megaphone didn't disappoint: Ruth surrendered a single and a base on balls to start the ninth, but Bullet Joe Bush came in to close out the Cubbies on a sacrifice and a game-ending double play.

More hats were thrown, and the pigtailed girl leapt into Zeb's arms, planting a steamy kiss full on his mouth as he was still whoopin' and hollerin'. Startled, he almost dropped her, but she pulled back and smiled the biggest smile he'd ever seen. "Pleased to meet you," she said. "I'm Lucy McCrae. What do you say we go to the carnival tonight?"

Zeb hadn't known what to say. Lucy was small, but that kiss had been hotter than hell... and she was cute as could be with those pigtails and freckles. Zeb had them too, and kids had always made fun of him for them until he started growing—and kicking the tar out of anyone who dared to mess with him.

He felt a kind of kinship with her. It had counted for a lot that she knew who he was, and stuck up for him with Mister Smartypants. Zeb could fight his own battles, but it was nice to have someone else back him up for a change. Marcus was just a tagalong. He used to be one of the kids who teased Zeb—before he realized he was better off cozying up to him. Lucy seemed to really like him. He'd never seen her at school before, and it turned out she'd dropped out during her senior year. That was three years back, which meant she was actually 21, even though she looked like sweet sixteen.

Zeb didn't mind. Her being older meant she knew how to kiss like Theda Bara in *A Fool There Was*. She also had ways to get booze, even though the Temperance League was lobbying for a national ban. But moonshine would always be available, and her uncle had a still hidden out in the woods by Cabin Creek. She promised to bring a couple of jars if he would help her smuggle them into the carnival, and that was the clincher. It was a date.

She even paid for the tickets.

"Step right up and try your luck against Hurricane Hannigan!" the talker called out. "Win a prize for your girlie if he doesn't strike you out on three pitches, and a gen-u-wine Louisville Slugger signed by the Babe himself if ya hit it past him. Just a dime for three pitches! Step right up!"

"Well, would you look at that?" said Marcus, who had somehow heard about their date and managed to get a ticket on his own. He was like a pesky flea from the flea circus. He'd latched onto Zeb, and the Sandlot Sensation just couldn't seem to shake him off. "You gonna try to win a dolly for Lucy?"

Zeb bristled. "I ain't gonna *try* to win no doll," he scoffed. "I'm *gonna* win that bat!"

Marcus stifled a laugh. "Zeb, that ain't no chump out there. Didn't ya hear? That's Hurricane Harrigan? He goes around the country pitching blindfolded, and the only guy ever to lay wood on him was the Bambino himself. A foul ball!"

"Well," Lucy teased, wrapping her arm tight around Zeb's. "If the Babe can connect, you can too, right? I want that dolly over there." She pointed to a Raggedy Ann dolly suspended near the entrance to the attraction. "I think I'll call her Annie-Belle!"

Zeb glared at her. "I'll win you a prize at another booth," he said. "I got my eye on that Louisville Slugger, and I'm gonna have her!"

A smile crept across Lucy's face beneath her nearly black eyes. "Go do it!" she said. "I have faith in you, Babe."

He couldn't tell whether she meant that affectionately or was expressing her faith in him—that he could do something George Herman Ruth could do, maybe better.

"Gimme that bat!" he said, slapping a dime down on the wooden board by the entrance.

"I'll give you six balls for a quarter," the jointee offered, but Zeb shook his head. "I only need one."

"Do your worst," the jointee chuckled as he lifted a wooden board across the front and ushered Zeb inside. Lucy and Marcus stepped up to the counter and leaned in, watching as Zeb spit on his hands and took a firm grip on the bat handle. It wasn't a Louisville Slugger; just a run-of-the-mill sandlot bat. *All the better*, he said to himself. It was just like the one back home.

He stepped up to the plate, which looked just like home plate at Fenway, and pictured himself facing Grover Cleveland Alexander. He tapped the plate hard with his bat twice, and on cue, the jointee pulled back the curtain in front of him, putting him face-to-face with the man. The legend. Hurricane Harrigan. He wasn't blindfolded. No one had said he would be.

Zeb didn't care.

His eyes locked in on Harrigan as he launched into the exaggerated windup that had given him his nickname. It was meant to disorient the batter; to catch him off guard when the pitch finally came.

Zeb didn't flinch. A half smile that was close to a snarl curled up the left side of his upper lip as he waited calmly for the release. Harrigan had a tell. Zeb could see it coming. Right before the delivery, he kicked high and threw his head back, gazing up at the sky in silent petition to the gods of baseball.

Zeb waited, then watched as the curveball, Harrigan's money pitch, came toward him and then danced away, tailing off and down toward the far side of the plate. Zeb held the bat high and waited until the ball was just a few feet in front of him, then stepped on the plate and unleashed a mighty swing that created a thunderous sound as he connected. He tore the hide right off the ball as it sailed like a shot over Harrigan's head and far past the end of the joint, bouncing once before it slammed into the side of an open-mouthed horse riding high on the carousel.

It was, fortunately, riderless, but the kids on the other gaily colored mounts screamed, and one pigtailed little girl fell off, arms flailing, onto the moving circular platform. When she tried to get up, the back hooves of her wooden horse came down at the same moment, slamming into her head. She fell again, dazed, and tried to roll away from the line of demon animals, but in doing so, she reached the edge of the carousel and, before she could stop herself, went tumbling off backward. A loud crack greeted the ears of those who'd stopped to witness her distress. Mesmerized by the spectacle unfolding before them, not one of them took a single step forward to catch her. The crack was the sound of her skull hitting a rock that happened to be sticking up beside the merry-go-round, and the little pigtailed girl went immediately still.

"Is she...?" someone cried out.

Her mother, who had been watching from the other side of the carousel, rushed to kneel beside her, cradling her daughter's tiny, now dust-covered head in her lap. "Somebody get a doctor!" she shouted, nearly wailing. "Who's a doctor here?"

But the vultures, having seen what they had flocked to see, scurried away, each worried that they might somehow be blamed for the little girl's death, or for failing to help her.

As the sea of humanity parted, the girl was left lying there on the ground, suddenly forgotten by everyone except her mother, who knelt there with her, sobbing. By the time Adoline arrived, there was no help for her. She checked for a pulse and, finding nothing, shook her head sadly and escorted the grieving mother to her tent.

"Holy moly! Did you see that?" Marcus grabbed onto Zeb's arm and shook him.

Zeb jerked away. "That's my pitching arm, fool."

Lucy looked up at him.

"Hey, that wasn't my fault. The idiots put the carousel too close."

"Your fault? It ain't your fault. You killed it," Lucy enthused, oblivious to her unfortunate choice of words. "Just don't forget your prize."

In all the commotion, Zeb had almost forgotten the gen-u-wine Babe Ruth Louisville Slugger. "Where's my bat?" he demanded.

"Uh..."

"Where's my bat, Mister?" He pulled in closer, leaning across the wooden counter that separated them and raising a fist.

"I gotta... go get it," the jointee said. It was clear he didn't *have* a bat to offer, because he never expected the Hurricane to lose.

"You do that, mister *man*," Zeb snarled. "And make it quick. I'll be right here waitin' for ya."

The man hurried off, leaving the joint unattended and a growing line of disgruntled customers in his wake. They'd seen Zeb beat the Hurricane, so they knew it was possible, and they were arrogant enough to think they could do it too. It seemed unlikely that the jointee had *two* autographed bats in his possession. The way he'd run off— and now was taking his time returning—it was starting to seem like he didn't even have one.

Zeb started beating both fists on the counter, shouting, "Bring me my bat! Bring me my bat!" like a five-year-old, and the crowd began clapping and stomping their feet in unison.

Just then, the jointee returned, carrying a Louisville Slugger. Beaming proudly as though he had accomplished some great feat, he handed it over to Zeb, who was quick to inspect it for the Babe's signature. To his surprise, it was there, and appeared to be authentic: Zeb had seen it on a Goudey card in a friend's collection (a card he had tried to purloin), and had memorized it for just such an occasion. He could not have known that the Slugger was nothing more than a common bat, and that the signature had been forged in defiance of Artemus' rule against such subterfuge.

But who would know?

"What now?" Marcus asked, trying to keep pace with Zeb and Lucy.

Zeb was sauntering down the Midway like he owned the place, a preening cock in his own personal henhouse.

Lucy gripped his arm tightly, unwilling to part with her prize for even a moment.

"Maybe Zeb should try the milk jug toss," she said slyly.

"Yeah," Marus agreed. "That'd be keen, Loos. Then he can show *everyone* he's the next Bambino, right Zeb?"

"Already showed 'em," Zeb growled.

"But if you do this too, you'll be a legend," Lucy cooed.

Zeb looked down at her with a grimace that melted into a smile when he saw the look in her eyes. "Sure, doll," he said. "I'll do it. Child's play."

They made their way to the joint, a small stand surmounted by an immense wooden sign. Black paint ran down from the letters that formed the words "SPILL THE MILK," with a slightly lopsided baseball beside them.

"Step right up," the jointee barked. "Win big! All you gotta do is knock down these three bottles. Nothin' to it. I'll show ya."

He stepped outside the counter and picked up a baseball, rearing back and letting it fly at the targets, set neatly at the back edge of a table with a gingham cloth.

The three bottles flew apart like bowling pins and disappeared behind the table. "See?" the jointee crowed, raising both hands in triumph. "Easy as pie. Now, who'll be next?"

He scurried back behind the table and retrieved the pins, placing them neatly in a pyramid where they had been.

A bunch of hands shot up and tried to push their way forward, but Zeb used his bat to shove them aside, leaving bruises on kneecaps and shins where necessary. "I'll be next," he announced. "Gimme a ball."

He plunked down a nickel on the wooden counter, and the jointee placed two baseballs in front of him.

"I'll only need one," Zeb growled. He picked one up and hefted it in his hand. It felt like regulation; he'd heard of carnival games being rigged, and even though Carnivale Darke prided itself in not allowing gaffed games, he didn't trust it. He didn't trust anyone or anything except his arm and his bat.

Zeb tossed the ball up and down twice, then let it settle in his palm. He shifted it so it nestled between his thumb and two largest fingers, gripped it loosely, and set his eyes on those three milk bottles. He wouldn't need a high kick for this one. Once he'd sized up the target, he took a slide step, and delivered.

The ball went crashing into the direct center of the three bottles, the heart of the strike zone. The top one went flying, and one of the bottom two teetered and fell over, but the other just skittered sideways and came to a stop, still upright.

"Impossible!" Zeb shouted. "Gimme another."

The jointee placed another ball on the counter, and

Zeb snapped it up, glaring at him angrily.

"Step back!" he commanded, and the crowd reluctantly gave him space. This time, he would use his high kick to be sure he had enough force behind the pitch. He reared back, looking up toward the heavens just the way Hurricane had, then focused on the bottles as he came down and let fly, adding a little backspin this time for good measure. Again, the top bottle flew back behind the table; the left bottom bottle fell sideways more quickly, but the third bottle only teetered before coming to rest again on its base.

Zeb lost it.

He grabbed his bat and started swinging it around willy-nilly.

"Whoa, man! Chill out! It's only a game. It's not like you're actually the Babe. You still beat Hurricane Harrigan." Marcus snickered as he held his hands out in a placating gesture.

Zeb turned on his heel, bat over his shoulder, poised to swing. When Marcus came into view, he lashed out mightily and connected with the side of his head, the loud crack rising above the noise of the crowd. As he followed through, he caught a passer-by, just above his eyebrow, on the backswing.

The young man who'd been struck ran away, blood streaming from his face.

A woman cried out when blood flew off the bat and splattered on her face and several others in the mob of people.

The side of Marcus' skull bore the imprint of the bat. His brain was exposed, with bits of skull projecting from the wound. Marcus stood there looking stunned—silent and motionless, a blank expression frozen on his face—before slumping to the ground in a heap. Blood pooled in the dirt around his head.

"Finally, he shuts up! I've wanted to do that all day," Zeb exclaimed, his face beaming with pride.

The woman clutched a handkerchief in her hands, dabbing off the drips of blood from her son's forehead. "Help! Help! There's a madman on the midway!"

Zeb locked his eyes on her, storming over to stop her caterwauling. The little boy saw him approaching, rage in his eyes.

"Look out, mama!" the boy yelled, as he ran behind her skirts to hide.

"You stop right there, young man! Put that bat down!"

Zeb looked around to find out where the voice had come from. He saw a squat man, holding his folded-up belt in his hand, standing in front of the throng.

"Oooh! You going to whip me?" Zeb mocked.

The man's bravado had already begun to fade. As Zeb approached, he looked around for someone to back him up—instead he found that all the people near him had run for cover. "I don't want no trouble, young man. You're going to be in enough trouble yourself when the police arrive. I suggest you put that bat down."

"Do you, now? Where should I put it? How about down here?" Zeb slammed the bat into the man's right kneecap, An audible crunch resounded across the midway. The man moaned and bent down to hold his shattered kneecap. "Or maybe down here?" Zeb brought the bat down on the back of the man's neck.

The man's head flopped down limply. Zeb prodded it with the bat. It dangled like a sheet fluttering in the breeze. "Will ya look at that, people?"

Zeb looked around and realized he'd lost sight of Lucy. She'd probably run away when he'd gone off on his tirade.

Forget her! She may be a good kisser, but she was starting to annoy me.

Zeb remembered the woman who'd been screaming for help and turned around to look for her, but she was nowhere to be found.

Stupid bitch!

The crowd parted when they saw his glare, and there she was, with that sniveling little snot crying at her feet. Zeb marched over with an evil grin on his face.

"Don't hurt me. I have a child."

"This one?" Zeb gestured toward the boy, pulling him away.

"Don't touch him," the woman screamed as she stepped toward them.

Zeb held the bat out, stopping her forward motion.

"Batter up!" he boomed, just before he swung the bat, connecting with the boy's chest.

The child flew back ten feet and fell to the ground quiet and still, except for the slight stilted rise and fall of his chest. A hush fell over the midway—Zeb could hear a tiny wheezing whistle as the child fought to breathe.

"Oh, my God! Timothy!" The woman tried to run to her fallen child. Zeb grabbed her by the hair and slammed her face down on a bench. Blood spewed from her nose and a cut on her cheek. He dropped her to the ground, unconscious. "Another one down. Who's next?"

Zeb stalked over to the milk bottle game, determined to beat it. That idiot carny was still standing there, wide-eyed and hyperventilating. "Give me all the balls." The man set the basket of balls on the counter and backed up. Zeb threw one ball after another—connecting with that one bottle on the bottom right over and over—but never overturning it.

"That's it."

Zeb placed his hands on the counter and vaulted over it. He snatched the milk bottle up, and recognition dawned on him immediately. The bottle was heavy and filled with concrete. That shyster must have switched it out when he went back behind the table. The game was rigged! He raised the bottle over his head and turned to the carny. The man fell to his knees, crying, "It's not my fault." Zeb was about to crack the carny over the head when someone grabbed his hand from behind.

A booming voice said, "Drop it now, or I'll break your wrist. We're gonna wait right here for the police." The voice belonged to Oliver Pierce, a burly roustabout who'd been with Carnivale Darke since it opened. Most people knew not to mess with Oliver, but Zeb's fury had banished all sense of caution. And the insanity that fueled his adrenalin made him just as dangerous—if not more.

Zeb spun to confront the large man, but Oliver was relentless, keeping pressure on his wrist.

"Watch out!" a woman nearby screamed.

Oliver realized the danger only a second before Zeb's other hand jammed the end of the bat into his throat, crushing his windpipe. Oliver turned purple, clutching at his throat, trying desperately to breathe... to no avail. Zeb watched gleefully—the once-throbbing pulse in the man's thick neck slowed and then stopped.

During the scuffle, the carny running the milk bottle fraud had disappeared. Zeb looked down at his bat and saw that Babe's signature had smeared. The ink had still been wet.

That bastard! Another fraud, of course! I should've realized that sooner.

Zeb headed back over to batting game, ready for retribution. The operator's eyes grew wide as he saw the young man returning, covered in blood.

"He-hey there, slugger! C-come back for more? 'Fraid there's only one grand prize per... per... per... person," the man stumbled through his spiel.

"Don't even try it, asshole! 'Louisville Slugger signed by the one and only Babe,' my ass! You're not fooling me." Zeb's tone grew darker and his voice louder as he reached the stand, vaulting over it with ease. "Wanna see me try this bat out?"

"I'm sorry, son. Nobody's ever won before. I mean... it's Hurricane Hannigan, after all. I never expected to need one. I didn't know what to do. You were so insistent about getting your prize."

"It's all good. You can make it up to me."

"Really?" the batting cage operator asked, surprised.

"I wanna test the strength of this bat. I can really wallop them balls, you know?"

"I do! I saw you earlier. I assure you that, while it may not be a Louisville Slugger, it is a quality bat."

"Is that so? Let's see," Zeb replied with a wicked grin.

Without warning, Zeb swung for the fences, landing the bat squarely in the man's face. The man dropped to the ground, gurgling as blood poured down his throat from his broken nose. Broken teeth and blood oozed from his mouth. Even if he'd been conscious, he couldn't have seen Zeb preparing for his next blow through the crimson flood running into his eyes.

"Not bad. Let's try again."

Zeb brought the bat down on his face three more times until it snapped in half. The man's head was a pile of soupy mush. The walls of the stand were covered in blood and brains. Chunks of bone and teeth had been flung onto the wall and were sliding down. Zeb saw one of the man's eyeballs lying to the side, where it had landed after being forcibly ejected by one of the catastrophic blows. He placed one booted foot on it and stomped, crushing it, with an audible pop.

Zeb, enthralled with the carnage before him, never saw Jimmy launch at him from the side. He looked up to see a fist coming at his head and tried, unsuccessfully, to block the blow. Zeb's reign of terror had come to an end. Willis and Joe, who'd come with Jimmy, helped tie up the unconscious young man while they waited for the police to arrive.

Adoline stood by while the police questioned the onlookers and found out about the gaffed games. She watched as Artemus deftly handled the payoff, while assuring the chief that he never sanctioned grifts at Carnivale Darke. The carnival was officially shut down and would be leaving town, but there were still a lot of lookie-loos hanging around. Adoline knew she had to make a statement for the sake of the carnival's reputation and to ward off any other fraudulent operators.

Adoline walked over to the Superhuman Heroes tent and asked Larry the Lumberjack to bring his enormous axe with him. She explained to him what she needed done as they returned to the midway. Adoline climbed on a wooden crate. "I'm putting everyone on notice. In case, you've forgotten the contract you signed when you joined Carnivale Darke, our carnival is *one-hundred percent authentic*. No fakery."

Adoline nodded at Larry. He chopped down the batting stand, followed immediately by the milk bottle game. He cleaved the "SPILL THE MILK" sign in two with a single blow.

"When we load the train cars tonight, do not board if your game or act is fraudulent. We have a zero-tolerance policy. Henceforth, I will be performing random checks at every stop."

Artemus came to her side when she had finished. "I think we're going to find ourselves short on employees tomorrow. Three gaffed games in one day is suspicious. I think we've finally heard back from Harold on his promise to 'get us.' But his attempt to sabotage us will never see the light of day: He can't compete with Carnivale Darke."

Lucy was tired when she left the carnival. It had been exhausting putting on such an emotional show for the authorities. The next morning, she sent a telegram:

> *Success! The word is out that Carnivale Darke has gaffed games. Literal carnage ensued. They'll never recover from this.*

Adoline was busy the next few months replacing the midway operators who had left and those she'd fired from the carnival on that fateful day. She asked Jimmy for suggestions, but his heart just wasn't in it. Oliver, who hadn't survived the attack, had been his best friend, and his mood alternated between despondent and enraged. He kept sneering about how he meant to have revenge on Zeb for killing Oliver, and that he wouldn't rest until he'd done so.

Zeb Douglass, however, was in custody on 24-hour watch, and therefore out of reach.

Adoline watched the newspapers to find out what would happen to the crazed young man who had killed five people—including a child, and injured two others.

Zeb eventually pleaded not guilty by reason of insanity. While he managed to avoid prison, she was relieved when he was sentenced to life at Danvers Insane Asylum in Boston.

THE LIFE

have rarely granted interviews with the press, but when I do, one question is a constant: "How have you maintained your success all these years?" They want to know my secret, as though my success were the result of some secret regimen or elixir. I always give them the same answer: The carnival life is, by its nature, transient. The trick (and it is really no trick at all) is to remain pliant when confronted with external changes while staying true to one's core values.

My core values have always been to present the absolute best show possible and to be honest about it. No flim-flams and no sleight-of-hand. When coin-operated fortune-telling machines were introduced around 1910, operators like Zim, Sells Bros., and Barnum purchased them immediately, fully aware that these kismet machines were no more reliable than a flipped coin or a fortune cookie. I had nothing to do with them. If a fortune was to be told, it had better be accurate. I was not about to subject my customers to worthless contraptions, and I was not about to let go of a bona-fide psychic who could actually deliver the goods.

Why buy a machine to squash pennies when my strongman could do the same thing between his thumb and forefinger, inducing the crowd to pay a premium for the "full experience"?

My attitude was the same to the love-tester machines that came along in the late '20s. A salesman who came around to hawk one of these seemed to have been taken in himself by their "amazing" ability to predict whether the user was "bashful," "dreamy," or "hot stuff."

"Try it yourself!" he enthused. "It really does work."

To humor the man, I gripped the handle and held it, leading it to conclude that I was "BLAH!"

He fixed me with a sympathetic gaze and shook his head. "I'm sorry, Mr. Darke," he began. "Perhaps you have been too wrapped up in your business to explore your... amorous side."

I glared at him, then told him: "Allow me to make one more attempt."

I then proceeded to jog in place for a couple of minutes as he watched, entirely baffled at my behavior. When I felt myself starting to break a sweat, I stopped and grabbed the handle again. Like magic, it shot straight to the top, indicating I was "hot stuff."

The salesman shook his head, looking perplexed and a

little worried. "I must apologize, Mr. Darke. This model must be defective. I assure you that I will have it looked into and repaired, and should you decide to purchase any love-testers, they will be delivered in optimal working condition."

I smirked at him. "There is nothing wrong with your machine."

For a brief moment, he looked relieved, but then he realized the implications of what I had said: The machine itself was inherently flawed. "I assure you...," he began again, but I raised my hand to forestall him from continuing.

"Your assurances mean nothing to me," I said. "This machine of yours does not measure love or passion. It merely responds to the user's heartbeat, body temperature, and level of perspiration. In any case, Carnivale Darke is not about love; it's about entertainment. Legitimate entertainment. And I will allow no fly-by-night electrical scams on these premises."

I picked up the so-called love tester and threw it out of the room, with the salesman following fast on its heels.

My principles were simple and unshakable. Within their parameters, however, I had considerable latitude to adjust my carnival to match changes in the social fabric and meet new demands from attendees as they arose. New contraptions were always being invented, new advances were being made, and the nation's economic fortunes rose and fell.

But through it all, I stayed one step ahead of the latest developments by keeping my ear to the ground and my eye on the prize. I was in this business to make money, and nothing was going to keep me from doing just that.

Flush Times

It soon got easier—a *lot* easier.

The Great War came and went, ushering in an era of high times like nothing seen before. Prosperity put the final nail in the coffin of the horse-drawn transport, which had been limping toward the glue factory for more than a decade. Babe Ruth went from star to legend when he nearly doubled his own previous record with 54 home runs in 1920 and topped himself with 59 the next year. F. Scott Fitzgerald wrote *The Great Gatsby*, and radio became the latest sensation. Prohibition and the G-men made things a little harder, but not much: There were ways around such brutish restrictions, and nearly everyone with a taste for whiskey found them.

Yes, the Twenties really did roll in with a roar on the heels of flappers doing the Charleston in their Mary Janes. Young couples were drawn to our jazz band and the new portable dance floor we installed. Flapper girls and dapper young men boogied the night away to the beat of a bass drum and the blare of the brass section. Dance marathons had become strangely popular, and people would spend weeks out on the dance floor for the chance to win a few hundred dollars—bewildering behavior at a time when money was plentiful.

We didn't hold any dance marathons, although we would change our tune when the Depression came along. Such hard times, though, seemed inconceivable to the customers who flocked through our gates in the Roaring Twenties. Flush with cash, they came to each show just itching to spend it, whether it be thrill acts like knife throwing, the globe of death, or fire eating; or new games and rides, like a tethered hot air balloon.

Each attraction now cost extra, of course.

We had a family friendly entertainment tent featuring a contortionist and a ventriloquist. After the conclusion of the magic act, women and children were funneled to a Punch and Judy show, while the men were led to a live hoochy-coochy show for a *mere* $2 a head.

Young love was served on the midway, where many a young man would spend an exorbitant amount of money trying to win a stuffed bear for his sweetheart before taking her on a romantic ride on the Ferris wheel, hoping to steal a kiss at the top when the ride stopped to let people off.

Meanwhile, we expanded our sideshow acts.

In 1925, we opened an extreme oddities tent with acts too harsh for women and children's delicate sensitivities. Three times a day, tattooed, pierced, and scantily clad performers paraded across the stage, stopping briefly to eat glass, lie on a bed of nails, suspend heavy objects like bricks from nipple piercings, hang from large sharp hooks embedded in their backs, and pierce their bodies with a bevy of needles like pincushions.

And the main sideshow tent was no longer just a Ten-in-One. My scouts were out scouring the globe for unique, never-before-seen human oddities to excite and titillate the crowd. Each of these prodigies had their own personal collector card with a short bio and picture of them for customers to collect, at a nominal fee of course. Souvenirs had become big business. Customers lined up to buy our stuffed animals, balloons, tin and celluloid toys, and Kewpie dolls.

Times were so good, in fact, that I was forced to rethink my business model. Up to that point, it had always been my policy to run off the rag-tag vendors who tried to piggyback on our success by setting up pit shows, selling souvenirs, and holding sporting events outside our gates, without getting my express permission first. I had obtained the permit—let them get their own.

But now, with the increased demand for more and newer attractions, I decided to offer those outside acts and vendors a piece of the action. Rather than chasing them away, brought them into the fold—in exchange for half their take.

We soon had pit shows with enormous snakes and alligators on the grounds. From the time the gates opened until we closed for the night, lines of customers stood waiting to walk up the stairs and look down on a man wrestling an alligator or struggling under the weight of a fifteen-foot boa wrapped around his neck. They also set up clandestine gambling operations within small tents where cock fights and boxing matches were held. We even had a small variety show with a cat and rooster orchestra that played for a troop of acrobatic poodles.

Our new vendors, meanwhile, included a tattoo artist, a tinker, and a glass blower who had followed us around from place to place. They would always set up shop, and we'd have to chase them away, but they just moved a little farther up the road, and it had taken up too much of our security team's resources to run them off. Once, in Little Rock, the local cops had showed up and taken *their* side, blaming *our* roustabouts for creating a public nuisance.

They didn't like panhandlers, but they liked us even less.

"Take your girlie shows and your riffraff somewhere else," they told us. "This is a law-abiding, god-fearing county."

They shooed the independents away too for blocking the road, but they just followed us to Jackson and on to Tuscaloosa.

Working within the carnival grounds, I thought, would be a good deal for everyone. They'd be protected from the cops, we'd get half their profits, and neither one of us would have to waste time tussling with the other. But the one thing I would not compromise on was authenticity. That had only been reinforced by the bloodbath in Boston. Our new vendors had to meet rigorous guidelines. The rice writer had to pass unannounced inspections verifying that what he claimed to have written upon a grain of rice was truly visible. Adoline supervised the glass blower to make sure he only sold items that he had created at the carnival—no passing off items bought from a supplier.

The first glass blower we hired had tried to run a pickbox scam, where both simple and fancy, intricate glass objects were on display. The customer would buy a ticket, hoping for the swirled glass bowl, and instead always win a simple glass figurine the glass blower had made during demonstrations. The finer items had been bought from a supplier and were only *truly* available for purchase. It turned out he had received nothing more than a rudimentary glass-blowing education and thought he could run a grift in my carnival.

He found out soon enough that he was wrong.

I had never wanted to take on the hassle of running food booths, so I had always contracted with people to sell the usual carnival fare. But business kicked up so much I had to expand those operations to keep up with the demand. That meant more hot dogs, more popcorn, more candy apples, more peanuts, and more cotton candy.

Then there were those most odious of confections: circus peanuts. I never could fathom why anyone would want to ingest something made of marshmallow that looked like a peanut and tasted like a banana, but the kids loved them, so who was I to argue. It turned out, however, that there was at least one other drawback to these disgusting "treats." That became apparent when one young trouble-maker threw a whole handful of them at the spider monkeys while they were performing their trapeze act.

The commotion and the smell of the things distracted the simians so completely that they became wrapped up in the highwires as they tried to reach the ground. One crazed monkey pushed another from a platform to its death, its skull cracking open like an egg when it hit the concrete head-first. Another became so badly entangled in

the wires that it was unable to free itself. In its panic, it began thrashing around, but only managed to get itself more hopelessly trapped in the line—which became knotted around its neck and constricted more each time the monkey flailed.

The crowd that gathered to watch the gruesome spectacle pointed and gawked as the creature gasped and sputtered high above the concrete while the others dashed here and there below, tackling or swatting their competitors for the precious circus peanuts.

Another miscreant child took the opportunity to throw some more circus peanuts at the monkeys, trying to hit them in the head, which added to the frenzy. By the time we were able to restore some semblance of order, three monkeys had died, several more had suffered broken bones or gashes, and the act had to be shut down for the day.

The circus peanuts, however, sold more briskly than ever.

The Human Regurgitator

The strangest act we welcomed during the 1920s was the Human Regurgitator. He swallowed just about any object from mice and goldfish to colored ribbons, coins, and pocket watches. Then he would bring them all back up, one by one—in the order they had been swallowed or by the designation of audience members. He'd heard through the grapevine that I was hiring the most extraordinary acts fit for The Show to End All Shows, and he was ready to move on from his current position at another carnival. He arrived unannounced at the gate, requesting an audience with me. When Adoline introduced herself as the vice president of operations and inquired about his business, he made the most ambitious, arrogant claim she'd heard, so she'd felt compelled to arrange an audition for him.

I'd been busy planning out our stops for the next few weeks when I heard her rap on the sign posted outside my tent.

"Artemus, I'm sorry to disturb you, but I've arranged an impromptu performance for a prospective employee. I can't quite put my finger on it—either he's a complete shyster, or we have the chance to steal one of Zimmerman's most treasured acts," Adoline said with a glint in her eye.

"And what's so special about this act of his?"

"He calls himself the Human Regurgitator, and..."

"I've heard about him! I've been trying to contact him. Where is he? We can't lose this opportunity. But wait! Why would he want to leave Dr. Zim's Carnival of Oddities?"

Adoline shook her head, a frown on her face. "*Doctor*

Zim's?"

"Oh! Haven't you heard, dear sister? He's renamed himself Dr. Zim. I'm not sure quite where he gets off calling himself a doctor. Probably wants to make himself sound more important than he really is, like that 'Doctor' Couney with his baby incubators. And as for the Zim part, I don't know if he wants to sound more exotic and mystical or because of discrimination."

Whether Harold had rebranded himself out of arrogance or fear, it was no skin off my back either way. But why would this man leave Harold's employ? Zimmerman was our fiercest rival. None of the others, not even Barnum, came close to the success of our carnivals."

"Now I understand what he was talking about. I'll let him explain it to you. He's waiting for us in the magician's tent with Ozymandias. If there's anyone we can trust to help us discover a man's chicanery, it's him."

I smiled. There was a reason I'd hired her.

When we arrived at the magician's tent, the man was in deep conversation with Ozymandias.

"Artemus, may I introduce you to Ralph the Human Regurgitator." Ozymandias rose and held out his arm toward the smart-looking gentleman dressed in a charcoal grey suit. He looked more suited to be a door-to-door salesman than a carnival performer.

"Hello, Mr. Darke. I'm pleased to make your acquaintance. Thank you so much for agreeing to meet with me."

"Delighted," I replied with a curt nod. "Now let's get down to brass tacks. Why are you here? Are you spying for Zimmerman? If so, let me be clear: There are no weaknesses in our operation. You can just take your leave now and tell Harold to piss off."

The man raised both hands, palms out. "Sir, I assure you that is not the case. He doesn't know I'm here, and to be honest, I prefer it stays that way until you hire me." He raised his eyebrows, an arrogant smile spreading across his lips.

"Pretty sure of yourself. And just why would I hire you?"

"Because I'm the real deal. No trickery involved. You've never seen a *real* act like mine, and you won't again anytime soon."

"If you're so amazing, why would you want to leave Zimmerman's? Does he not pay you enough?"

"I'm sure you've heard that he's called Dr. Zim now and about his Carnival of Oddities. All he cares about are his 'creations.' The rest of us are just filler. He doesn't give a damn what we do. I'm a man, not a man servant. I refuse to bow down to him and that *thing* he calls a son."

"Slow down. I'm not sure I'm following you. He has a son? And why would you call him a thing? What creations?"

"The 'Carnival of Oddities' is his freak show. He treats these monstrosities like royalty. He calls his carnival an employee-owned company, but they're the only employees. They share in the profits, while the rest of us get paid peanuts. When their performances are over, they rest in their berths. The rest of us are responsible for all of the other duties, including set-up and teardown."

"I've never heard of such a thing. But that still doesn't explain the rest of what you said."

"I was getting to that. He has a few freaks that he's found around the world, just as you have. But he's *created* the majority of them himself. A man will walk in off the street looking for work and come out of his 'laboratory' as some bizarre creature. Don't get me wrong. I have nothing against people with medical disabilities or deformities. But these aren't natural. They don't exist in the real world. He turned Bobby, a down-on-his-luck young man, into The Count. He has wings... real true wings. When people approach his stall in the tent, he flies out over their heads, sweeping from one end to the next and doing loops before swooping down toward the women to make them scream."

"My God! You can't be serious. That sounds just like what he was trying to do with poor Rose Daniels! And his son? He's a creation as well?"

"He's the worst of all. They call him The Brain. His head is enormous, nearly two-and-a-half times normal. It's like he doesn't even have a skull. The skin covering his giant brain shows every fold and furrow of its surface. The blood vessels throb and pulsate as he completes complex math equations in mere seconds. He's just 9 years old, but he's already joined his father in the laboratory, and the creations are only growing more twisted and horrifying to behold. I can't stay there any longer."

"I see. I never expected Zimmerman to go that far. Has Adoline or Ozymandias explained my policy regarding true feats of wonder? I accept no trickery in Carnivale Darke."

"I assure you that you have no worries in that regard."

Ozymandias rose and strode over to a small table on the stage. "I made some preparations in advance of your arrival, Artemus. I have a couple of marked Carnivale Darke souvenir coins, my old engraved pocket watch, and two goldfish from the midway, one red and one white with red spots. Adoline, my assistant Alara and I will be watching from the other three angles while you observe him from directly in front. He has assured me that he can bring up the items in any order we desire, and I will verify their authenticity."

"Perfect, Ozy. Thank you for your attention in this matter."

Ralph walked to the table and removed his shirt and pants. Clad only in shorts, he turned to Adoline, "I hope you don't take offense, Miss Darke. I don't want there to be any concerns that I might be hiding the objects on my person. Any particular order you wish them to go down, Mr. Darke?"

"As you wish," I replied with a nod.

Ralph picked up the pocket watch and placed it in his mouth. With a small sip of water, he washed it down in seconds. Then he plopped first one coin down his gullet, followed by the cup containing the red goldfish. With a large gulp of water, he swallowed the second, larger coin chased with the white goldfish. Ralph let out a small belch and then smiled.

"Ladies first, I presume. What would you like, Adoline?" Ralph asked with a small bow.

"Logic dictates the first to go down should be the hardest to produce first. The pocket watch please, Ralph."

With a quick slap to his belly and a few shimmies of his hips, Ralph leaned forward and then stood up tall, small undulations rippling through his abdomen and then up his throat. A few seconds later, with a small gag, he opened his mouth and produced the pocket watch with a short string of saliva trailing from it. He placed the watch in the handkerchief in Ozymandias' outstretched hand. The magician pressed the little release button at the top and held it up to show the engraving: "To My Dearest Ozy."

"Impressive, Ralph. Now, can you produce the two goldfish at once?" I asked with a dismissive wave of my hand.

"One moment, sir."

Once again, he repeated the shimmy, and seconds later opened his mouth over one of the small cups. A stream of water filled the cup seconds before the two fish emerged, right next to each other. They dropped into the cup and swam around, checking out their new surroundings. "I assure you, they are quite fine and ready to go home in some child's grubby little paws."

I fought to control the broad smile that was trying to creep across my face. If I stole this act, it would be a coup. Ralph was the talk of the carnival circuit. Whether Zimmerman knew his worth or not, I surely did.

"I guess that leaves only the coins then, Mr. Darke. What order?"

"Drink that water in the pitcher over there. Then do a handstand for one minute so everything gets all mixed up in there. If you can produce the large coin first without regurgitating any of the water, the job's yours."

Ralph left the stage to grab the pitcher of water. He downed it in one long swallow. "It's a pleasure to join your carnival, Mr. Darke," he replied with his hand extended.

"We shall see," I returned, my eyes twinkling. I couldn't help but admire his cockiness. It matched my own.

He returned to the stage, placed his hands on the

ground and kicked his legs up. With a small waver, he assumed the position and waited for the time to be called. When Adoline announced it was time, he stood up without a word and, with barely a noise, produced the large coin, followed by the small one, with not even a single drop of spilled water.

"Welcome to Carnivale Darke, Ralph. How soon can you start?"

"I stashed my carpetbag out in the bushes near the ticket booth. How about this evening? Can someone point me to the cookhouse? I'm famished."

Ozymandias let out a sonorous laugh. "You're going to fit right in here. I'll show you the way."

I returned to my tent and wrote out a short note for Adoline to take to the telegraph office: "You're a peach, Harold! Thank you for sending us, Ralph. He's a welcome addition to Carnivale Darke." I knew that would burn Zimmerman. He hated to lose... especially to me.

An Elephant-Sized Problem

When the Depression hit, everything changed. Fortunately for me, I had more than enough money to survive the hard times without slowing operations. While other carnivals gave up the ghost, I soldiered on, all but cornering the market—even though that market was vastly smaller.

The Great Crash of '29 didn't hit me as hard as it did some, but that didn't mean I was immune to its effects. As the Depression wore on, I faced a slew of unforeseen troubles that changed my carnival operations yet again.

Hoovervilles housing out-of-work men dotted the landscape across the country, usually along the rail lines just outside of towns. More and more hobos rode the rails in search of work. Stowaways were nothing new to Carnivale Darke. Historically, we had allowed them to sneak aboard our boxcars and ride from one location to the next, giving them a bit of bread and coffee in exchange for helping us set up at our next stop.

What changed was the number of hobos expecting us to house them. To deal with this new influx, I started expanding their duties to allow more men to receive the help they needed without becoming a burden. Some helped with set-up, while others cleaned up messes and dumped trashcans throughout the day. Those I deemed suitable were put to work performing more complicated tasks or used as roustabouts to chase off those hobos so drunk they couldn't stand; people who tried to set up pit shows with those loathsome, so-called "geeks" outside the fairgrounds; or poor children who ran the grounds picking the pockets of my patrons.

It all seemed to be working until one day when I found I could only trust those important tasks to my paid employees—the same day that I had a problem with one of the outside vendors I had contracted to work within the carnival.

That problem forced me to reverse course and stop hiring any outside contractors at all. From that day forward, all operations for Carnivale Darke fell under my personal employment. My roustabouts were ordered to chase off all vendors if they tried to set up outside our grounds. Food concessions were a hassle, but the liability for improper food handling far outweighed those concerns.

It all started one fateful morning with a commotion in the field a few hours after we arrived. We had set up to open at the Kansas State Fairgrounds in Hutchinson for the weekend. My tent had been pitched, and I was hard at work while everyone set up the carnival to open late that afternoon.

The animals were being unloaded, and Susie, one of the caretakers, rushed into my tent in distress.

"Mr. Darke, Big Bertha is dead!"

I had been deep in thought. I raised my head, squinting at her as I tried to decipher what she'd said. "Who's dead?"

"Big Bertha, the old elephant we took on from that circus back in 1910."

"Well, that's hardly a surprise. That was over twenty-

five years ago. Go find some of those hobos that rode in with us, the ones I put to work inside the grounds. Tell them to dispose of her. There must be a dump around here somewhere. I'm sure they'll know where."

Susie sniffled and rubbed her nose on her sleeve. "Ok, sir." She stood there looking up at me from her downcast gaze, rocking back and forth from foot to foot.

"Is there something else, Susie?"

"I'm sorry, sir. I'm just very upset. I hate to throw her away like garbage."

"Is that not what she is now? She'll no longer be earning her keep. Soon she'll be a stinking heap chasing our customers away. What else would you have me do?"

"I... I... I don't know. I guess. Never mind. But what about the show tonight?"

"Do you have something else to tell me? Do we not still have five other elephants?"

"Uh... yes, of course. I just thought they might be upset. And Big Bertha's always led the show."

"So you want me to hold a funeral for the other elephants and you to mourn? That's preposterous. They're just animals. They get paid in peanuts and hay. I suggest that if *you* want to get paid—and them to get fed—you should go figure out how to run the show with another elephant in the lead." I clapped my hands brusquely. "Now off you go!"

Susie scurried out of the tent, and I thought that would be the end of the matter.

Little did I know the scope of the problem that was about to descend on my head.

The carnival opened just after lunch. Not surprisingly, traffic was slow—times were hard and money was scarce. People straggled in throughout the day, but we did have a decent crowd for the evening circus performance under the big top. It all started normally enough—parents sat with their bouncing, happy children, oohing and aahing at the equestrian act and giggling at the clowns.

But then it all changed.

The unmistakable sound of a child retching.

And then the scream from the woman in the row below when she was soaked to the skin in vomit.

We were always prepared for this kind of contingency. A day spent filling up on rich foods and then boarding stomach-twisting rides sometimes led to such unfortunate occurrences. One of the roustabouts ran up with some towels to clean up the area and escort the family to a more appropriate location.

But then—before he could reach them—the sound of more retching filled the air. From all around the tent. Both children and adults. It had become a vomitorium. The smell of sweat, animals, and manure, common to any circus, changed to the sour, tear-inducing stench of bile. People were pouring out of the tent to escape the smell and then becoming overcome themselves outside. Trails of dark, foul-smelling liquid ran from the legs of the patrons as they streamed toward the gates. The whole fairground had become an outhouse of disease. Cries of "They poisoned us!" rang out from the departing crowds. Those who weren't sick ran to their cars and drove off in a rush, and I gave the order to close all the shows and begin breaking everything down. We would depart within the hour.

We rushed to clear the fairgrounds and pack up the carnival. Adoline and I ran around overseeing the work, and I soon found the cause of the illness. The elephant that I had ordered to be disposed of in the dump was instead a rotting, butchered carcass hidden under a tarp in one of the barns on the lot.

I bellowed from where I stood, my voice ringing out across the open space. "Who did this?"

Two of the hobos I'd taken on to work that day disappeared into the darkness. Mikey, a new young man I'd employed to oversee them stepped forward nervously. He stared down at the ground, twisting his flat cap in his hand. "I'm sorry, Mr. Darke. I thought it would be okay. They assured me it was fine. Normal practice and all. And I needed the money... to send home to my wife. She's expecting our first child."

"*Who* assured you *what* would be fine?"

"The hot dog vendor. He said money was tight, like it is for all of us. And with the rationing, he's been having trouble getting meat to make the hot dogs. They said they could use the elephant to make more hot dogs." Mikey's eyes welled with tears as he realized the gravity of the situation.

"So, you're telling me they fed a dead, rotting elephant to my customers?! We don't even know how long she was dead when we found her. The meat had certainly gone bad, and now we've given food poisoning to half the town. Where is that vendor? I want to speak to him now!"

Adoline ran off to find the vendors I'd entrusted to feed my customers. She came back in a hurry to announce they'd left.

"How convenient of them to disappear," I growled, "when the sheriff is probably on his way here as we speak."

At that moment, the sheriff and his deputy pulled into the fairgrounds, red beacon flashing and siren blaring. Adoline ran to meet them and escorted them to my tent where I had retreated. This situation called for finesse.

When Adoline entered with the sheriff and his deputy in tow, I rose to greet them. "Hello, Sheriff..." I leaned forward to read the name embroidered on his chest. "Adams. I'm sorry to meet you under such unfortunate circumstances."

"Care to elaborate?"

"Yes, it's a dreadful situation. I only just found out about it myself. I contracted with a..." I looked down to consult my notes, "a Mr. and Mrs. Andrew Williams out of

Topeka as food vendors for my carnival. Everything seemed above aboard. I followed all the required procedures and verified they had a license for food service.

"Unfortunately, we lost one of our elephants this morning... old age, you see. I told my people to see about disposing of her in the dump. Apparently, those scoundrels, the Williamses, paid my people to give them the elephant carcass to make hot dogs. I don't know how someone could conceive of such a thing."

"You're saying the citizens of my town were fed meat from a dead elephant?"

"Sadly, yes. It's horrifying to even contemplate. I've since fired the employees who took the bribe from those awful criminals. I wish I could tell you where they are, but they took off before I even found out what had happened." I picked up a slip of paper from my desk and handed it to the sheriff. "I do have their address back in Topeka. I'm sure they couldn't have gotten far since they were on foot, you see. Maybe sitting back in Hutchinson even as we speak, waiting to catch a bus out of town."

"Are you saying you don't hold yourself accountable for what happened to the poor people of this town? They came to your carnival to forget their troubles for a few hours. They spent what little hard-earned money they had, and you sent them home ill. I scarcely believe any but a handful of them could afford a doctor if they needed one."

"Well, it surely is not my fault. That unscrupulous couple was *not* employed by *me*. They were outside contractors who came in to do a job. But I'm not a heartless chap by any means."

I reached over and picked up a thick envelope, my thumb carefully brushing the flap open to reveal a large wad of cash as I handed it over to him. "I feel it is imperative that I reimburse you for your time. Make use of that as you see fit."

The sheriff took the envelope and tucked it in his breast pocket. "Well thank you kindly, sir. That's very gracious of you. We'll inform the townspeople of the situation. But I do recommend that you be out of here before sunup."

Adoline returned to my tent after seeing the sheriff and his deputy to their car. "What do you want me to do now?"

"Send all the outside vendors packing—no exceptions—after you collect our percentage of their profits. We'll no longer have anyone here who is not an employee of Carnival Darke. Put the word out that we'll no longer tolerate freeloaders. No more hobos riding in our train cars, either. Put Sophie to work at the ticket booth the next few weeks while you make arrangements to hire our own food vendors and any others that need to be replaced. Pull Mikey from his position. He has one last chance with our operation, but he'll be shoveling shit in the animal cars."

Wrath of the Phantom Nun

The Great Depression brought its share of challenges, but true to form, we persevered and even thrived where others failed.

The same was true during the war years that followed.

The Great War was supposed to have been "the war to end all wars," but now here we were, immersed in another, even more calamitous conflict. FDR's radio address proclaiming December 7, 1941, a day that would live in infamy rang in all our ears as America began battling the Axis powers in two far-flung theaters.

Unlike the indebted Ringling Bros. operation, which was given special dispensation to use the rails by Roosevelt himself, we were obliged to switch our manner of transport to trucks. We purchased buses to carry carnivalgoers to the grounds where we would be putting down stakes on any given day.

Coffee, sugar, and meat were being rationed, and with so many men being sent overseas, new sources of labor had to be found. We employed older men, the disabled, and even children to tear down after the show was done.

Society at large was much the same. With able-bodied men busy defending democracy, their wives took their place in factories, assembling tanks, guns, aircraft, and other essential military hardware. It wasn't just Rosie the Riveter, either. With professional baseball rosters depleted, women filled the gap there as well. Carnivale Darke was among the first to stage softball and baseball exhibitions between all-female teams, leading directly to the formation of the All-American Girls Professional Baseball League in 1943.

A good friend of mine, Phil Wrigley, wanted to keep America's pastime front and center while major stars like Joltin' Joe, Teddy Baseball, and Stan the Man were busy fighting overseas. I signed on as a silent partner in this endeavor, in exchange for which he agreed to promote Carnivale Darke across the Midwest and give us space on billboards across from Wrigley Field.

When our show came to town, we staged tryouts and

exhibitions in places like Kenosha, Racine, South Bend, and Rockford, all of which wound up fielding teams in the league. It didn't always go well, though. During a stop in Kenosha, we set up our carnival along Lake Michigan in the shadow of a girls' boarding school called Kemper Hall.

It turned out to be a poor choice of venues. A senator named Charles Durkee had the hall built as a mansion in suitably gothic style during the early 1860s. It was donated to the church a few years later for use as a school for troubled girls. A nunnery was added after the turn of the century.

The girls there were unruly, many of them from poor families in Chicago; as determined to defy authority as the nuns were to impose discipline. The tension and the incipient madness on both sides were palpable. It finally burst into its full flower during the winter of 1900 when a nun named Sister Augusta vanished without a trace. The Hall told newspapers that she was safe in Missouri. But that was blatantly false. A few days later, two young children noticed black robes floating near the beach. When investigators arrived, they found them clinging to the lifeless body of Sister Augusta.

Its intended coverup having failed, the Hall administration set about impugning the nun's reputation. She had, they lamented, become "mentally deranged from her work, which had been exceedingly hard during the last few months." In simpler terms, she had cracked, proving herself unworthy of God's grace.

She wasn't the only one, either.

Another nun at the convent had gained a reputation, not for madness, but for cruelty. She forbade the girls at the boarding school from engaging in any form of recreation; games were expressly forbidden, and punishment for the smallest infraction was met with a switch across the bare buttocks and the top of their legs.

This continued until it became intolerable. One day, when she was standing at the top of a five-story spiral staircase, she felt a presence. Half a dozen girls had crept up soundlessly behind her. One gave her a shove, and when she turned, trying to right herself, another gave her a swift kick to the gut that sent her hurtling down the stairs. Her head hit the wall with such force that her neck broke, and another flight down, the now-flopping cranium became lodged between two spindles on the banister. There was a terrible crack and a sudden spurt of crimson blood, whereupon the head stayed stuck where it was and the rest of the body continued to the very bottom of the stairs.

The girls ran off and were never heard from again. The nun, meanwhile... became as stuck in its own haunted purgatorium as her head was between those two unyielding spindles. This was of little interest to me, as I chalked both these stories up to local raconteurs with an eye toward scaring children and titillating tourists. I did, however, find the stories intriguing, and thus committed the details to my memory.

Our spirits were high when we pulled into Kenosha in 1943. Business had picked up considerably since the start of the war, and our patrons were happy to overlook the absence of cotton candy and candy apples due to sugar rationing. Everyone was keen to do their part in supporting the boys, and everyone was just as eager for an escape from the dire news of more death overseas. Horrors like the Blitz on London and Hitler's relentless expansion were in the past, but every new dispatch from the front brought news of more death in what had become a war of attrition.

Like any successful business, we dedicated ourselves—visibly and loudly—to the war effort.

"Buy bonds!"

"Support Uncle Sam!"

"Dig for victory!"

"We can do it!"

"Do with less—so they'll have enough!"

Those were our battle cries. To support the bond effort (and draw paying customers), we hosted celebrities like Hope and Crosby, Bette Davis, Red Skelton, and Desi Arnaz at every opportunity. In Kenosha, we'd arranged for an appearance by no less a star than Marlene Dietrich, who was also to sing the national anthem before the All-American Girls exhibition.

We welcomed more paying customers that Saturday than on any single day we'd ever been open, all of them braving a light rain and brisk zephyrs blowing in from Lake Michigan. Our guest of honor had just finished singing "The Star-Spangled Banner," and curious fans had filled up the temporary stands we had set up for an exhibition game between two newly christened teams: the Kenosha Comets and the Racine Belles from just up the road.

It had all the makings of a fierce rivalry, but before a single pitch could be thrown, a headless figure in a black-and-white nun's habit strode out onto the field. The teams, acted like they thought we'd set up some promotional stunt, tried to ignore the intruder until she placed herself directly between the mound and home plate. The pitcher just stood there, unsure what to do, as the nun approached and stopped no more than a foot away.

"I warned you, impious whores: I will tolerate *no games* at Kemper Hall!" The nun reached underneath her robes, produced a paring knife, and thrust it into the pitcher's throat.

Blood fountained out and down onto the dirt as the pitcher collapsed. Members of both teams shrieked and began running off the field, while fans stampeded down out of the stands. The weight of them moving all at once caused one of the wooden support beams underneath to buckle and give way, sending half the bleachers slumping and sliding at a crooked angle, then crashing to the ground. Bodies were thrown downward, tumbling over one another and the ruined seats, which splintered and stabbed one falling body after another. Some of the spectators were rendered unconscious, and others were run through. Those who escaped these fates were faced with the sight of the headless nun, rushing madly toward them, now raising a battleaxe over her head that she could not possibly have hidden under her robes.

Only one entrance to the field had been left open, and they all scrambled toward it, only to be met by six young girls armed with cleavers and pistols and meat tenderizers. They rushed toward the madding crowd, which turned them back toward the nun. The six girls hacked and slashed and pounded their way through the fleeing spectators from one side; the nun swung her axe back and forth in wide swaths on the other. Men, women, and children fell to the ground motionless. But it was clear that neither the nun nor the girls cared a whit about their victims. They were bound and determined to reach *each other*—and when they finally did... they all just vanished.

So did the spectators. So did the players.

Then the applause began. It came from the section of the bleachers that hadn't collapsed, where I had strategically instructed our ushers to escort the flesh-and-blood spectators. I had promised them a show, and that is what I had delivered. My magnificent illusion was based on Nikola Tesla's MasterView technology, as enhanced by my late and lamented magician Magnus and a genius named Albert whom I had put on contract—surreptitiously, and at considerable cost. Albert had released Pandora from her box, taking the MasterView out of its viewing stations and unleashing it on the world at large. He had developed a projection system—one that didn't need a screen—to superimpose the MasterView's "alternate dimension" onto the real world. Projectors were placed at strategic positions around the ball diamond, creating phantom players, the headless nun and her murderers, the collapsing stands, and the resulting melee.

I had memorized the details of Kemper Hall's ghost stories not because I had come to believe in them, but to render my illusion all the more believable to others.

The entire presentation was a rousing success. Marlene Dietrich returned to the field and sold more war bonds than anyone else had ever managed to sell at a single event. Once word got out about my illusion-maker—which I christened the Virtuality Maker—the crowds got even bigger, and profits soared. I scrapped my original MasterView stations altogether; they were obsolete now, and made plans to deploy my Virtuality Maker at every stop on the circuit.

When Zimmerman Jr. got wind of it, he paid me a personal visit to accuse me of violating my own principles by faking the whole thing.

"You're a fraud, Darke!" he shouted, shaking a fist in my face. "I knew it all along. You like to pretend you're better than we are, but you aren't. You're worse! Claiming to be all squeaky clean and on the level... You pompous ass. You're no better, Darke! No better! Do you hear me?"

Harold Jr., or The Brain as he was more aptly named, was just as monstrous as Ralph had described. The skin on his head pulsated sickeningly and swelled until, at one point, it appeared as if it might burst. Hoping to incite just such an event, I just shoved his fist aside and laughed in his face. "Oh, but that's where you're wrong," I said. "I *am* better than you. We've *both* been showing movies at our carnivals since the days of the Nickelodeon. But do you have anything like my Virtuality Maker? Of course you don't! You're still just showing two-dimensional movies and peep shows at your carnival or freak show or whatever you're calling it..."

"Doctor Zim's Carnival of Oddities."

"Whatever, Zimmerman. You don't impress me. Everything you've ever done is just a cheap imitation of what I've already accomplished. We *create* a new reality while you're busy playing connect-the-dots. We took out patents for equipment sophisticated enough to make your cheapo projectors look like old-timey flipbooks. And you're not even a doctor, either, unless your real name's Victor, as in Frankenstein."

Zimmerman raised his fist again but, true to form, couldn't muster a proper rejoinder. Instead, he just said, "You'll pay for this, Darke. I swear on my life you will!"

But the more Zimmerman tried to besmirch my name, the more publicity my Virtuality Maker received. One day, I got a call from a physicist named Oppenheimer who was working on a top-secret project for the government. He wouldn't tell me what it was, but he did say the Pentagon wanted to use it to scare the Japanese so badly they'd shit themselves; they'd come to us just begging to surrender. He implored me to let him use my Virtuality Maker as an alternative to whatever he was working on, but he said it would have to be on a scale large enough to make it appear as though we were wiping out an entire city.

I told him there was no way we could operate the VM on that scale. The logistics would be impossible. We would have to station projectors around the city itself, for one thing, but he was undeterred, suggesting that the projectors be directed downward from aircraft.

"How would that be feasible?" I asked. "The aircraft would have to remain stationary, which would make them sitting ducks for anti-aircraft guns."

He even had an answer for that: "We could use other projectors to 'cloak' the planes themselves: make it appear as though they aren't even there."

This sounded like a nightmare to me. Too many things could go wrong, and I would not be responsible for the lives of American pilots. If word got out, as it surely would, that my device had been responsible for the failure, my reputation would be ruined.

"You can't have it," I told him flatly.

But he continued to press. He asked me for the schematics so he could do it, himself. I declined again, but he continued to persist, and I knew it was only a matter of time before he sent the feds poking around to confiscate the VM if I didn't do something to secure it.

So I did.

Reluctantly, I gathered up the equipment I had used in Kenosha, had my roustabouts smash it all up and bury it in a landfill. I had destroyed all my MasterView stations, but I still had Tesla's original prototype, which he had made in the form of a headset for Magnus and Cassandra to "perfect," but I couldn't let them get their hands on that, either.

So I put it away for safekeeping, where I was sure nobody could find it.

When the bombs fell on Hiroshima and Nagasaki, I considered that I might have been—at least indirectly—responsible for killing 200,000 innocent people. But no one knew about it, and my reputation was intact.

That was what mattered.

STEPHEN H. and SHARON MARIE PROVOST

Now, for My Last Feat...

Beauty is in the eye of the beholder, or so the saying goes. This may or may not be true of mere aesthetics, but of magic, it surely is. Men have spent centuries using sleight-of-hand, misdirection, and chicanery to hoodwink audiences into thinking they're seeing something truly magical. That, however, was never my way. Why settle for tomfoolery when one can have the real thing? As with any rare treasure, however, true magic must be guarded closely, lest it fall into the hands of the unscrupulous and the untrained. Before us now, we see two such men, eager to wrest magic from the hands of the skilled and use it for their own selfish purposes. The chaos that ensues illustrates the very reason I always insisted on authenticity... inside the gates of Carnivale Darke.

—Artemus Darke

1922

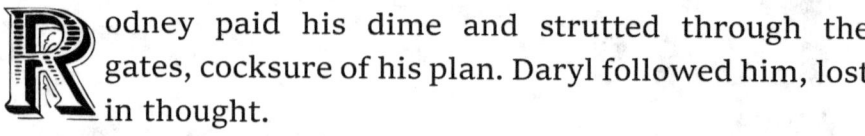odney paid his dime and strutted through the gates, cocksure of his plan. Daryl followed him, lost in thought.

The carnival had stopped for a weeklong stint at the fairgrounds in Knoxville, and the two Smoky Mountain moonshiners had been planning this caper for several months.

"Are you sure this will work?" Daryl asked, for what must have been the hundredth time.

"Of course. I know what I'm doing," Rodney replied.

"But what if she doesn't know?"

"She'll know. She has to know. Why do you think magicians call them 'tricks'? Do you even know what it means to trick someone, you dunce?"

"Don't call me that. 'Course I do. It's like when we pissed in that empty beer bottle and gave it to Alan."

"Exactly. It's a cunning act intended to deceive someone." Rodney had looked the word up in the dictionary that morning so he could spout it off and sound more confident than he felt. He knew his theory was right, but that didn't mean it would work.

"So what's your point?"

"I mean the magician doesn't actually saw someone in half, idiot. There is some trickery involved, and the assistant must know what the magician does. I'm sure he doesn't even pick a random person from the audience like he says he does. The person is probably a plant."

"A plant? Like a rose bush? That doesn't make any sense."

"Not a literal plant, shithead. No wonder the only job you could get was picking up the trash. How'd you ever graduate from school anyhow?"

Daryl looked down at his feet. "I didn't."

"That explains a lot, except for why I'm friends with you."

"Probably because I'm the only one who drinks as much as you do and will tolerate your asshole attitude."

"You may have a point there." Rodney shrugged and chuckled. "Anyhow, a plant means putting one of their own people in the audience who knows the trick."

"Ahh. That makes sense."

"Why would his assistant tell us the trick though? Wouldn't she be afraid of losing her job?"

"Well, we'll just make her more afraid of what we might do to her if she don't tell us."

"Whoa. I'm not down with hurting no one, 'specially a dame."

"Neither am I, but she don't need to know that."

Daryl looked up with a smile. "Now I get it. But how are we going to keep from getting caught?"

"We'll wait till the evening show when it gets dark, and kidnap her from the tent when no one's around."

"You sure the magician will still do the show if she's missing though?"

"As they say, the show must go on. Who knows? He probably has someone to fill in for her too. I mean, people get sick or take days off work, right?"

"That's true. We going to wear masks so she can't identify us?"

"Nah. Tonight's the last night of the carnival. They'll be pulling up stakes after the last show in the big top ends at 8. They won't stick around to get the police involved. Don't you know that carnies try to avoid dealing with them?"

"You really did think of everything."

"I know," Rodney said, with a cocky grin.

Rodney and Daryl hid in the darkness of the copse of trees near the magician's tent. A man carrying a satchel walked out of the back and headed toward the midway.

"Now's our chance. The show starts in an hour. She's probably in there getting ready. You know how long it takes dames to do their face," Rodney whispered.

The two men waited for the coast to be clear, then ran, hunched over, to the tent and slipped through the opening.

The woman walking around in a silk robe didn't notice Rodney slip up behind her—until Daryl caught her attention when he stumbled over a small rock on the ground.

"What are you doing in here?" She clutched at her robe, pulling it tighter around her. "Get out!"

Rodney wrapped one hand around her waist, pulling her up against him with one hand and using the other to cover her mouth. "Keep quiet and do what we say, and you'll be fine."

Tears fell from her eyes, and she nodded. Daryl pulled a gag out of his back pocket and shoved it in her mouth, tying it tightly in the back. Then he helped Rodney bind her wrists with the belt from her robe.

Daryl looked outside and didn't see anyone around. Rodney scooped her up and carried her into the darkness, with Daryl close behind. The two men took her to an old unused outbuilding about a half-mile away.

Rodney set her down on a wooden crate while Daryl lit an oil lantern. "Let's establish some ground rules here. Do you want that gag out o' your mouth?"

The woman nodded.

"If I take it off, no screaming. No one'll hear you over the noise coming from the carnival, and we're too far away anyhow. No trying to escape. I don't want you to get hurt, and I won't be able to stop him," Daryl tilted his head, indicating Rodney, "if you do anything stupid."

Rodney gave her his best maniacal grin, tossing a knife back and forth in his hands.

The woman's eyes grew wide, welling up with more tears.

Daryl untied the gag.

"Please don't hurt me. What do you want?" the woman whispered.

Alara entered the tent in search of Ozy. He should have come down to the performance tent ten minutes ago so they could prepare for the show.

"Ozy, are you ready? The show starts in thirty..." she called out as she entered the back of tent. She looked around, but he was nowhere in sight. His long-tailed tux was still hanging on the rack. This wasn't like him. On her first day working with him, Ozy had told her, "If you're not twenty minutes early, you're late."

Alara trotted out of the tent and ran over to Charlie, one of the roustabouts, standing nearby. "Have you seen

Ozy?"

"No, ma'am."

"Uhh... okay."

"Something wrong?"

"I'm not sure. I can't find him. Do you know where Melanie is?"

"I just saw her sitting by the sideshow tent about ten minutes ago."

"Thanks."

Alara ran toward the tent, checking with everyone she saw along the way to see if anyone knew where Ozy was.

"Melanie!" she cried out as she neared the tent.

A woman emerged, concern on her face. "Alara? Are you okay?"

"Yes... no. I'm not sure. I can't find Ozymandias. We're due to be on stage in less than twenty minutes. He was supposed to meet me at the tent early to eat first, but he never showed."

"That's not like him."

"I know. I have a big favor to ask you. I'm going to keep looking for him. You helped him with his act before, when I was sick. Can you go to the stage and be ready to act as his assistant if he shows up there, and I don't get back in time? My costume is backstage, so you can get dressed there."

"Sure, doll. You know I'd do anything for you."

It was five minutes before the act, and neither Ozymandias, nor Alara had shown up. Melanie put on the costume and fiddled with the long tassels hanging from the skirt. It was the first time she'd gotten to wear it since Adoline had convinced Artemus to update it to look like a flapper dress. She didn't know what to do if they never arrived. Adoline had already come by to check on them and had been irritated when she didn't see Ozymandias ready to go. She had assured Adoline he'd be here, but she didn't want to be held responsible for his absence.

Melanie peeked out from behind the curtain to see a full house waiting for the show to begin. A little girl squealed when she saw her. "Look Mommy! She's so pretty!" Melanie waved and backed up, squealing herself when she bumped into Ozymandias, who had just appeared.

"You ready to go?" Ozymandias asked her hoarsely, out of breath.

Melanie tilted her head, squinting at him. Ozy seemed off, but there was no time to worry about it. It was showtime.

She waved at the roustabout off to her left, signaling him to raise the curtain.

"Welcome to Carnivale Darke and the Wondrous World of Magic with Ozymandias show. With no further ado, please let me introduce the world's most famous and accomplished magician, Ozymandias Pendragon!" Melanie stepped to the side with a sweeping gesture to her right, and Ozymandias appeared in a puff of smoke.

After all the times she'd seen or performed the act, this was the first time she'd seen him step into view from behind the curtain. He *really* must have been sick for his timing to be off.

"Now for my first feat of wonder. Melanie, please hand me the rings." Ozymandias held out his hand, pointing in the opposite direction from where Melanie had set out his usual props.

She paused only for a second before she saw a set of three metal rings on a wooden crate just offstage. She grabbed them and handed them to Ozy with a flourish.

"As you can see, I have three solid metal rings here," Ozy spun the rings on his arm, then clacked them together to show they were real. "Here, young lady. You want to hold one and verify its authenticity?"

Ozy held a ring out to a young girl in the front row. The young girl ran up, giggling, and tried to spin the ring on her hand. It fell off and bounced across the floor. Her mother jumped up and handed it back to Ozy, nodding and apologizing.

Ozy made a show of spinning the rings on his arms once more, then slid them against each other before clicking them together one... two... three times, and they were magically connected. The crowd cheered and clapped.

Next, he performed several close-up magic card tricks—another surprise for Melanie. This wasn't a part of his regular act.

When Melanie turned to retrieve the box for the next trick, he nodded. She returned a few seconds later with a large wood box on a rolling table with several latches sealing the lid.

Melanie called the audience's attention to the latches, then pointed out a split in the center of the box, which could be separated when the two halves of the rolling table were unlatched. Ozymandias spun the two halves of the box so the audience could see they were empty, then put it back together again with a flourish. He flipped open the lid and directed Melanie to position a small set of steps next to the box.

"Now, for my last feat... Any guesses what it might be?" Ozymandias asked.

Melanie looked over at Ozy to see if she'd heard right. This wasn't usually the last trick. Maybe he was too sick to do a full show.

She heard a couple of whistles from the audience before a loud male voice from the audience called out, "You're going to saw your assistant in half!"

Ozymandias held up his finger. "Close but no Kewpie doll. You've probably never seen the trick this way, or how else could I call it a feat of wonder?"

Several people cheered and leaned forward, excited to see what he had in store for them.

"For this feat, I will need a volunteer from the audience. Do I have any takers?"

A flurry of hands flew up in the air.

Ozymandias stepped down from the stage and grabbed the hand of a dark-haired beauty with delicate finger waves framing her face, dressed in a black flapper dress. She was tipsy and unsteady on her feet, so he helped her get onto the stage, before leading her up the stairs to climb into the box.

She almost fell when she hesitated a little at the top, but Ozymandias took her hand and gave her a reassuring nod.

Once the woman was inside, Melanie closed the box and latched it. Usually, the two of them would spin the box all the way around several times to show it was closed. But she was afraid she might make the young woman throw up, so she only turned it once.

Ozymandias stepped offstage and returned with a large saw in his hand, brandishing it for the audience to ogle.

"What's your name, my dear?"

"Bette."

"And what do you do for a living, Bette?"

"Why, dance and drink at the jazz clubs, of course," Bette said with a hiccup before lapsing into a fit of giggles.

A volley of whoops and cheers arose from the men in the audience, while the older women looked at the volunteer with disdain, shaking their heads and covering their children's ears.

"Water, you mean, I'm sure," Ozymandias said with a wink to the audience.

"Pure unadulterated giggle water," Bette tittered.

"Well, my dear, I hope you're plenty hydrated. Are you ready for me to saw you in half?"

"Yes!"

Ozymandias held up the saw once again for everyone to see. Then he placed it in the split and began to make exaggerated sawing motions. After a few seconds, the sawing seemed to slow and even bog down as the magician struggled with the saw. Bette let out one loud, ear-piercing scream and then her head slumped to the side.

Ozymandias smiled, a few beads of sweat dripping down his face. "Guess the excitement was too much for her. Better finish before she wakes up." He continued sawing, and finally removed the blade—which was smeared with blood.

A woman from the audience stood up and screamed, then fainted into her husband's lap. Mothers covered their children's eyes and pulled them out of their seats, heading for the door.

The man who'd been so excited about the trick earlier stood up and approached Ozymandias menacingly, "You killed her!"

Ozymandias dropped the saw and raised his hands. "No, no, no! I didn't hurt her. She's fine. Tell them Melanie. She simply passed out. We all know she's had too much hooch today."

Melanie stood there with her mouth open, looking back and forth between Ozy and the men preparing to rush the stage. "Uh... umm," she croaked in a wheeze.

"It's a new trick. I took it too far. It was meant to be shocking. I didn't know that the red paint would be spread so much, or that the girl would pass out. She's new to the biz. She was nervous about her first performance and drank too much to calm her nerves."

"She's a plant. You tricked us?" the man in the front growled.

Ozy turned to Melanie and touched her arm gently. "Please wheel her to the back and find some smelling salts to rouse her." Then he turned back to the crowd with a weak smile. "I'm very sorry to upset everyone so. The talker will give you a refund at the door, as well as a voucher for a free hot dog for everyone."

Melanie weakly pushed the box to the back, her eyes glazed over. The man in the back closed the curtains behind her.

The man leading the charge stopped and appeared to be debating what to do. Ozy called to Arthur, who usually ran one of the kiddie rides, "Arthur, would you please take these good men to the cooch show?" He turned back to the men. "Please enjoy the show on me. I apologize for all the fuss."

The men in the back of the tent walked over to Arthur, and the others soon followed. When the last one left the tent, Ozy rushed into the back to find a pale Melanie, shaking in the corner.

"What happened? How could you do that? You're a monster!"

"Melanie! Melanie, it's me, Alara." Alara pulled off the wig and fake mustache, revealing her true identity.

Melanie's eyes went wide.

"I thought you'd recognize me."

Melanie was shaking. "I... I guess it's like Ozy always says: People see what they want to see."

"I guess."

"But that girl... that girl is *dead*! And you know we don't use fake blood. Or plants. Artemus would never tolerate that. What were you thinking?"

Alara lowered her head "I don't know what happened. I couldn't find Ozymandias anywhere. I didn't want to get us fired. I thought if I just pretended to be him that I could carry off the show good enough to get through. I thought the magic was in the props. Ozy has used that saw on audience members—and on us —how many times? And no one's ever been hurt."

"What are we going to do? Now we won't just get fired, we'll go to jail! Oh my God!"

"Melanie, calm down. I need you to run and find Artemus and Adoline now. Tell them it's an emergency. I'll handle the rest."

"Let's have it," Rodney said, brandishing a switchblade. "Now."

The woman had been resistant to telling them anything about Ozymandias' act and tried to attract attention, so they'd dragged her over to an old boxcar parked on an abandoned rail spur. They'd used it before in conducting the business of selling their hooch.

They used a piece of copper wire they'd found in the car to secure her hands and another to bind her feet.

"Why not start with the Sinister Saw, when that magician saws you in half?" Daryl suggested. "Ain't never been able to figure out how y'all do that."

"I told you," the woman said. "I don't know how he does his tricks. A magician never reveals his secrets."

"I don't believe you," Rodney said, spitting on the ground at her feet. You're part of the act. You *have* to know what he's doing, how the tricks work, and who the plants are..."

The woman sat up straighter. "There are no plants, and there certainly are no tricks," she said haughtily.

Rodney smacked her across the face with an open hand. "Stop lying, bitch," he said. "You're not very good at it."

The woman turned her head back around slowly to face them, fixing them with a determined look. "Why do you want to know, anyway? Who goes around kidnapping people just to learn a magician's 'trick,' as you so callously put it?" Then, answering her own question under her breath, she said, "Hillbilly trash."

Rodney stiffened, but it was Daryl who answered. "Look here, missy," he said, "you're in the Smoky Mountains. You might be thinkin' we're dumb as doorknobs or whatever, but we're people with feelin's an' everything."

"And we *ain't* dumb!" Rodney spat. "We were makin' the best moonshine in the Smokies before them big-city types moved in an' demanded a piece of the action. We told 'em we'd sell to 'em, but we didn't take kindly to them demandin' a piece of *our* action. So they sent their goons to come in an' bust up our still, and that was the end of it. Said they was makin' an example of us. It ain't our fault we're in this perdicament."

The woman opened her mouth to speak, but Daryl cut her off.

"Like Rodney here said, we made the best moonshine in the Smokies, an' now we wanna put together the best magic act in America."

"Which is where you come in," Rodney said, wiping his knife methodically back and forth against his jeans. "Everyone knows Ozymandias has the best magic act out there now, so we wanna know how he does it. Then we're gonna snatch him too. We don't take kindly to competition."

Rodney's face darkened as an amused smirk spread across the woman's face. "What's so funny?" he demanded.

"It's just that people always see what they want to see. What they're expecting to see. When confronted with the unexpected, they don't know how to react. You expect to see a trick, so you're not prepared for real magic. And you're right, Ozymandias *did* teach me some of it... like this!"

Rodney and Daryl jumped to their feet simultaneously.

"Where's she go?" Daryl said, looking frantically around the boxcar.

"Hell if I know!"

"There! I heard something over there!" Daryl pointed.

"I heard some rustlin' in the hay."

The air looked like it shimmered, barely perceptibly, but it was hard to tell in the dimly lit boxcar.

"Them's just shadows, you dimwit!"

Just then, some hay on the floor of the boxcar blew up into Rodney's eyes as though it had been propelled by a dust devil. The door to the boxcar, however, was shut, and the air inside had been stale and dead—until now.

Rodney began coughing and wheezing as he raised both arms to his eyes, dropping the switchblade as his arms flailed against the hay and dust. Before he could focus, he felt a sharp pain in his gut, as though someone had kicked him, and doubled over, falling to his knees. Then came a heavy blow to the back of the head, and then another, knocking him out.

Daryl stood watching, transfixed, trying to see what was happening. He rubbed his eyes as a piece of loose copper wiring appeared to untie itself and wrap itself around Rodney's throat.

Rodney gasped as he came awake suddenly, reaching up with both hands to grab the copper, but it was already wrapped too tightly around his neck for his fingers to get any purchase. The indenture in his neck deepened until blood began oozing out over the wire. Rodney's eyes bulged as he choked and sputtered. The wire dug in even more, and the blood began to flow more freely until Rodney's hands fell to his sides. His eyes closed, and the sputtering finally ceased.

It was then that Daryl saw Rodney's switchblade, apparently hovering in the air. He saw that faint shimmer again, almost like camouflage that matched the boxcar's interior perfectly. Then the knife came forward suddenly, and he felt the stab of cold metal into the side of his throat, followed by the warm flow of blood gushing out. He fell to his knees, thrashing around.

The last thing he saw was the door to the boxcar open of its own accord and heard a voice call back through the entrance: "Never dealt with a strong woman, have you? I may wear a dress, but you better not mess."

Artemus, with Adoline on his heels, burst through the curtains in a rage. "What the hell is going on? What's this about a girl being sawed in half?" As he finished his sentence, the scene before him finally sank in. Blood had pooled in the dirt underneath the box.

"Dear God! Who is she?" Adoline asked breathlessly.

"I don't know. Some drunk flapper named Bette that I picked out of the audience."

"You? Alara, what in the hell are you doing dressed as Ozymandias? You're his assistant. You hand him the props, you don't perform the magic. Or should I say *murder* in this case."

A woman came running into the tent, flushed and out of breath and stopped in front of Artemus. "Artemus! I killed them! They gave me no choice."

Artemus' crimson face appeared ready to burst.

"*Who*, may I ask, are you? And who did you kill?" he bellowed in her face.

She looked around at everyone else, then her eyes settled on the dead girl in the box and Alara standing next to her. Alara gave her a mournful look before casting her eyes down to the ground.

"It's me, Artemus, Ozymandias. It appears that I have a lot of explaining to do. But what happened here?"

"I tried to fill in for you. I looked everywhere for you. People were getting angry that you weren't here ready for the show. I didn't know what to do. I couldn't let us get fired. I didn't know how to perform any of your magic, but I did know a few tricks from a magician I worked for in the past." Alara averted her eyes as she pointed to the box, "But I'd seen, or been a part, of this one countless times. I thought the magic was in the box, but I was wrong."

"You performed fake magic tricks for my audience?" Artemus demanded.

Alara nodded, tears falling from her eyes.

The woman claiming to be Ozymandias came forward and wrapped Alara in her arms. "I'm so sorry."

Alara gasped when she saw her up close. "You're covered in bruises, and you're bleeding. What happened to you?"

"Would someone care to explain to *me*, Artemus Darke, about just what happened here?"

"Artemus, my real name is Ophelia Penn, but you've known me for the last seventeen years as Ozymandias Pendragon."

"And why have you hidden your true identity from me?"

"Everyone knows how difficult it is to get a job at Carnivale Darke. You insist on authenticity and only the best. I knew you wouldn't hire me as your magician if I was a woman. The world isn't ready for a female magician. We're only seen as fit to be the assistant in the skimpy costume." Ophelia held out her open hand toward Melanie."

"So much for authenticity," Artemus grumbled. "And who is Alara then?"

"This is Alara Clearwater, my partner, just as you've known her from the start." Ophelia put her arm around Alara's waist and gave her a soft kiss on the lips."

"I see," Artemus replied.

Adoline gave them an understanding nod. She knew how difficult relationships could be in the carnival life.

"And why weren't you here at the show tonight so that this whole mess occurred with Alara?" Artemus asked. "You mentioned killing someone... *more than one person,* if I recall correctly. What happened?" His impatience was growing.

"About an hour before the show, two men entered my tent and kidnapped me. Apparently, they wanted to know the secrets behind my tricks, starting with this one." Ophelia pointed at the box. "They thought I was the assistant and that I would know. When I wouldn't tell them, they hurt me. The one man named Rodney... I thought he was going to kill me. I killed them in self-defense. I came running back here as fast as I could, hoping the show had just been delayed."

"Adoline, please see Melanie to her tent before she drops." Turning to Melanie, Artemus continued: "Don't tell anyone what happened here tonight. Adoline and I will speak to you again in the morning when you've recovered."

Melanie nodded weakly and followed Adoline out.

"What do you know about all of this?" Artemus asked Sammy, the roustabout standing in the corner of the room.

"Nothing. I was just manning the curtain," he replied.

"Anybody else know what happened here?" Artemus was looking directly at Alara.

"Arthur was here. I had him take the men to the

coochie show. I made sure they all got a refund, and I gave them vouchers for a free hot dog. I think some of the wives are pretty hot though."

"Sammy, go find Arthur and bring him back here. I have a job for the two of you." Artemus turned back to Alara. "And just how did you explain what happened here to the audience?"

"I told them it was a new trick meant to be shocking, but it just got out of hand. I said she was a new employee who got drunk and passed out."

"And they *bought* that sorry excuse?"

"Seemed to. Nobody argued it. She appeared to be here alone, and I don't think that anybody knew her."

Adoline re-entered the tent, with Sammy and Arthur right behind her.

"Adoline, I need you to work the ticket booth for the rest of the night. If anybody complains about the magic show, apologize and give them a refund. Get the word out to the staff that we're getting out of here as soon as possible tonight."

"Got it." Adoline touched Ophelia's shoulder gently, "It'll be okay," and then turned to leave.

"Sammy and Arthur, I need you to get the wagon and take this girl's body a few miles down the tracks, and leave her on them. Make sure you remove any identifying information, and burn her clothes in the rubbish bin. When the 9:30 train comes through, there'll be nothing left to find."

Sammy walked out and found an old canvas cloth to bundle up her body. When they separated the table, blood and loops of intestine poured out onto the ground. The sour, fetid smell of feces and bile filled the room. Alara turned away and gagged, tears filling her eyes. The two men carried out the bundle and rode off into the night.

"Alara, you made this mess. Clean it up. I need to speak to Ozy... what's your name again?"

"Ophelia."

"Ophelia then. Leave no speck of blood behind. There's to be no sign that anything untoward happened here. Is that clear?"

"Yes."

"We'll discuss your future later."

Alara nodded and went to work. Artemus pushed through the curtain and led Ophelia out to the main part of the tent.

"What about these men that you killed? Is there anything to link you or, more importantly, Carnivale Darke to their murders?"

"No, sir."

"How did this happen?"

"What do you mean?"

"How could she have cut her in half?"

"From the moment I came here, you insisted that all my magic be authentic. No tricks to deceive the viewer into believing something happened if it didn't. My magic is just that. I can make the impossible happen, just as Magnus did for you in the past. It's not linked to my props. The saw in Alara's hand did just what it should have... ripped through that woman's flesh and bone, killing her."

"But not when..." Artemus looked bewildered.

"A magician never reveals his—or her—magic. You've seen me do it. You know that Alara or Melanie or whoever I choose from the audience is in two halves when I'm done. Healthy, happy, pain-free, and fully functional but cleaved in two—until such time I return them to their natural state. I won't explain my methods, but they are authentic. You know that, Artemus. You provided me with that saw, did you not?"

Artemus nodded. "I shall forgive this trespass because of the peril you faced. However, I cannot stand for this fraud to continue."

"But..."

"No buts. Your magic is real. *You* must be authentic as well. You may go by Ophelia or whatever name you like, but from now on, my magician is female. Is that clear?"

Ophelia was dumbfounded. "Yes, sir, but won't that be a problem?"

"Carnivale Darke is what *I* make of it. If people don't like it, they can go see one of the tricksters down the road. As for Alara, however, her deceit cannot be tolerated."

Ophelia stiffened. "If you send her away, I'm afraid I shall have to leave as well. Society may not tolerate us, but we refuse to be separated, even if that means I have to live as a man forever."

"I didn't say she had to leave. The two of you may continue as you see fit. That is no concern of mine. However, she will no longer be in my employ and will receive no salary from me. If she doesn't cause any more trouble, she is welcome to travel with the carnival—but at *your* expense. I'm assuming you're agreeable to that."

"Yes, sir."

"Now go make sure that all traces of foul play are disposed of. This tent and everything in it needs to be ready for showtime tomorrow in Asheville."

STEPHEN H. and SHARON MARIE PROVOST

A Monstrous Proposal

Some derided them as freaks. Others glorified them as prodigies. Call them what you will, these performers were mainstays of carnivals and traveling exhibitions from the 19th century onward. Many visitors came to see the Bearded Lady or the Elastic Man simply to gawk at and ridicule those who were different... and, in their narrow minds, inferior. I was not unaware of this impulse, but I did not share it. I treated my prodigies the same way I did all my acts: as human beings worthy of being handsomely paid for their unique talents—as long as everything was on the level. I, of course, reaped my own financial reward from their efforts, just as any employer does. But there were showmen for whom this was not enough, men who would dress their carnies up in wigs, plastic appendages, and ridiculous masks that made them seem more clownish than marvelous. At least one such charlatan decided to go even further—to actually create monstrosities out of unremarkable animals and people. When this loathsome individual showed his true colors, it was clear he had no place... at Carnivale Darke.

—Artemus Darke

1933

Adoline drummed her fingernails on the wood as she waited for someone—anyone—to come buy a ticket. Crowds of fairgoers had been few and far between as of late, but it had gotten especially bad as they traveled through the Plains states. As if the Depression hadn't hit the country hard enough, the drought and dust storms in the area had turned Burlington and all of eastern Colorado into one large ghost town.

Artemus liked stopping in out-of-the-way places like Burlington because, he said, "There's no competition. People are starved for entertainment there; they spend months just waiting for the circus to come to town."

Most of the time that worked, but not here in Colorado. The dust had taken enough of a toll here that many had moved on to (literally) greener pastures. Against that backdrop, the man Adoline saw approaching stuck out like a sore thumb—as if he needed help in that regard—with the hitch in his step inexorably drawing all eyes to him. He looked like a visitor from a distant land in the long brown hooded cloak he wore, despite the sun's rays beating down.

He slapped a dime on the counter. "One please," he said gruffly, his head hung low.

"Here you go. The show in the big top starts at 7. Carnival rides are to the left, the Ten-in-One and other acts are to the right, for an additional dime," Adoline replied with a smile. She stooped slightly in an effort to see under his hood, but he never lifted his eyes to meet hers.

"Thanks." He entered the carnival without a look back and headed toward the shows.

Adoline perched on her stool and pondered the strange man's demeanor. Was he trying to hide from the law? Artemus wouldn't appreciate that—the last thing they needed was some sheriff poking his nose around for no reason. But then again, maybe he didn't want trouble any more than they did. He sure wasn't doing a good job of avoiding scrutiny.

The man walked up to the sideshow tent, but the talker wasn't up on the bally stage. He poked his head inside and called out, "Hello?"

A dwarf poked his head out from behind a curtain. "Come back later. Show's closed till 1:30."

"Excuse me. Might I speak to you for just a moment?"

"Come back at 1:30!" The dwarf disappeared behind the drape.

The cloaked man walked into the tent and poked his head into the back. "I hate to bother you, but I really must speak to you about a matter of some importance."

Adoline hadn't been able to get that strange man out

of her mind, and she felt compelled to go investigate.

She called out to Fannie, who was just returning from the cookhouse. "Can you watch the ticket booth for a few minutes? I'll send Martha to relieve you when I find her so you can get to the show."

Fannie nodded, and Adoline scurried off in the direction the stranger had gone. The sideshow tent was empty, and she was about to walk past it toward the thrill acts tent when she heard voices inside coming from the back, one of which was rough and unfamiliar. Adoline leaned in close, pressing her ear to the fabric, straining to hear the conversation...

The dwarf rolled his eyes at a young girl with long curly hair sitting awkwardly on a stool. Her knees bent backward, almost like the hocks of a four-legged animal. "And they say *we* are disabled. Are you hard of hearing, sir? I told you to beat it! We'll see you at 1:30."

The girl giggled and leaned forward, her hands

coming to a rest on the straw-covered floor before walking on all fours over to a wooden crate where a plate of food sat. "My name's Ella the Camel-Legged Girl. Don't mind Sal over there. He's grumpy when he's hungry, but he's right. The show will be back in just about 35 minutes."

"I need to speak you in private though."

Sal and Ella peered at him curiously. They hadn't seen him say anything. "You got someone else with ya?" Sal grumbled, moving over to sit on a hay bale beside Ella.

"No," the man replied, as he pulled off his cloak to reveal a head that bore not a single face but two.

Sal's eyes widened just a little, and he nodded approvingly.

"Well, actually, yes," said the second face, which was looking at them from the large mass protruding from the top of the man's head. He made a grand, practiced bow. "Allow me to introduce ourselves. Our name is Rob...," he said as he pointed to his chest before pointing at his head, "...Bert. Rob-Bert! Pleased to make your acquaintance, Ella and Sal. Now, may I have a moment of your time?"

"Of course you may," said Ella, smiling brightly.

Sal nodded in agreement. "You're one of us."

"Very well then," said Bert. "I'll let Rob do most of the

talking."

The conversation shifted to what seemed to be the primary, more developed head of the two. "I'm the more loquacious of our pairing," Rob laughed. "But I'll cut straight to the point: Bert and I have come here to extend you an invitation. We would be honored if you would consent to join us..."

"Join you where?" Sal interrupted, a skeptical look in his eye.

"Don't be so suspicious!" Ella said. "I think he's inviting us to dinner," Ella said. "I do hope it's a filet with some nice red wine. We never get anything fancy here." She winked at Rob... then winked again, meaning it for Bert.

"That's exactly why I'm here," Rob said. "But I'm inviting you to more than just dinner. What if I told you that, where I come from, we eat filet mignon every other week, and a different meal every night? Fried chicken, chicken-fried steak and potatoes, rib roast with au jus... It's not like *some places*, which only give you slop or hot dogs the customers didn't eat."

Ella frowned. "Well, it's not quite that bad here," she said.

"Pretty close," said Sal. "We had beans and cornbread three times last week, and okra with tomatoes two others. And we *did* have stale hot dogs just yesterday."

Ella lowered her eyes. She couldn't argue. Even if the servings were always generous and the hot dogs weren't actually stale, she'd never had a filet during her two years at Carnivale Darke.

"How do they treat you here?" Rob asked. "Like second-class citizens, I bet. You're not big-top stars, you're just side acts to keep the crowd entertained until it's time for the big show. When that talker calls 'All out for the big show,' suddenly they don't love you anymore. They never did. They think of you as freaks because that's how Darke bills you. And that's how he treats you, too, isn't it?"

"Damn right," Sal scoffed.

"It's like that movie *Freaks*. You're kept out of sight until it's time for the show so you don't 'alarm' anyone, and the point of the show itself is for people to gawk at you. You know what they're saying to themselves, don't you?"

"Sometimes they say it out loud," Ella said, looking crestfallen.

"That's right!" Bert said.

"And," Rob continued, "they'll keep right on treating you that way unless you fight back. You're *stars*, not 'freaks,' and you need to be *treated* like stars."

Sal shot him a derisive look. "Fight back? You're full of it. Artemus Darke is one of the richest men in the world, and he doesn't give anyone a second chance. If you make problems, you're out on your ear. That's it. There's no coming back. He can always find someone else."

"Oh, but there's a bigger picture," Rob said.

"Dr. Zim..." Bert said.

Sal shot up out of his seat. "Zim? What about him?"

Rob put his hands out, palms down, in a calming gesture. "I'm sure you've heard a lot of lies about Zim from Artemus and his minions. They're famous for spreading shit, and it's all because Artemus holds a grudge against Zim for going out on his own... and creating a better show, built around people like us!"

"We don't care about that," Sal said. "Bossmen can fight all they want as long as it doesn't affect us."

"But it does, my friends, it does! That's what I'm telling you. Dr. Zim has come up with a system to celebrate people like us. We're invested in our work because we're invested, financially, in the company."

"You're shareholders?" Sal asked, incredulous.

"Exactly! Each of us actually owns a small stake in Dr. Zim's Carnival of Oddities. But don't just take my word for it. The invitation I'm offering is an invitation to come with me and visit our showgrounds. You can see for yourselves. We're just an hour or two away in Kit Carson. And we're serving filet tomorrow night." He winked at Ella.

"That sounds wonderful," she enthused, but Sal put up a cautionary hand.

"If you'll excuse us, we'll have to discuss this," Sal said. "Come back in a few minutes, and we'll give you our answer."

Just then, the tent flap was drawn back, and Jean-Jacques entered. A veteran performer, Jean was spending the twilight of his career with Carnivale Darke, showcasing a physique like none other: Known as 'The Double-Bodied Man,' he'd been born with a vestigial twin, Jacques, protruding from his stomach. The two shared the same circulatory and nervous system, and Jacques could even move his appendages—though he was not actually conscious.

Rob-Bert nodded slightly at Jean-Jacques as they passed at the entrance.

"Who was that?" Jean-Jacques asked, standing in front of them, "and what is it we need to discuss?"

"That's Rob-Bert," Ella said. "He wants us to come for

a filet dinner tomorrow!"

"Allllll right...," Jean-Jacques said. "I haven't heard of any steakhouses around here."

"Zim sent him," Sal said. "He's trying to recruit us."

Jean-Jacques nodded knowingly. "So *that's* why he's running his carnival just up the road in Kit Carson. He certainly didn't schedule a stop there because business is booming. Frankly, I can't understand why Artemus chose this place himself. It's deader than a doornail."

"Which means he won't miss us if we take Rob-Bert up on his offer," Sal said.

Jean-Jacques shook his head slightly. "I still think there's more to his invitation that meets the eye."

"You're such a killjoy," Ella said, rolling her eyes. "I

say we do it. What do we have to lose?"

"Our jobs?" Sal said with a snort. "Not that they're really worth keeping."

Jean-Jacques spoke up again: "Adoline just told me she's giving all of us the day off tomorrow. I think Thomas convinced her to do it. But that's doesn't mean..."

"See?" Ella said. "Now we don't have any reason *not* to go."

Sal gave a quick nod. "You've convinced me. Rob-Bert is right; we've been sitting here, just taking it, for too long. It's time to fight back."

Jean-Jacques held up his hand. "Let's not decide just yet. We still have the night to think it over."

Adoline couldn't wait any longer. The carnival was finally starting to pick up, and her help would be needed soon. But first, she had to let Artemus know what was going on before they ran into trouble.

Adoline charged into Artemus' tent, out of breath and flustered. "Artemus, we have a problem."

Artemus looked over the top of his spectacles at her. "Besides the fact that you left Fannie at the ticket booth when she was needed in the sideshow tent? We can't exactly give Fannie the Bigfoot top billing and then not have her show up, now can we?"

"I know, I know. I'm sorry about that. I didn't expect to be gone so long."

"No excuses needed. I solved that little predicament. But what has you in such a dither, my dear sister?"

"The problem I mentioned: That's what distracted me. I sold a ticket to a strange man in a dark hood today. He looked like he might be up to no good, so I followed him and overheard him talking to our performers in the freak show. He works for Dr. Zim, and he was trying to lure them away. He was very convincing, and I heard them talking about it afterward. They are considering going up to Kit Carson to check it out. It sounds like they're thinking seriously about jumping ship."

"That's preposterous. We pay our performers much more than they would earn at any other carnival or circus, including *Doctor* Zim's. Don't you remember what Ralph told us back when he came here?"

"I do. I just don't understand why he would want our freaks when Ralph told us he was making his own. All the news I've heard on the circuit seems to confirm that he has come up with some unimaginable creations."

"No doubt Harold is trying to damage our reputation and steal our acts—and therefore our audience—away. Times are hard, and I'm sure he's struggling, like they all are. Like we would be if not for my money. In fact, I recently heard about three more circuses going bankrupt in the last two months."

Adoline's expression grew more concerned. "We can't let them go, Artemus. I will not let Harold use them as pawns in his game of destruction with you. You may just see them as employees..."

"Highly paid and well-treated employees."

"I know. But they're family to me—the only family I have—other than you. We've given them a home and a way to make a living. Raise a family even, if they want. They're kept safe from the riffraff of society who might seek to harm or exploit them."

"I'm well aware, sister, of what we provide. I believe I'm the only carnival owner with a doctor on staff to treat the ailments of my employees. We wouldn't be able to care for them or stage The Show to End All Shows if I wasn't a good businessman. I protect my investments. Who knows about all this?"

"He was talking to Sal and Ella, then Jean-Jacques came in at the last minute."

"Who was this man anyhow? Did he give his name?"

"Umm... Rob Bert, he made a point of accentuating the two names, like he was two people, yet he appeared to be alone. But—and I know this won't make sense—I could have sworn there was someone else with him."

"Hmm. Well, we can solve this mystery by talking to our performers. Go round them up and find out if they've told anyone else. With luck, it hasn't spread to all of them yet since their performance won't be finishing for about five minutes."

Adoline returned 10 minutes later with Sal, Ella, Jean-Jacques, and Fannie in tow. Artemus raised his eyebrows at Adoline as she came in with Fannie. Adoline shrugged, "She is Sal's wife after all. You know he would have told her right away."

"I see," Artemus replied. "So is this everyone then?"

"Not exactly, but you can think of us as the 'board' making the decision in this matter," Sal replied with a smug smile. "All of us *freaks*...," Sal spat the word out with utter disdain, "are in the know now or soon will be. No one's going to be pulling the wool over our eyes. We've received a very lucrative offer to join Dr. Zim's Carnival of Oddities."

"You know I see all of you as my prodigies. The Ten-in-One may be known as the freak show, but that is purely for the purpose of dragging in the masses to see your performance."

"We know how all you *normal* people see us. Freaks... malformed... simpletons... undesirables. Unfit for polite society and only worthy to be seen at a 'freak show' so they can laugh, point, and make fun of us. Rob-Bert told us about that movie *Freaks* and confirmed everything we already knew."

Adoline stepped forward with a gasp, her hand over her mouth. "I could never think that!" Fannie placed her arm around Adoline's shoulders as a tear slid down her face.

Sal looked over at her with warmth in his eyes. "I didn't mean you."

Artemus stepped forward, a look of amusement on his face. "We all know about you and Thomas, Adoline. No one would believe that is the way you think." Turning back to Sal, Artemus continued, "You're right about the rest of the uncouth wretches in this world, but that's not true of us here at Carnivale Darke. Thomas may be called the Half-Man, but he is all man to my sister. That is all that matters. Why would we spend every moment together on the circuit for seven months out of the year, then winter together in Florida? Not in Gibtown, like the others. I built an entire community just for you. For us. Why would I pay every single employee of Carnivale Darke far more than you'd earn at any other carnival, circus, or at Coney Island? It defies credibility to suggest that Zimmerman's offer is somehow more lucrative. I insist on authenticity. I hire only the best, and I pay you accordingly."

"You say you pay us well, but how do we really know?" Fannie asked quietly.

"Ella—you can confirm—and several of the others came here because they weren't satisfied elsewhere. Who had the affrontery to travel here and present this so-called offer?"

"His name was Rob-Bert. He was really quite exceptional," Ella gushed with a big smile.

"How so?" Artemus was deep in thought, his brow furrowed.

"He had this big lump that jutted out from the top of his forehead, and there was another person, or should I say a face, there. It could talk and everything."

"She's right," Jean-Jacques affirmed. "I saw him leaving just as I arrived. It was like my parasitic twin attached to my abdomen, but instead of a body, it was only the head attached to *his* head." He looked dejected. "How could I ever compete for attention with that? Jacques has to wear a diaper, and Bert can speak in full sentences."

"My point exactly! And more importantly, just as I suspected! If you talk to Ralph the Regurgitator, he can confirm everything I'm about to tell you. Doctor Zim, as he calls himself, used to be plain old Harold Zimmerman. He was a partner in this very enterprise before I bought him out, and he opened his own carnival. It features a large freak show, that is, in fact, the centerpiece of his spectacle."

"Spectacle? And you say you're different?" Ella gasped.

"I say 'spectacle' because his so-called freaks are just that, not prodigies like you."

"What d'ya mean?" Sal groused.

"There are a few true oddities such as you, but the majority of them are Harold's creations. He fancies himself Dr. Frankenstein, and he's taking so-called 'normal' people and turning them into monsters. He does it purely for shock value and to feed his own ego when people are horrified by what they see. He even did it to his own son—turned him into The Brain."

"I still have nightmares about the way he described him," Adoline said, nodding.

"Turned a man into a bat and called him The Count. Apparently, he flies around the tent." Artemus snarled.

Ella gasped and wrapped her arms around Fannie's enormous leg.

Adoline rubbed her head. "These people are not authentic oddities. *They're* the real freaks, not you. They haven't experienced the pain, suffering, scorn, and humiliation that you have. They don't have true medical maladies that require treatment and special accommodations for their comfort."

"She's right," Artemus put in. "They're nothing but attention seekers! Those are the only people he really cares about. The true oddities he has on display are purely filler, at least until such time he comes up with a suitable creation to replace them."

Sal balled up both fists. "That's insane!" he nearly shouted. "You're making this shit up. Think we're too stupid to know better?" He turned away angrily and stalked toward the exit.

"I'm not!" Artemus said, and Sal stopped reluctantly and turned around, a fiery look in his eyes.

Artemus ignored his theatrics. "Look, I'll agree to let three of you visit Zimmerman's sick excuse for a carnival at my expense, so you can scope out the situation. Then you come back and tell me your decision. I trust you'll be back presently."

"How do we know that you're not going to fire us in the meantime?" Fannie asked. "Everyone knows you don't give people a second chance." She looked around at the others to back her up.

"Forget him. We don't need him if he does." Sal was growing more fired up by the minute.

"I'll overlook that." Artemus turned away from Sal and addressed Ella and Fannie. "You have my word. You trust Adoline, do you not?"

The two of them nodded.

"I suggest our delegation consist of level-headed individuals who can *control* their emotions." He shot a sidelong glare at Sal, and continued. "Ella, Fannie, and Jean-Jacques, are you interested?"

The three nodded enthusiastically.

"You'll be off in the morning then. Adoline will make all the arrangements."

The four of them walked out of the tent, Sal grousing the whole way. Adoline turned to leave as well.

"I need to speak to you for one moment, Adoline." Artemus sat down at the table. "I have a special mission for you as well. But first I need you to find Ophelia. Zimmerman is up to something. It's not an accident that Zimmerman parked his carnival so close to ours. We just need to figure out his endgame."

True to his word, Artemus had a car waiting the next morning to take Ella, Fannie, and Jean-Jacques 60 miles up the road to Kit Carson.

"Where's Adoline?" Ella asked as she climbed into the back seat.

"She's busy with a food-service issue. She's sorry she couldn't see you off. I'm sure you'll see her tonight when you return." Artemus said.

The trip, using gravel and occasionally paved roads, took them over a landscape far different than what most people thought of as Colorado. The Rocky Mountains occupied only the western half of the state, with the eastern part consisting of flatland and prairie.

Occasional barns and fence lines were the only things interrupting the sameness of it all, and the three were relieved when they finally arrived at Dr. Zim's carnival just outside Kit Carson. Rob-Bert had obviously been expecting them, as he was there to greet them at the gate.

"I'm so glad you were all able to come," he enthused. "I'll take you over to the Human Oddities tent to introduce you to all the other performers. Dr. Zim will join us there in a bit."

The trio followed Rob-Bert to the center of the showgrounds, where they saw two large tents marked "Oddities." They entered the bright red-and-black tent, the newer of the two, excited to see what Dr. Zim's had to offer. "This is the main performance tent," Rob-Bert said, "It is outfitted with ten curtained stalls, one for each performer. All of our performers have fancy costumes; and each stall is adorned with a soft armchair and lush décor."

One of the oddities, a half-man, quickly approached Rob-Bert, gliding across the floor on his hands. "Sir, I need to speak to you for a moment."

"Can't you see I'm busy here?" Rob-Bert hissed.

"I'm very sorry, sir. It's a matter of great importance."

The half-man climbed onto a nearby hay bale, and

Rob-Bert leaned down to listen to what he had to say in hushed whispers.

When they had finished their exchange, Rob-Bert turned back to his guests. "That's Johnny Eck, from that movie I told you about. He would never have gotten his big break without Dr. Zim! I wish I had time to introduce him formally, but I have to go attend to something," he announced. "Feel free to explore on your own. I'll be back in a few moments." Then he rushed off, following the half-man.

"Let's start over here." Fannie led the group to the first stall on the left. "It says it belongs to Sasha the Elephant Woman." Fannie expected to find a woman with greatly oversized legs and Bigfoot-sized feet like her own. But she and the others were all shocked to find a woman whose legs looked like they belonged on an *actual* elephant. The stocky pillars were covered in gray, wrinkled skin with small half-circle toenails painted pink.

Jean-Jacques was at a loss for words. He grabbed Fannie's hand and motioned for Ella to follow as he led them to the next stall, labeled "The Count." The man had long, sharp canine teeth, just like Dracula's fangs. His enormous wingspan exceeded the size of his stall. Ella saw Fannie turn pale and gulp as she lurched away.

Stall after stall revealed more of the same. A mermaid swimming in a pool. Siamese triplets. A lobster boy with sharp claws that could sever a man's arm. One grotesque, fake freak after another, just as Artemus had described.

But where were the real freaks, those like themselves?

The visitors stumbled out of the tent and tried to calm one another's frayed nerves.

"We have to find the real freaks," Jean-Jacques said, leading the others over to the second tent. "Maybe they're in there."

Jean-Jacques heard Rob-Bert calling out to them just before they entered, and turned to answer him. Fannie turned with him. Ella, walking on all fours, had surged ahead of them and was now blocked from view. Fannie gave a slight wave of her hand behind her back, motioning for her to continue inside.

"Where's Ella? And where are you two going?" Rob-Bert asked, his brow furrowed.

"We were going to visit the next tent while Ella saw the rest of the carnival. She's still a young girl, eager to explore. You know how it is," Fannie replied.

"There's nothing to see in there."

"Where are the rest of your freaks? I thought you wanted all of us from Carnivale Darke to join your show. There doesn't appear to be room for us in there." Jean-Jacques raised an eyebrow.

"They're all in there, as would you be." Rob-Bert motioned toward the tent behind them.

"I thought you said there was nothing to see," Fannie replied coolly.

"Right now, I meant. Nothing to see right now. They're on a break, eating lunch. We stagger performances."

"I see," Fannie said.

"Well let's go back to the other tent, and I'll introduce you to everyone. How will Ella find us?"

"She's resourceful. I'm sure she'll be back soon enough," Jean-Jacques said with a shrug.

When they returned to the tent, lunch was just being set up for them to dine with Dr. Zim and the Oddities. Roast chicken, potatoes, and wine were being served. Mysteriously though, the other freaks never joined them.

Ella hid behind the tent flap quietly until Rob-Bert had moved off with the others. Once they were gone, she continued across the floor to see what Rob-Bert was trying to hide. To her astonishment, she found ten legitimate freaks. They each had their own stall, but without all of the comforts she'd seen with the others.

224

There was Eleanor the Four-legged Girl, who had two normal legs on the outside with a pair of tiny semi-functional legs in between; Bobby the Human Caterpillar, who had been born without arms and legs; Sally and Lily the Siamese Sisters; Topper the Pinhead; and Arthur the Rubber-necked Man, among others. They were sitting on bales of hay in the center of the room eating a simple meal of peanut butter sandwiches and water.

Ella, never a shy girl, came up and started a conversation with them. "Hello. I'm Ella. Do you like working here?"

She heard a rustling noise from behind her and turned to see the Half-Man approaching her quickly. "You were with those others. What are you doing?" he asked her in a breathless rush. "You're not supposed to be here."

"What's the big secret?"

"Just leave it alone. You're going to get us all in trouble."

"Why aren't you in there with the other 'oddities'?" Ella asked, wiggling two fingers on each hand in the quote motion as she balanced herself on her elbows.

"We're not good enough," Bobby snapped.

"Shut up!" the Half-Man yelled.

"You shut up, Johnny! Think you're so special just because you were in a movie?" Sally cracked. "Dr. Zim will treat you the same as the rest of us when the novelty wears off." Lily finished her sister's statement: "All he cares about are those monsters he made."

"Think I don't know that? I intend to get out of here before he replaces me. Once he comes up with an idea to top your disability, it's a one-way ticket out of here. And it ain't to Poughkeepsie! But in the meantime, I intend to enjoy myself." Johnny turned away angrily, but his expression softened as he turned to face Ella. "I've got to get ya outta here, girlie," he said. "Now come on!"

Johnny scooted across the floor at surprising speed, forcing Ella to catch up. He led her back into the main Oddities tent and showed her to her seat. Rob-Bert gave him a questioning glance.

"I found her by the rides and brought her over for lunch," Johnny winked at Ella and disappeared quickly.

Adoline had seen Ella, Jean-Jacques, and Fannie follow Rob-Bert deep into the showgrounds upon their arrival. She had gotten to Dr. Zim's Carnival an hour ahead of them, undetected by anyone. Artemus had Ophelia cast something like an invisibility spell on her early that morning before she left so she could investigate unseen.

She started with the Oddities Exhibits. Harold's penchant for manufacturing fake oddities had led to his falling out with Artemus. She slipped through the opening of the tent and found exactly what she had expected to see.

Except it was different this time.

On display were stuffed eight-legged calves, a skeleton of Siamese lambs, another of an animal that appeared to have the head of a horse on the body of a goat. He hadn't just sewn on limbs procured from another animal... they were all part of the same creature. Zimmerman must have started experimenting with animals, not always successfully, and then moved on to people.

As evidence of this, there were live animal specimens as well, including a four-legged chicken and a three-headed pig. Each head of the pig was devouring food while it wiggled its curly tail happily.

The last section of the tent was devoted to humans. It was there that Adoline found the most disturbing exhibits of all. There appeared to be no limits to Zimmerman's depravity. He was clearly willing do whatever it took to make his creatures, even if the cost was someone's life.

One of the most sought-after treasures for a carnival oddities exhibit was the skull of a child with craniopagus parasiticus. This extremely rare condition was found exclusively in children because it always proved fatal, usually within the womb or very shortly after birth. Collectors and showmen considered such an object the crown jewel among conjoined or parasitic twins: two people connected at the skull, one with a fully developed body, while the other's body was vestigial.

Adoline approached a large glass case where the skeleton of a grown man was on display. Jutting from the top of his head was the *full-sized* skull of another person. This could never have happened in nature. Zimmerman, in his arrogance, appeared to have tried the impossible—and killed someone in the process.

Adoline knew he had to be stopped. But she had to find proof of his misdeeds before she could call the authorities. She hid in the shadows and waited for Zimmerman to appear. With any luck, she could follow him to his tent or wherever he did his experiments.

While everybody was distracted eating lunch, Ella told Fannie and Jean-Jacques what she had discovered. When the meal had concluded, Dr. Zim excused himself to attend to some carnival business.

"Thank you so much for coming to meet our little family, and that's just what we are here... family. I do hope you will decide to join us. I'm not sure if Rob-Bert explained it to you, but the Carnival of Oddities is an employee-owned operation. That means there are no employees, no salaries. Everyone shares in the profits."

"Does that include everybody who works here?" Fannie asked with a smile.

Dr. Zim swept his arm across the room, indicating everyone in attendance. "It includes all of you... my treasures. The Oddities. The backbone of my operation."

"If you have any questions, please feel free to ask Rob-Bert. He will take you out now so you can enjoy the carnival, and you are welcome to join us for dinner as well before your car arrives at 9. I hope to see you all again soon."

Rob-Bert led them out to the rides and invited them to enjoy whatever they'd like free of charge. Fannie took Ella over to the midway and ordered her some cotton candy. As they waited in line, Jean-Jacques came up and pointed out that Rob-Bert was deep in conversation with some of Zim's other oddities off in the shadows.

"If Rob-Bert asks where I am, tell him I went to the bathroom," Ella said. "I'm going to see if I can sneak over there and catch what they're talking about" Without waiting for a response from the others, she moved off toward where the conversation was taking place.

"Shouldn't we stop her?" Fannie asked, concern etched on her face.

"She can take care of herself. Let's go on the Ferris wheel. With any luck, he'll think she's on a ride too." Jean-Jacques linked his arm through her elbow, leading her away.

Fannie watched Ella creep away in the shadows, staying low to avoid detection.

Adoline saw two men carrying a large, rectangular box toward a black tent behind Zimmerman's own. This must be the place. Ophelia had put what the magician called a "glamour" on her so she could walk through a place unnoticed and unmolested. It didn't make her invisible... not exactly. But the result was the same. She didn't know exactly how it worked, but Ophelia had compared it to a putrid smell, like a skunk's spray, that would send people scurrying away before they paid too much attention. The only difference was that it affected the vision, not the olfactory nerve.

Adoline was careful not to follow the men too closely; the magician had told her the glamour only went so far: "It will do nothing to shield you from being discovered if you make a loud noise," Ophelia had told her, "so you'll still have to remain quiet."

Creeping up behind them, she heard them muttering. "Why is this thing so goddamn heavy?" the one at the rear of the box complained. "What do you think is in it?"

The other man turned his head and whispered over his shoulder. "How the hell should I know?" he spat. "They don't tell me nothin', just like you. All I know is we're just supposed to deliver it to the Zims."

"In *that* tent."

"Yeah, the lab tent. I know what's in there, dumbass."

A narrow smile crossed Adoline's lips, then quickly vanished. She was in the right place. But she had no better idea what was in the box than they did. It looked a little like a coffin, but coffins weren't made of metal, and usually weren't that wide or deep. Could it be Big Betsy, one of the few freaks Zimmerman kept on after he started trying to "create" more outlandish creatures like his son, The Brain?

She'd heard The Brain was helping him now, tapping into his own superior intellect to come up with even more grotesque specimens for the crowd's "enjoyment."

She crept up closer to the two men as they neared the tent, and entered just behind them before the flap closed. They placed the container on an elevated table and departed. It made her nervous to rely solely on Ophelia's glamour, so she moved off into a shadowy corner to be sure none of the four men in the room would spot her. She identified them as Zimmerman, his son, and two attendants, all dressed in black gowns, surgical gloves, masks, and goggles that made them look like barnstorming pilots.

An electric generator thrummed and whirred in one corner of tent, powering various medical devices that had been placed in the tent.

What on Earth?

The men were standing around a large woman, who lay naked and strapped down to a table: Big Betsy. But if she was here, then who—or what—was in the box? Betsy appeared to be conscious. Cannulas had been attached to her head in several places. A mask, fitted firmly over her nose and mouth, was connected by a tube to a machine powered by the generator and what looked like an oxygen canister. The machine forced air in and sucked it back out as Betsy struggled to keep up, filling her lungs so full that it looked like her chest might pop open. She was sobbing and trying to move, but she was held so tightly to the table that it was useless.

She moaned something through the facemask that sounded like, "No, Zimmy, please. I love you. You said..."

The elder Zim turned away. Adoline recognized him and noted how much he seemed to have aged. The Brain was standing next to him. It was impossible to miss him with that huge, malformed cranium.

"Shut up!" The Brain shouted at Betsy, who began whimpering softly. Then he whirled to face his father and grabbed him by the shoulders, turning him back around. "This is what you get when you get involved with the carnies. And a freak at that!"

Zim fixed him with a glare. "You presume to lecture *me*, boy? She's nothing to me."

The Brain glared at him but held his tongue. His father's dalliance with Betsy had not been public knowledge.

"Are you sure this is going to work?" Zim asked.

"No, I'm not. I've never done this before. You're the one who's always telling me we don't need tests. We could have tried this with a mouse and a bat, but you wanted to have Pigmalia ready for opening day."

"Don't call her that."

"You just said she was nothing to you. And you were the one who came up with that name."

"I didn't know it would be her, though."

"She was the only candidate—the only one on our staff with O-negative blood. We need to minimize the possibility of rejection."

As Adoline watched, she felt bile rising in her throat. She choked it back down, but in doing so felt a sudden contraction in her throat, followed by the inevitable sound of a hiccup.

Dammit!

The Brain turned to one of the two assistants, who was standing between him and Adoline's shadowy corner. "Get out of here now! Go drink a glass of water or something! We need steady hands for this procedure." He didn't wait for the man to leave but turned his attention back to the table.

The man stood still where he was, looking mystified.

Adoline hauled in a deep breath and held it, shutting her mouth tight. Her grandmother had taught her a sure-fire cure for the hiccups: downing a spoonful of sugar followed by a glass of water. There was, however, no water available, and she was unable to prevent a second hiccup.

The Brain didn't bother to turn around this time, shouting. "I told you to get the hell out of here. Now!"

The man regained his composure and hurried toward the tent entrance. Adoline had only one recourse left: She took her index finger and pressed it hard into the base of her throat, which made her gag. She opened her mouth as if to wretch but somehow managed to stay silent and avoid vomiting. She was relieved... and even more relieved to find the hiccups were gone.

The assistant returned, announcing he had "cured" the hiccups he'd never had in the first place. It was easier than trying to argue with The Brain, which never got him anything except more abuse.

The Brain, however, was ignoring him entirely. He was rushing around the head of the table where Besty lay, checking each of the half-dozen cannulas. "Sugar delivery in place," he muttered to himself. Betsy moaned louder as he moved to the facemask and breathing tube. "Oxygen secure."

When he was satisfied that everything was in place, he turned back to the assistants. "Now, you two," he barked, "bring the cooler over here and open it."

Something that looked like fog or steam rose from inside when the lid was removed, and a sudden chill filled the air.

Adoline watched as the assistants removed all four sides of the container to reveal its contents: the headless body of a pig packed in dry ice, which they hurriedly removed. Plastic tubes had been affixed to the creature, sticking out of its neck, and a large electric heater was brought over near it, presumably to thaw it out.

"Time is of the essence!" The Brain shouted. "We'll have less than a minute to complete the procedure once it is initiated. The oxygen and sugar will only buy us thirty seconds at most. Are you ready?"

"Yes, sir," the assistants replied in unison, as one took his place beside the pig and the other put his hands firmly on either side of Betsy's head.

"No! Oh, God, no!" she wailed, gagging on her own saliva as tears streamed down her cheeks.

The other assistant picked up what looked like an axe and raised it above his head, its razor-sharp blade glinting for a moment in a narrow beam of light shining down from a hole in the top of the tent.

Adoline caught her breath in horror as the man brought the axe down on Betsy's neck and severed it from her body in a single clean cut and the other assistant snatched the cannulas from her head. The head blinked its eyes once and glanced frantically, its mouth still open to produce a scream that died suddenly on the air. The eyes fluttered as the assistant, in a single pivot, moved Betsy's head to the table and set it there, where the porcine body was waiting. In a flash, The Brain began connecting the head to the tubes protruding from the porcine neck, almost dancing as he flew back and forth around the head of the table, securing the two ill-matched parts of his new creation.

"More heat to the body!" he shouted as he kept working, his hands moving at lightning speed. "It's still too cold!"

The elder Zim reached over and turned the heat to maximum, and the coils glowed so brightly that their orange light reflected off the pig's flesh.

At a signal from The Brain, one of the assistants leaned in with a vacuum and sucked up some of the excess blood that was seeping from the severed head. Only about half a minute had passed, but the Brain looked on the verge of panic as he attached the two spinal cords and signaled for his other assistant to begin pressing the head onto the pig's body as he guided the tubes so they would stay in place.

In a few blinks of Betsy's still-fluttering eyelids, the head was securely in place, and The Brain applied clips to hold it in place as he sutured it on faster than Adoline would have thought possible.

She looked at the pig, then back to Betsy's head, then at the pig again.

She thought she saw a leg twitch and then, incredibly, the pig's chest expanded ever so slightly and contracted again. It happened again an hour later, only this time it was more pronounced. The Brain was clutching both fists to his chest, his eyes fixed upon his greatest creation, as his father looked over his shoulder, an inscrutable expression on his face.

Betsy's head closed its mouth then, and opened it with a sickening gulp sound.

"Can you hear me?" The Brain asked, bending over her.

"Glurp," was the only response. It was somewhere between a burp and a gurgle, like the sound one imagined a giant fish might make if it were out of water, gasping for air.

The head rose in a giant convulsion, then dropped back hard on the table, but it hadn't moved of its own accord. The pig's body, now fully revived, was thrashing about wildly. Conflicting neurons from its own latent reflexes and Betsy's oxygen-starved brain sent it into violent convulsions.

"Glurp." Betsy started to drool, then a disgusting brew of blood mixed with vomit, bile, and half-formed fecal matter from the pig's digestive tract started pouring like lava out of her mouth. The connection had been a success, but The Brain hadn't counted on this.

"Vacuum!" he shouted. "Or she'll drown!"

The assistant put the vacuum to her mouth, but that only made her gag even more.

"Not so close, idiot! You're choking her!"

The assistant pulled back, but more of the pig gunk poured out of Betsy's mouth, faster now, and began seeping through the sutures connecting her head to the pig's body.

"Somebody make that pig lie still!" the elder Zim

shouted, and the assistant with the vacuum dropped it and ran to join the other in an attempt to hold the pig body down.

"Not you, fool!" The Brain screamed as the gunk began flying out of Betsy's mouth and seeping through the sutures, loosening them until, before anyone knew what was happening, they gave way under the pressure and the head fell away from the body. It rolled off onto the floor, covered in pig vomit, as the pig body thrashed a few more times, then finally fell still.

Pigmalia's short life had reached its end.

Ella recognized most of the people talking to Rob-Bert except for one. However, it didn't take much thought to figure out who he was... The Brain, Dr. Zim's son. Sally and Lily stood behind the group, holding a tray of drinks for them.

"Do you think they bought it?" The Brain asked.

"Hook, line, and sinker, especially that quadruped girl." Alex slapped his claw against Rob-Bert's shoulder, snickering. "Am I right?"

The Count nodded his head.

"Wonderful! Father... I mean Dr. Zim... will be so happy to hear that. He's been looking for a way to take Artemus down for years, and now, victory is near! He won't have anyone to draw in the crowds if his whole freak show abandons him. The rest of the acts will be sure to follow."

"What if some of the freaks don't come right away?" Alex asked.

"We'll string these others along long enough until they all jump ship. Then we'll dump them," The Brain replied.

"But what will happen to them? How will they survive? Nobody hires people like us," Sally said, gesturing toward herself and Lily.

"That's not my problem," The Brain scoffed. "Or yours. I'd worry more about where your next meal's coming from if I were you."

"I'll drop them at the soup line. Problem solved." Rob-Bert cracked. "I better go check on them. Their car will be here anytime."

Ella backed up into the shadows. Sally noticed the movement and shifted her position, with Lily in tow, to cover the girl's escape. Ella trotted off toward the main Oddities tent. She had one last task to accomplish before they returned to Carnivale Darke.

Fannie and Jean-Jacques had just stepped off the Merry-Go-Round when they saw Rob-Bert approaching.

"Where's the Camel Girl?"

"Camel-*legged* girl! She went to the restroom. She should be back any moment." Fannie looked around, hoping not to show her anxiety.

Just then, Ella appeared at her side. "You guys ready to go? I think I saw our ride pull up."

"Perfect. I'm quite tired from all the day's excitement, and I want to get a good night's rest. The next few days are going to be difficult."

The three visitors from Carnivale Darke proceeded toward the gate with Rob-Bert behind them. As they neared the ticket booth, they heard sounds of a disturbance back near the tents, followed by the scream of "Fire!"

"I apologize for not seeing you off, but I must go check

on that. We'll see you back here soon then?" Rob-Bert gave them a questioning look.

"Undoubtedly!" Ella said with a devious smile. As Rob-Bert ran off, she looked over to her companions. "I think we should hurry up and get out of here."

"I'll second that," Fannie replied.

The three of them jumped into the car and looked back at all the activity. Flames could be seen billowing from the large red-and-black tent.

"Did you start that?" Fannie looked at Ella, shocked.

"Yes, I did. But we've got bigger fish to fry," she replied.

"We certainly do," Adoline agreed from the front passenger seat where she had suddenly appeared. "Wilson hit the gas. We need to talk to Artemus immediately."

"Where did you come from?" Jean-Jacques exclaimed.

"I'll tell you on the way home."

When the group returned, they proceeded immediately to Artemus' tent and reported what they'd seen. Sal was already there waiting for them.

"So, it was just as I told you?" Artemus asked, not waiting for a reply. "Am I safe to assume you'll be staying here where you are appreciated?"

"Yes!" came the resounding reply from the group.

"I'll go talk to everyone else and let them know. Thank you, Artemus, sincerely," Sal said, reaching out to shake Artemus' hand.

Artemus nodded and turned toward Adoline, dismissing them with a wave of his hand. "You look like you still have more to say."

"Artemus, we have to stop him. He's the monster, not his creations—although they need to be dealt with too.

He's killing people with his sick experiments. If only you'd seen that poor woman! How she must have suffered in those few moments!"

"I know, Adoline, but there's nothing we can do. No one would believe us if we told them. Harold is undoubtedly covering his tracks. We just need to be careful. I'm sure we haven't heard the last of Zim and his tricks, or from that son of his."

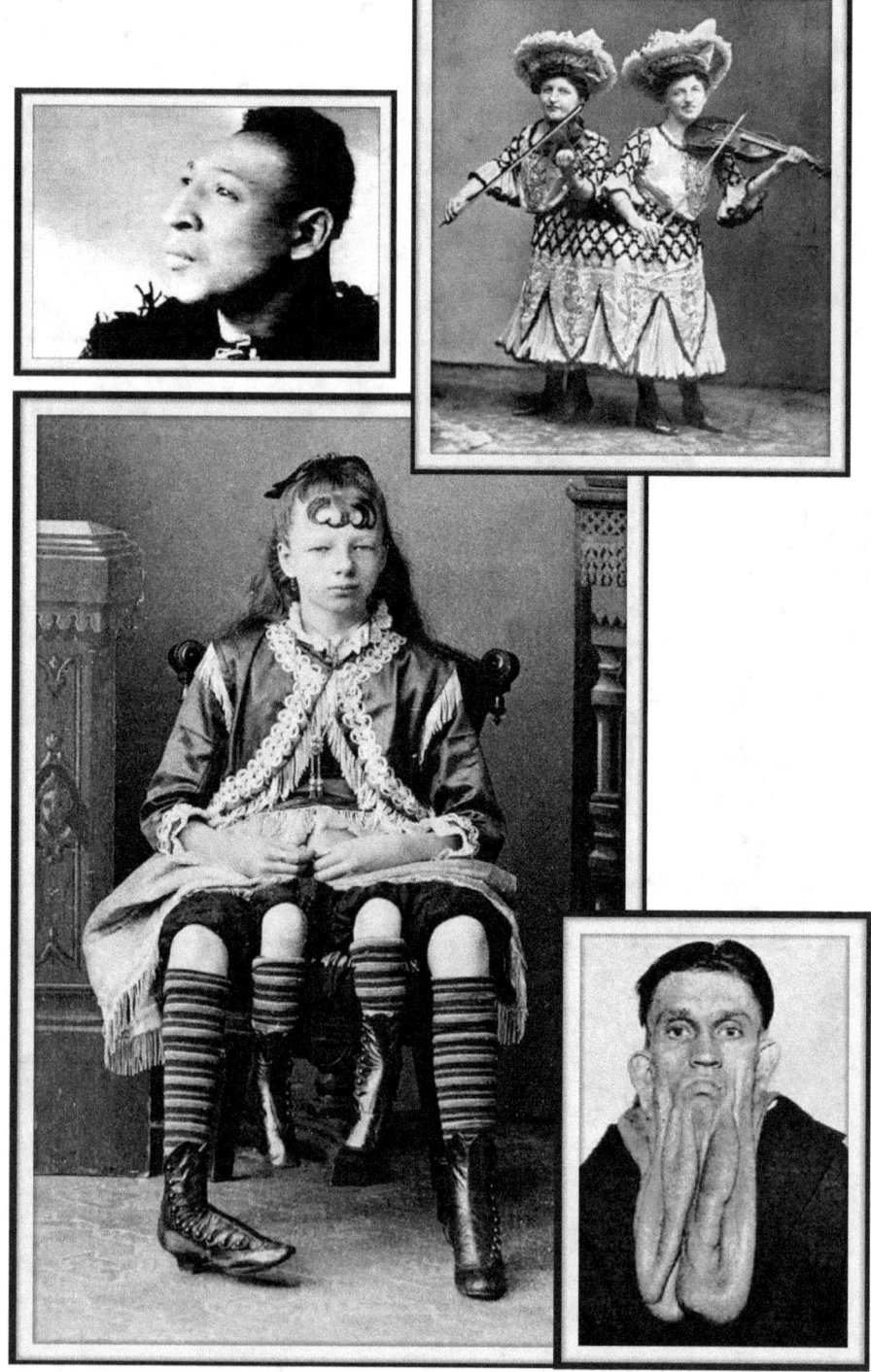

DANCING FOR DOLLARS

Men become their best when times are at their worst. An associate of mine maintained that this was true, and in doing so, ignited a lively conversation. I argued that, to the contrary, it is only the best of men who are prepared to survive such trying times. Consider, if you will, the Great Depression. A catastrophe to some, it awakened an indomitable spirit in others. Despite having lost everything, they clung to that ephemeral lifeline we call "hope" with all the tenacity of a pit bull terrier. Some

241

walked hundreds of miles on dusty highways, searching for a new start in California; others danced in slow, delirious circles on ballroom floors, hoping to win big money by being the last ones standing. Hooverville has-beens and breadline beggars tried their luck at these dance marathons, which paid money to those who could last the longest. These weren't dance contests as much as wars of attrition. It might take days or weeks or even months, but the conviction that they could survive pushed them far beyond the limits of their endurance—and, sometimes, of their own moral code. Such dreary spectacles were not to my taste, so I took it upon myself to liven things up and sweeten the pot. Witness now a pair of down-on-their-luck Texans, shuffling their way along Route 136 to a little piece of nowhere called Spearman. It is there that they and many others will soon converge, drawn like flies to a filthy stable, hoping to find redemption and a new lease on life... at a place we call Carnivale Darke.

—Artemus Darke

April 1935

our feet kicked up dust as they scuffed their way up the highway northward. Highway 136 was their yellow brick road; that's how Leland and Maybelle Rodgers saw it. They'd left Amarillo behind for greener pastures outside of Spearman. Not greener, exactly. That was a figure of speech. Most of the pastures around Spearman were dusty flatlands. The crops there had lost their grip on the hard, parched earth, blowing away as surely as the Okies had fled to California.

Spearman wasn't quite on the Panhandle, it was close enough. Leland didn't want to talk about that. He was a

Texan through and through, going by the most common nickname in the Lone Star state "Tex." But he and Maybelle were anything but common, even if they'd lost their home like half of everyone in North Texas. If it wasn't the Depression, it was the Dust Bowl. The thirties got you one way or the other, leaving you with nothing but the clothes on your back and the shoes on your feet.

The bank had foreclosed on the Rodgers' little two-bedroom home in Amarillo, and they'd taken their Model A less than a month later. That's why they were walking up Route 136 toward the little town of Spearman. Conditions weren't any better there. In fact, one-third of the population had departed when the dust storms started in '34. So why go to Spearman?

Because that's where the Darke Dance was happening, a marathon contest being staged by Artemus Darke, owner of the world's most famous traveling carnival. Darke had chosen Spearman as the site of his opening show on the '35 circuit, which might have seemed peculiar to most people—as it did to Tex and Maybelle. But Darke had somehow stayed a millionaire, even after Black Thursday, and was known to make shrewd business decisions others didn't always understand. As for Tex and Maybelle, beggars couldn't be choosers, and with a $3,500 prize being offered to the winner, they figured it couldn't hurt to throw their hats into the ring.

"I think I'm a-gettin' a callous on my heel," Maybelle complained as they were coming into Stinnett. It was the county seat of Henderson County, with a grand courthouse... and not much else to speak of, two-thirds of the way to Spearman.

It's natural for travelers to lose a little spring in their

step when they see a town appear on the horizon ahead. They might be on their way somewhere else, but even a town of a few hundred people seems like a destination, especially when you've walked sixty miles and you've got another thirty to go.

Just a mile before they hit town, Maybelle sat down in the middle of the road and removed her shoes, rubbing her feet. "Callouses," she muttered again.

"Your shoes're comin' apart, Maybe," Tex said, using a nickname she'd never found quite as funny as he did. "Look at them soles comin' loose. We need ta get 'em fixed up afore the contest."

"No duh, mister smarty-pants. That's what happens when ya been walkin' fer a week an' a day." She put her shoes back on, hauled herself up to her feet again, balled up her fists and started walking.

Leland stepped in front of her and stopped, forcing her to stop. "Now, Maybe, ya know there weren't no other option," he said, half sternly and half apologetically.

"But how're we gonna dance in this, Tex?" She took her left shoe off again and held it up in front of him, waving it—with its half-detached sole flapping around like a chicken wing—in front of him. "It ain't just comin' loose, it's got a hole!"

"Then I guess we gotta get some new ones." Tex reached into his pocket and jangled some coins.

"That money's fer the entry fee, Tex, an' fer food. How're we gonna get through the contest it we cain't eat?"

"Holy smokes, Maybe! I'm trying ta help here!"

"Well y'aint doin' a very good job of it, *Leland*. I'm sore an' I'm hungry, and one feelin's just as irksome as t'other."

Tex put his thumb and forefinger on the bridge of his nose. "Irksome to you, woman," he muttered. "Aggravatin' as hell to me."

Maybelle stood up straight and got on her tiptoes, so she was staring Tex right in the eye. "If you ain't got no good ideas, I do," she said, and waved her left hand under his nose. The tiny stone on her wedding finger sparkled with red and gold and blue in the sunlight. "How much did ya pay for this?"

"Maybe! That's..."

"How much!?" she interrupted, raising her voice.

Tex stared down at his feet and scuffed them on the ground. "A hunerd bucks," he said.

"*A hundred bucks*?!" Maybelle shouted. "You can't buy a proper diamond fer that! What is it? Glass? You cheapskate sonofabitch! I oughta..."

"Quartz," Tex muttered. "Not glass. Quartz."

"And when were you gonna tell me about this? I'll tell you when. Never. I figured we could get a thousand bucks for it, but noooooooo! You had a lot of guts givin' me this... this... *fraud*! If we coulda sold it for a thousand bucks, like I thought we could..."

"Then we wouldn't be needin' that prize money, Maybe. And you wantin' to pawn it. It hurts, Maybe. It just hurts."

She slapped him in the arm. "Now don't you go trying ta make *me* feel sorry for *you*. It don't work *like* that, Leland. It just don't. I oughta toss this worthless ring o' yours away here an' now. But as 'tis, we can pawn it for fifty bucks, that'll give us enough to get my shoes fixed and have somethin' left over for a better meal at this place comin' up here. I bet they at least got a diner hereabouts somewhere."

Tex shook his head sadly. "I promise ya, Maybe Baby, when we win that contest, I'll buy ya a proper ring."

"Like hell," his wife said. "You'll buy me a proper *house* before anything. Then you'll get to work and earn the money to get me a *diamond*. A real one. Got it?"

Tex nodded. "Sure, hon. Whatever you say."

Maybelle growled under her breath but bit her tongue. She was hungrier than she was mad, which was saying something, considering how furious she was. She walked on ahead of him, reinvigorated by that anger, and more determined than ever to win that damn contest.

"This makes no sense." Seamus McPhee paced back and forth, trying to make sense of it.

Adoline watched him, her eyes following him as if he were a ball bouncing back and forth in a tennis match. "It's not your job to make sense of it, Seamus," she said. "We pay you to do one thing: Get the word out. You're very good at that, by the way, but don't think you know better than Artemus. He's the one who knew enough to pull his money *out* of the bank before the panic hit in '29."

Seamus stopped pacing and faced her directly. "Because he had inside information," he said slowly.

Adoline shrugged, raising her palms upward to face the ceiling, then tilting her head back and running both hands through her thinning, graying hair. At 63 years of age, she didn't have the patience to debate the likes of Seamus McPhee, even if he was the best promoter they'd ever hired. "What if he did?" she said wearily. "Maybe he has inside information *now*. It is not your place to know what it is. It is only your part to follow his directives. You aren't working for that idiot Zim anymore. It isn't as though you have a stake in this company. But we do pay you handsomely, so..."

Seamus took the hint and sat down opposite her. Unlike everyone else, except Artemus, of course, she had her own tent, with straw laid down instead of just dirt, a queen-sized bed with a brass frame, and matching chairs with claw feet and brass arms that rose up and crested in swirls on the back, like waves caught in suspended animation before they could batter the shore. The chairs, like the bed, were raised on wooden pedestals to spare them from being soiled should rain send mud in under the sides of the tent.

Adoline drew a deep breath. "I do, I suppose, owe you an explanation," she said finally, "at least as much as I have of one. Artemus doesn't even tell *me* everything, you know. But knowing what he has planned will help you properly promote the Darke Dance, I suppose."

Seamus bowed his head slightly. "Thank you," he said. "What I don't understand is why he chose this place. It's so far away... from everything."

Adoline smiled. "He sought out this location precisely *because* it's so remote. They've banned this sort of 'entertainment' in New York, Pennsylvania, Seattle..."

"And Texas. We're in Texas, boss lady."

"Barely. No one's gonna enforce the law way out here in the sticks, and Artemus... well, let me put it this way: Money is no object." She winked. "Besides, in these times, people are desperate. Setting up out here feeds that desperation. The poor and the destitute will do anything for a chance to get back what they lost. To have a reason *not* to quit. We're giving them that." She noticed the skeptical look on his face. "Mark me," she said, leaning forward, "they'll flock from miles around—*hundreds* of miles around for a chance at redemption. They've lost faith in their god, faith in themselves. We give them something to believe in. Is that so bad?"

"I suppose not."

"It's your job, Seamus dear, to take that hope and that desperation, and transform them into a potion that's... irresistible: something that won't only draw contestants, but an audience. A betting audience. One that will pay to live vicariously through the men and women torturing themselves on the dance floor. We will have some unique rules for our competition, Seamus, which I will now reveal so you can make the appropriate preparations."

Adoline told him the particulars, and he nodded, a smile forming on his face as her plan became clear.

"I understand, ma'am," he said when she had finished speaking. "You've inspired me indeed. I have the perfect idea to draw people in, but your potion lacks one crucial ingredient."

"And what might that be?"

"Hate."

"Chicken-fried steak, two orders, please." Tex handed the menu back across the counter to the waitress, whose nametag read "Beatrice." He wore a smile for the first time in memory. He'd come to terms with the loss of Maybelle's wedding ring, turning his attention to the possibilities that lay ahead.

"Coming right up, dear," the waitress said.

"He's nobody's 'dear' but mine," Maybelle growled.

"Well 'scuse me, hon, but I don't see no wedding ring." She turned on her heel and walked away briskly.

The man sitting next to them finished his coffee, plunked down a dime, and folded up his newspaper, leaving it there on the counter.

Maybelle pulled it over toward her and opened it.

"MORE STORMS ON THE WAY," the headline read in all caps.

"Ain't we had enough of that?" Tex muttered. "Maybe we better go back. At least we got a little money now, and..."

"You'll just spend it on chicken-fried steak and Coca-Cola."

"Maybe if you'd quit those damned Lucky Strikes before we went broke, *Maybe*."

"So now you're blaming me for losin' your job? And why do y'all gotta keep callin' me 'Maybe' for, like y'aint made up your mind about me or somethin'? Is that why you got me that fake diamond? Any other man, a *real* man, would call me Belle. It means 'beautiful' in French."

But Tex had buried his nose in the newspaper.

"Leland, are you listn'in' ta me?"

Tex put the paper back down on the counter and pointed at a half-page ad on Page 3. "Look there."

Maybelle's eyes followed his finger.

$5,000! BIGGEST PRIZE EVER!
Artemus Darke is pleased to announce that he has
increased the size of the top prize for the Darke Dance,
which has received official sanction from the Dance
Society of America as the official WORLD'S
CHAMPIONSHIP for 1935.
Last Couple Standing
Up to 48 Hours of Dancing
No breaks

This is NOT a walk-a-thon!
ANYONE who can't keep up with the music will be
ELIMINATED

Maybelle's eyes looked like a couple of full moons placed side-by-side. "Tex!" she said, shaking his shoulder. "We just gotta win now!"

Tex smiled broadly at her. "You know we're gonna," he said, patting his shirt pocket. "We got our secret weapon."

"Five-thousand dollars!" Adoline shot out of her chair like a rocket, tossing the newspaper ad to the floor.

"Yep," Seamus said, beaming and puffing his chest out. "I got posters printed up and had my boys hang 'em up in Stinnett, Amarillo, Dodge, Lubbock... I even got some sent out to my friends in KC, Dallas, Tulsa, an' Denver."

Adoline was shaking now. "Who authorized this?" she demanded.

The glow vanished from Seamus' face, and his chest went from puffed out to caved in. "Why... you did, ma'am."

Adoline slapped her hand on the small table beside her. "Are you mad? There's no way on God's green earth I would... That's as big as the *entire pot* for the New York world's championship in 1928—*before* the world went to hell. Did you talk to Artemus about this?"

Seamus drew himself up a bit. "You yourself said, and I quote, 'With Artemus, money is no object.' If he can't afford it, you shouldn't have said so."

Adoline was at a loss for words. "I... I... Of course he can afford it! That's not the point. But no matter. What's done is done. If it's a success—a *financial* success—you can keep your job. You can figure out what'll happen if it isn't."

The billboard poster plastered on a telephone pole in Tulsa captured the attention of a man waiting there at the bus stop. He cocked his head to one side and thought a moment. Five-thousand dollars was quite a payday, and for someone who'd been crowned a world champion endurance dancer, it was hard to deny the appeal.

Mike, who was living in Hammond, Indiana, at the time, had never danced better than he had with Anne Gerry. The Chicago woman had danced 700 hours in Milwaukee back in '28 but had been forced to drop out after her partner, a middleweight prizefighter, fell asleep and didn't wake up. Ann was one tough gal: She'd kept on going by herself all the next morning and into the afternoon until she was disqualified for dancing without a partner.

Mike and Ann had been magic together. They'd won the $2,650 top prize at the 1930 world's championship in Chicago two years later, setting a record of 2,831 hours on the dance floor.

Over 117 days.

But that hadn't been enough, they'd wasted no time in entering another Chicago marathon, at the White City Ballroom, the following year.

They'd placed second there, but it hadn't been good enough for Mike, who blamed Ann for "bein' weak" and "givin' up." She fell asleep on his shoulder and started snoring, and he tried to wake her up with a good shake. When that failed, a radio man happened to notice and brought a microphone over to capture her snoring. The crowd went wild, but Mike felt humiliated. It didn't matter that her body temperature hit 103 and stayed there for three days.

That's when he'd ditched her for a new partner, a chick from Milwaukee named Frenchie. He entered a contest at Erie with $2,000 on the line. But Frenchie decided she couldn't go the distance, so she quit. Mike flew into a rage, and the cops had to rush in and pull him off her. He was put behind bars without bail, and it looked like his dancing career might be over.

Until now that he'd seen that poster. Five-thousand smackers was too much to pass up... the only problem being he didn't have a partner. Frenchie was out of the question: She was a loser, and she probably still wanted to get him back by popping him in the eye.

But Ann... Ann was another matter. Things had never gotten physical with her, and she *had* been a winner at the world championships. He'd gotten more riled up over that second-place finish than he should've, especially seeing she'd gotten sick. If she was feeling tip-top, the two of them would be a shoo-in for the big prize. All he had to do was get in touch with her and arrange for her to be down here by the day of the competition.

So he walked over to a nearby payphone, dropped two pennies in the slot, and dialed the last number he had for her.

"Hello?"

It was her, all right. Goldilocks. He'd never forget that voice.

"It's Mike," he said. "Got any plans for the weekend?"

"Mike who?"

"Mike," he said impatiently. "Your dance partner, toots. Fancy another few twirls around a parquet floor?"

"Go to hell, Mike."

He smiled, then dropped the bombshell. "Top prize is five large."

"Mike, I ain't going nowhere with you for $500. I'd rather..."

"Five LARGE, doll. As in five grand. You mean to tell me you ain't interested?"

There was a long silence on the other end, then, "Where?"

"Place called Spearman, up in the north part of Texas by the Okie panhandle."

"Never heard of it."

"Well, we're gonna make sure everyone's heard of it by the time we're done. We're gonna put little ol' Spearman on the map—and make five grand in the process. How does that sound to you?"

"Sounds like you've got yourself a partner."

"Who the hell is *that*?" Morgaine asked between puffs on a cigarette. The magician's assistant was sitting with several other carnies on crates near the showground entrance.

"How should I know?" Geoffrey the Clickety-Clack Clown said. "Never see 'em before. All I know is I don't take kindly to being upstaged by a bunch of bad dancers." He got to his feet and jumped up on his crate, treating the others with a sample of his tap-dancing prowess.

"You should enter the contest yourself, Geoff," said Val N. Tyne, so named because of the unusually heart-shaped curvature of her body. She had a crush on Geoffrey that he didn't return, though half the other carnies did. She was, as Rollo the Strongman called, "a dish."

The object of their attention was a couple arriving in a cherry-red Packard convertible. The woman was driving, and the clean-cut, doe-eyed man next to her was standing up, waving to the crowd.

"Looks like he thinks we oughta know who he is," said Morgaine. "Even has his name embroidered on that sweater-vest of his. What does it say?"

Geoffrey squinted and craned his neck. "Cal, I think."

"Wait," Val said. "I know who it is!"

"Well don't hold out on us, then! Who?" Adoline said, strolling up behind them.

"It's Callum DeVillier, the world champion!" Val gushed, and just for a moment, Geoffrey felt a twinge of jealousy that her attention had been turned elsewhere. He might not have a crush on her, but he liked her having a crush on him.

"Oh, really?" Adoline said, her tone suspicious.

"And that has to be Vonnie Kuchinsky!" Val said. "Do you know they danced longer than anyone in history in Massa-two-shits back in '33. He's been in twelve marathons, and he's never lost. Ever. Oh, and get this: He's married her in the middle of a dance three times! Divorced her right after, though. It was all a put-on."

"Hmmmph," Adoline said. "We'll have none of that here, will we, Rollo?" She raised an eyebrow.

"We most certainly will not, ma'am," Rollo said, bowing slightly at the waist. "Shall I..."

"Please do."

Rollo pulled down the front edges of his gold-trimmed red vest and began sauntering over to the Packard, which had come to a halt just inside the entrance. Callum leapt out of the car without bothering to open the door, landing cleanly on the ground. A gust of wind kicked up, ruffling his close-cropped hair, as he turned to see Rollo walking briskly toward him.

"What's your business here?" Rollo asked gruffly.

"Why, we're here to enter the dance contest, of course. Don't you recognize..."

"I know who you are, and I don't care." He nodded his head toward Vonnie, who was still behind the wheel. "Is that one there your wife or ain't she?" he demanded.

"No, no, no. She was, but... Well, we can get married again during the dance if you'd like. Just some extra fanfare to send us off onto our 'honeymoon' before we win the prize." He lowered his head toward Rollo and gave him a knowing wink.

"Mister, do you know where you are?"

"Why, of course, this is..."

"This is Carnivale Darke," Adoline said, strolling up beside him, "and if you knew anything about us, you'd know that we don't tolerate fakery here. I suppose you want us to fix the marathon for you as well, make it just as fake as those weddings? How many of those twelve titles you've 'won'—won and never lost, I'm told—how many have you *stolen* on behalf of the organizers? Hmmm. Or maybe on your own behalf?"

Callum's face turned white. "I assure you, madame, every one of our victories is entirely legitimate."

"It looks otherwise to me, cupcake," Adoline sneered. "And I will not have even the appearance of fakery cast a shadow over our carnival. I would be most grateful if you would turn that Duesenberg..."

"Packard."

"Pile of junk around and leave immediately."

"You can't do this!" Callum protested. "We have an agreement with our sponsors to perform..."

"Sponsors? *Perform*? This is not a performance. It's a contest. And you won't be competing, sugar. Now, vamoose. If I can't convince you to leave, then I have a feeling Rollo will be able to."

Rollo stepped forward, tensing his arms at his side so his biceps rippled.

"You'll be hearing from our attorney," Callum snorted as he climbed back into the car.

Adoline chuckled. "Do what you want. We'll get a better lawyer and countersue you for defamation."

"Let's get outta here, Vonnie," Callum growled, and with a turn of the key and the accelerator down, the Packard peeled out, kicking up a cloud of dust in its wake.

Adoline smiled in satisfaction. She wasn't so much concerned with potential fraud—no show at Carnivale Darke was *ever* fixed—as she was with the pair depressing the profits. If the crowd caught wind that "The Incomparable Callum and Vonnie" were competing, they'd think the winner was a foregone conclusion, and they wouldn't even bother to show up. The wooden stands underneath the huge tent they'd put up would be empty of paying customers, and there wouldn't be any action on the dance, either. The few bets that *might* get placed would be skewed in favor of the champions, and with the carnival running the books, they might not even recoup that $5,000 prize money Seamus had promised.

Adoline kicked the ground, producing another puff of dust. There was nothing *but* dust in this place. Another gust of wind, this one stronger than the first, rushed through the midway, and Adoline couldn't help but remember the tornado of '96 that had leveled the carnival in Emporia, Kansas. She just had to hope the weatherman was exaggerating those predictions of a potential dust storm.

Regardless, however, it was too late to pull up stakes and cancel the event. Seamus had been right: People were streaming in from all over. And rain or shine, as she'd so often told her carnies, the show must go on.

"Look at all them people, Tex!" Maybelle's voice was shaking with excitement... and fear. Winning that $5,000 was going to be harder than she'd thought. It looked like the dance floor might not be big enough to hold all the contestants who were lining up to register for the marathon.

"Keep your places!" Rollo yelled. "Anyone tryin' ta butt in will be escorted off the property!"

But there was just one Rollo and a handful of other goony boys running this way and that, trying to corral the thousands of lot lice pushing their way toward the front. There they were, stomping on one another's feet and elbowing each other in ribs, chins, and groins, afraid the tickets would run out before they could secure a spot on the dance floor.

"Looks like they could use some help," Morgaine said, laughing at the sea of humanity churning around in front of them. "Jimmy ain't here—somethin' about his ma bein' sick—so I guess it's your job to step up."

"Do I look like a thug to you?" Geoffrey sniped.

Morgaine smiled sarcastically. "Under all that

makeup? Who knows what you look like! I ain't never seen you out of it. For all I know, you sleep in it. Or is it all tatted on?" She threw back her head and laughed.

"That's the point!" Geoffrey said, standing up and looming over her. "I'm a *clown*! Not a thug! If his majesty King Artemus didn't hire enough security, how is that my problem? It's opening weekend, and here we are just sitting around twiddling our dicks..."

"Speak for yourself, horny toad," Morgaine said, lighting a new cigarette from the embers of the last one, which she tossed down and stomped out before it could catch any loose hay on fire.

Keanu the fire dancer, who'd been listening in from inside one of the tents, kicked the dirt before sitting down with a thud beside Morgaine. "He's right, y'know," he said. "It's opening weekend, and here we are doing nada. Ain't no one comin' to see us, and we don't get paid if our acts don't draw. Ain't got no guarantees in our contracts like the so-called stars."

"Right," said Geoffrey. "They're all comin' for that damn dance! They're even puttin' it on in the big tent. I say let the lice all murder each other if they wanna. If the whole thing goes south, it'll be one-and-done for this Darke Dance bullcrap."

"Look there!" Val said, pointing.

A tall man with dark hair had just pushed the woman in front of him to the ground, but no one seemed to realize she'd gone down. They were kicking dirt into her open mouth as she lay on her stomach, gasping for breath, then walked right over her back. They pressed forward like a herd of buffalo, some tripping over her and falling, others trampling her as they surged forward.

Mike and Ann were right behind them, keeping a low profile after what had happened to Vonnie and Callum.

Tex and Maybelle were right behind them. This was their desperate last chance to turn their lives around before they wound up in a slum or on a poor farm somewhere. They'd get their number come hell or high water.

The mammoth tent stretched across a dance floor that was as big as two basketball courts placed side by side. Artemus Darke had set up dance pavilions for his patrons in the past, but nothing even approaching this scale. The floor itself was surrounded by wooden bleachers that had been assembled in record time: just two days.

A sign out front gave the admission price as a quarter; pay that, and you could watch as long as you liked. Small booths for taking bets had been set up underneath the stands; there, men in top hats would stand at the windows, ready to hand out wager slips in exchange for cash. The rules were simple: You had to dance—really dance. You couldn't just stand there and hold the other person up while shuffling your feet a little. Whether the band was playing "Minnie the Moocher" or "Puttin' on the Ritz," you had to keep up with the beat or be disqualified.

Maybelle beamed up at Tex, eyes wide. "Have y'ever seen anything like it?" she breathed.

"Looks like heaven's gate to me, with streets made of gold on the other side."

Maybelle got up on her tiptoes. "Is it time for our secret weapon?" she whispered.

"Not yet," Tex whispered back. "Wait till we really need it, then pretend to start sneezin' and snifflin' from all the dust bein' kicked up in the air. Ain't nobody can tell us not to use our med-i-cations."

"Won't it look suspicious if we sneeze at the same time?"

Tex paused. He hadn't thought of this. Then his face brightened. "You still got the last of that brownie y'ordered back there at the diner."

Maybelle nodded.

"Give it here. I'll cuff the thing while I'm eatin' the brownie for an energy boost. Everyone'll be so jealous about the food, they won't even notice me usin' it."

"Hey." She slapped him on the shoulder. "I was savin' that for myself."

"Fine," Tex whispered in a hiss. "Keep it, then. I'll do the sneezin'. But make sure you use it before you get too tired."

"Thanks, baby," Maybelle said.

He just sneered at her. "Whatever floats your boat, darlin'."

Artemus and another man stepped onto the bandstand and tapped on the microphone to get everyone's attention. The din coming from the enormous crowd, excitedly talking and laughing, sounded like a beehive. Adoline hoped it would die down once the music started; she already had a headache.

"Excuse me, everyone. Hello? Is this thing on?" Artemus called out and looked back at the band for confirmation. The volume was turned up, and Artemus rapped the microphone harder. Three loud taps and a rustling sound were followed by a feedback squeal that made everyone clutch their ears. "Attention!"

A hush fell across the crowd, and all eyes were fixed on Artemus.

"Thank you! I can't tell you how excited we are to hold the Darke Dance, the 1935 world's dancing championship with a grand prize of $5,000 on the line. I know you're all raring to go, but first there's the little matter of the rules. This is not your mama's dance marathon. Frankly, we don't have the time to keep it going for months on end. On the other hand, we can't just make it easy for you now, can we?"

The crowd cheered. Who didn't like a little friendly competition with that much money on the line?

"This dance marathon will go on for 48 hours..."

People yelled out "Easy!" and "No problem."

"You might let me finish before you get too cocky. Forty-eight straight hours... no breaks. No breaks of *any* kind. We will not be stopping for 15 minutes every hour, like you're all used to. There will no restroom breaks and no stopping to drink or eat."

"But we *have* to eat and drink. We'll drop from dehydration," a large man in the back yelled out.

"I certainly didn't mean to suggest we won't be providing the highest quality food and drink. You just cannot *stop* to partake. You must get your sustenance and eat without slowing your dance."

"Bullshit! That's impossible," Tex hollered.

"Well, if you were a professional, like us," Mike puffed out his chest as he gestured toward himself and Ann, "you wouldn't need to worry about such things for a mere 48 hours."

Ann elbowed Mike in the ribs subtly as she broke into a winning grin, nodding. "Don't be an idiot! We can't go without food and water for *that* long," she whispered angrily.

"I know, babycakes, but they don't need to know it. It's called intimidation," Mike whispered back, winking at her.

"But you can't stop us from using the restroom!" a girl of about 16 cried out.

"You've got me there. I cannot stop you. You must decide how to handle that situation yourself, should it arise." Artemus' mouth twisted in an evil grin, his eyes glinting.

"Ahem! Now if we can get back on topic." Artemus glared in response to the interruptions. "Speaking of pace and, more importantly, dancing. Unlike other marathons you may have seen, you won't be able to stay in the competition by merely shuffling your feet. You must actually *dance*, twirl, and jump to the beat, however fast or slow it might be. *At all times*. If you fall, you're out!"

"It can't be done." An older woman began to cry and walked off the floor,

Her partner ran after her, "Wait, Betsy! We've got to at least try."

"If anyone else has any objections, feel free to exit now." Artemus held out his hand toward the entrance, inviting dancers to leave.

Three other couples soon bowed out and exited the area quietly.

"Now that we have that out of the way, I'd like to introduce Stan Walker from the Dance Society of America to officially start the dance." Artemus backed up, clapping as Stan came forward to the mic.

"Hello, dancers. Everyone ready?"

The crowd cheered and clapped thunderously.

"Take your positions on the floor. It's going to be tight at first, but I'm sure you'll all figure it out. Let's get this started with "It Don't Mean a Thing..."" The band began to play the first few notes. "...If It Ain't Got That Swing," Stan finished with a smile. "And go! Start the timer."

The couples began dancing, pushing and shoving as they worked to establish their places on the floor. The first two hours flew by in a swirl of brightly colored dresses, skirts twirling, and feet keeping time to the beat. Swing dancing was the order of the day—progressing from the Lindy Hop to the Balboa, Carolina Shag, and the Big Apple. The audience in the bleachers couldn't help but tap their own feet to the music of Duke Ellington, Glenn Miller, and Benny Goodman.

In the third hour, a commotion arose near the back of the dance floor. The couples tried to keep dancing and ignore it, afraid that a momentary lapse in concentration could lead to disaster.

"Johnny, I've gotta *go*," a woman's voice whined.

"You have to hold it, Marge," a gruff voice replied.

"But I can't."

"Then do it. Just go!"

"Thanks, Johnny. I'll be right back."

"No, you bimbo. Give me your hand back *now*."

"But you said I could go."

"I meant relieve yourself."

"Right here? Right now? I'm not going to 'xpose myself in front of ev'ryone."

"We can't stop to let you pull down them granny panties anyhow. Just let it flow."

"I can't."

The sounds of a scuffle rose above the music. "Let me go! I won't do it. Please, Johnny!"

"Goddammit, Marge! So help me, I'll blacken yer eye!"

"Oh God! It's running down my legs. What'll I do?"

"Chill out, woman. There's nothing to be done about it."

Cries of disgust from other nearby dancers threatened to drown out the music.

"We gotta stop and get this mess cleaned up."

"They should be disqualified."

Artemus returned to the stage. The only people being disqualified are you... and you." Artemus pointed to the two couples who had stopped dancing to complain. "Dance around the mess. I'm sure it won't be the last of its kind."

"Well, I never!" A haughty woman, whose holier-than-thou attitude stood in vivid contrast to her tattered, out-of-fashion dress, pulled free from her partner and stormed off the dance floor.

As if to punctuate her exit, a loud groan arose from off in the distance. This was no human voice. It was as though some wounded titan were wailing in agony, having been cast down from Olympus by the younger race of gods. Or perhaps the gods themselves were mocking him from above. But this was no epic of Homer. This was happening now, in real time, a chorus to accompany a tragedy of a different sort being orchestrated with uncommon glee by Artemus Darke.

By the four-hour mark, more than a few of the couples had begun to slow, some of the women looking tired or pale. The monstrous groan came again, drawing the attention of dancers and spectators alike.

"What the hell was *that*?" Tex asked, his head spinning around as he dipped Maybelle low and drew her up again.

Maybelle didn't know, but the same question was on everyone's lips. The ominous wail poured forth in a long, lingering echo before waning and finally ceasing altogether.

Many of the dancers had fallen behind the music, craning their necks in an effort to determine what was happening—some involuntarily, others as an excuse to catch their breath. They were thwarted, however, when the beat of the music picked up into a frantic quickstep and a dance marshal rushed out onto the floor, barking a warning. "Lively dancing! Pick up them feet."

He gave them no time to respond before moving in and slapping them hard on the calves with a wooden ruler. "Kick up those heels!" he demanded.

A young blonde screeched and whirled on him with a glare. "You can't hit me!"

"Then you may see yourself off the floor," the man responded with a smirk.

"This is ridiculous, Martin! I've never heard of such a thing. I'm leaving." The blonde took off in a huff, her nose raised in the air, failing to notice the puddle of diarrhea from the other woman's accident. Her left heel slid out from under her, and she crashed to the floor, right in the pool of muck. The soupy fecal matter dripped and oozed down her dress, and she scrunched her face up, holding her breath and trying not to vomit.

"Disgusting!" she croaked, still trying not to breathe. "I'm going to tell the papers about this."

She jumped when she heard a crack of a flashbulb, and looked up to see a man taking her picture. Artemus came to her side on the dance floor. "I'll happily provide a picture for the story if you like." His mouth was turned up at the corner in a wry smile.

Her partner helped her to her feet, and she departed without another word.

As evening approached, stomachs could be heard growling—the volume of their discontent growing as the smell of food cooking wafted into the dance tent from outside. The tantalizing scents grew stronger as staff entered the tent with silver serving platters piled high with food; the clatter of saucers and dinnerware followed, as they were placed on tables set up along the edge of the dance floor.

When the band switched to a slow song, Adoline climbed onto the bandstand. "Dinner is served. But remember, you must not stop moving to the beat of the song. That means you must have one hand on your partner and dance as one at all times."

The silver cloches were removed from the platters to reveal barbecued ribs, bean soup, blueberry pie, and whole oranges. A collective groan arose from every corner of the room. The dancers' hollow stomachs ached. Acid poured in, burning their empty bellies. A chorus of voices could be heard:

"I haven't seen food that good in..."

"*Years!*"

"Or ever," Maybelle whined.

"It smells delicious, but how can we eat it?"

Adoline walked over to Artemus. "Where did you get that? We haven't eaten like that in ages. I thought it was nearly impossible to get meat and sugar, especially in such a large volume."

"Nothing's impossible if you're willing to throw enough money at it. Besides, I had to go all out for such an auspicious occasion."

"Go all out... or is it a scheme to knock people out of the competition?"

"I'll let you decide."

"You can't actually expect them to keep dancing while they try to eat soup, pie, and unpeeled oranges."

"Looks like we're about to find out." Artemus pointed toward Tex and Maybelle, who'd begun dancing a jig side-by-side, as they made their way over to the table.

"We can do this, Maybe Baby. Grab a rib... a whole handful even. We'll buy new clothes when we win that money."

The couple ignored the serving tongs and wrapped their hands around the meat. They cut back to the center of the dance floor, grateful for a slow song that had started. Tex shoved a whole rib into his mouth, pulling off the delicious, tender pork with his teeth. Flecks of meat and drips of sauce fell into Maybelle's hair as she stuffed her ribs in his pants pockets, chomping on one against his shirt.

Other couples soon began to follow their lead. Some ladled steaming soup into tall glasses. Others stuffed oranges into pants pockets or nestled them tightly into women's cleavage. Faces were buried into the palms of their hands, licking up the smashed pie slices they clutched.

A shriek pierced the cool twilight air. "Argghhh! It burns. Help me!" A dark-haired brunette with a bob stood near the back, her face and chest cherry-red. She'd been trying to dance the Lindy with her partner when his piping-hot soup splashed her. Blisters had already begun to rise on her skin.

"I'm so sorry, Belinda!" The man turned around, looking for help. "Is there a doctor here?"

Adoline escorted the couple off the floor and over to Dr. Samuels' tent.

The audience in the bleachers grew sparse as it grew late. The dancers might not be able to sleep, but the spectators knew they could return to check on their progress in the morning. The weather seemed to be worsening, and they knew better than to stick around under a canvas tent, no matter how sturdy, under the circumstances. They'd seen this kind of thing before. Sometimes it was nothing, but when the worst happened... well, this was why people had storm cellars.

As late evening gave way to midnight, a stiff wind picked up, burrowing under the edges of the tent and bringing with it a small cloud of dust that circled around the dancers' feet. As it grew stronger, the wind pushed its way upward toward the top of the tent, billowing it like a galleon's sail on choppy seas.

The dancers—those who remained—barely noticed. They were too busy trying to keep up with the ever-changing cadence of the music. Hoping to thin the herd, Artemus had ordered the band to switch frequently and abruptly from one style of music to the next. The Lindy Hop gave way to a waltz, followed by a foxtrot and the Carolina Shag. His devious tactic worked.

The changes in pace, combined with the dancers' deteriorating physical state, halved the number of couples by 3 a.m. Blisters, exhaustion, aches, and pains overtook the inexperienced, and even those who had endured more than one "ordinary" marathon were beginning to show signs of fatigue. By the 24-hour mark, the group was down to twelve strong, young couples. Mike and Ann danced alongside them, as did Tex and Maybelle. As their numbers dwindled, more of them began to engage in shrewd tactics designed to sabotage their rivals.

Groans and yelps punctuated the music regularly as couples threw elbows, kicked knees, shoulder-checked, and tripped each other. The trouble had begun when Tex accidentally led Maybelle into the back of another couple, causing her to stomp on the other girl's heel. The girl had stumbled and bumped into another couple, knocking the second girl down.

A fight ensued, and the other two couples were disqualified. The two men started throwing punches before realizing they'd both been the victims of Tex's clumsiness. Tex got a fist to the jaw for starting it all, but he took it in stride. He was accustomed to taking punches, and he and Maybelle kept going without losing a step. Jeannie, whose heel had been stomped on, was knocked out when another punch meant for Tex went astray as Tex deftly waltzed Maybelle out of the way. The other innocent girl, Josie, suffered a bloody nose when she tried to pull her husband away.

Through it all, Artemus watched with a smile.

"You're enjoying this too much," Adoline snipped.

"Isn't that why we have bleachers set up for the enjoyment of the masses? Would you exclude me from all this fun?" He rubbed his hands together eagerly.

Adoline shook her head and turned away.

"I don't see you leaving either."

"It's my job to oversee this *event*. Although, it's not quite the dance marathon I expected."

"It's everything I'd hoped it would be. See all those people over there placing bets? The action has grown ten-fold after last night's wipeout."

"I'm going to take a short nap. You can watch over this *circus*."

Artemus chuckled, then looked up at the top of the tent, concern in his eyes. The gigantic central pole and the sturdy ropes that held the sides remained unyielding, but he worried they might give way if the wind grew any stronger.

"Bethany! Bet, wake up!" A squat man, with a belly nearly as big as he was tall, struggled to hold up his partner, who'd passed out in his arms. He continued to slide her feet across the floor and even turned once, but he was slowing down fast.

When he saw the dance marshal approaching, he scooped her up in a Herculean effort and wrapped her around his shoulders like a mink stole. He held her hands in one of his and placed his other hand behind her legs to keep her from falling off. As he picked up the pace and tried to kick his feet, his face grew fire-engine red. Beads of sweat dripped from his brow, forming large wet spots on the front of his royal blue shirt. He began to huff and puff, his breaths coming in shorter gasps.

He stumbled over his own feet, nearly falling. His eyelids fluttered and his eyes began to roll back into his head as he slumped to the ground, dropping the woman right on her temple with a crack. Blood trickled from a laceration on her scalp. The dance marshal and one of the roustabouts ran over to the couple.

Dr. Samuels showed up a few minutes later to check them; they weren't moving. Crouching beside them, he picked up their wrists and felt their necks, checking for pulses, but found none. He lost no time in beginning chest compressions on the man, but after a moment, he stood up and shook his head at Artemus.

"They're both dead. Looks like he might've had a heart attack. She broke her neck in the fall."

Artemus turned to the strongman. "Rollo, remove their bodies," he hissed urgently.

The other dancers had slowed to watch the tragedy unfold, but Artemus barked at them: "You had best pick up your pace, lest we disqualify the lot of you."

Soon, the afternoon heat began to envelop the tent, intensifying the dancers' weariness. Two more couples were disqualified when one of the dancers passed out. Angry shouts rose from the audience as their favorites left the competition of their own accord.

"It's a fix!" one man shouted, throwing his wager slip on the floor. "I bet good money, and they're gonna be sure their favorites win!"

Four more couples voluntarily quit as dinnertime neared.

Adoline looked with dismay at the snake pit show tent, which had collapsed to the ground, unmoored from its stakes. She hoped that none of the snakes had gotten loose. Bits of hay and dust swirled around, and the horses in the show's temporary paddock were rearing up and whinnying, their forelegs thrashing at the air. One pair of hooves came down on another animal, tearing a long gash in its neck as it fell to the ground.

Adoline looked behind her. The skies back that way were ominously dark, but those weren't ordinary clouds. They were...

Adoline was jarred from her ponderings by a young boy who nearly knocked her down as he rushed past her. Artemus had hired the boy to spread updates about the Darke Dance, hoping to steer visitors who might have lost interest back to the big tent.

"Gilbert and Sasha about to be disqualified," he screamed. "Man turning purple."

Turning purple? Had she heard that right? Artemus had instructed the boy to make things sound interesting, but this didn't sound like hyperbole. The boy actually sounded shaken. Adoline ran down to the tent and arrived to see the couple stumbling through a slow dance. The man was gasping and clawing at his throat with one hand, while his partner pulled him along with the other. His face had turned a dark shade of purple.

"What's going on?" Adoline called out to Artemus. He was deep in a mob of people looking ready to riot, screaming at the couple.

"Don't you stop moving!"

"I bet $10 you'd win."

"Cough it up already. If I lose my money and that rib bone don't kill ya, I'll wring your neck myself."

Artemus pushed his way through the crowd and led Adoline up near the bandstand. "He was getting faint. He'd been trying to go without food, but when he finally gave in, he was in such a hurry to eat, he swallowed the rib, bone and all. But it stuck in his throat. Been choking on it for five minutes now, and he still hasn't given up. Almost makes me want to reward him for his effort. Almost."

With his last gasp, the man threw himself on the ground and leaned over, coughing. The hubbub around the tent died down to a whisper when they all heard "Huuuurrrkkkkk!" The rib bone flew across the dance floor, and Tex nearly fell when he stepped on it. The man on the floor, gasped as color returned to his face.

"You shit! I lost all the money I had in the world betting on your dumb ass." The bellow came from a tall, mustachioed man in overalls. He stormed across the dance floor, a shotgun leveled only inches from the weak man's face. "Damn you to hell, you bastard!"

BLAM! The sound of the shotgun blast echoed throughout the grounds.

The man's jaw and the lower half of his face were

obliterated. Stippling from the powder was visible around torn-up tissue that looked like raw hamburger. The shot had blown out the top of his skull when the bullet exited.

At the 36-hour mark, only four couples remained. The throng of onlookers had grown as the night progressed, and when news of the shooting spread, the crowd mushroomed so the tent could barely contain them. Everyone wanted to see if more blood would be spilled.

It had been only a matter of time before the chaos and bloodshed attracted the attention of law enforcement. Sheriff Ames arrived with two deputies, and they had to push their way through the crowd to reach the crime scene. "I'm going to need all of you to exit the dance floor immediately," he ordered—and stood there, hands on his hips, waiting for the dancers to comply. But it was as though they hadn't even heard him. They just kept dancing as if he wasn't even there.

Ames raised his voice and shouted to be heard over the din. "People, I'm not asking. You all must leave *now*, including all of you standing around looking at this mess."

The crowd moved in closer, and the couples continued to dance, even though the music had stopped: The band members had left the stage at the deputy's orders.

"This dance contest is over. Now leave!" Sheriff Ames bellowed. He stormed over to Adoline and demanded that the contest end.

She handed him the microphone. "Be my guest, Sheriff, but it doesn't look like anyone's going to leave."

The sheriff removed his gun and fired a shot in the air. "Disperse immediately, or I'll arrest the lot of you." His deputies looked at him, bewildered, wondering where they'd lock up the four couples, let alone the hundreds of onlookers.

The gunman who'd shot the young man only minutes before stepped forward with a large group of men behind him. "Let's get them, boys. We're not leaving until this is done."

The mob rushed the sheriff and his deputies in a fury, lashing out at them with fists, boots, and even knives until they were forced to retreat. Amidst the melee, the band returned to the stage and resumed playing for the dancers. Two of the couples had left during the riot, leaving only Tex and Maybelle and Mike and Ann on the floor.

As dawn arrived, Ann began to suffer from dehydration. She'd tried to drink water during the slower songs but had only managed to choke. Her steps were awkward as she fought the dizziness that had set in. She had started to mumble incoherently.

"What's wrong with you?" Mike snapped.

"Tired... drink... hey, Teddy," Ann slurred.

"Who are you talking to? Who's this Teddy? You need to focus on me."

Ann's head drooped. She snapped awake when her chin hit her chest.

"I've gotta go, Mike. I'm sick."

"Don't you dare pull that sick bullshit with me. Not again!" Mike backhanded her.

"Ouch! Leave me alone."

Ann stumbled again and started to drop to her knees.

"Get up, you bitch!" Mike yanked her to a standing position.

Maybelle nodded in their direction. "Look at that, Tex! They're losing it. We've nearly won. I gotta admit I'm getting awful tired myself," she said with a big yawn. "Where's that spray?"

Tex stuffed his hand in his pocket and fumbled around, trying to find their secret weapon. As he pulled the spray out, it caught on his waistband and fell, skittering across the floor and finally coming to a stop a few feet from a man Tex recognized. He was one of the men who'd been disqualified earlier thanks to Tex's bout of clumsiness.

The man jumped forward and picked up the bottle. "What's this? Benzedrine! They've been cheating. That stuff gives you energy," he shouted to those assembled.

"No. We ain't been cheatin'. Maybe has turrible allgergies and stuff. She gots it from a doctor."

Men from the audience who had bet on couples no longer on the floor gathered around the angry man, pressing forward alongside him, shouting insults and threats.

"What do we do, Tex?" Maybelle half-pleaded. "They seem awful mad."

The throng was distracted for just a moment by the sound of a fist landing on someone's jaw, followed by a cry of pain. Mike had finally lost his patience with Ann; it was clear he couldn't keep her in the competition as she repeatedly wobbled and went limp, then tried to pull away from him when he shook her awake.

"I have had enough of you!" he finally shouted, his fist pulled back as far as it would go.

Then, lightning quick, he hauled off and punched her in the eye, laying her out flat.

She fell to the floor with a thud.

Then, suddenly, a mighty gust of wind arose, jarring

the central pole loose and eliciting screams of terror from the crowd. The pole tilted at an angle, now held in place only by the weight of the heavy canvas. Roustabouts ran forward to secure it as spectators rushed toward the exit... only to find themselves battling that same fierce wind.

With the angry mob distracted, Tex tried to lead Maybelle away from them, farther up the dance floor. But he hadn't been paying attention to Ann, who was trying to haul herself up from the floor using her partner's pantleg. But she only succeeded in pulling his trousers down to his ankles and, thrown off balance, he fell in a heap on top of her, cursing at the top of his lungs.

Tex nearly stumbled over the pair, dodging to the side at the last minute and nearly dislocating Maybelle's shoulder as he yanked her along behind him. Somehow, through it all, he managed to stay upright and keep Maybelle moving as Mike got to his feet and stomped on Ann's wrist.

She cried out in agony, and Mike was prepared to deliver a heavy kick to her gut when Rollo and Geoffrey surged onto the dance floor, grabbing his arms and dragging him away.

An announcement over the loudspeaker confirmed that he and Ann had been disqualified.

Tex's mouth dropped open as realization dawned on him what had just happened. "Maybe Baby, we won! We did it!" he shouted, thrusting his fist in the air. His feet, however, were still moving. Unwilling to leave anything to chance, he was determined to keep on dancing, waiting until the official announcement was made.

Maybelle's eyes widened. "Tex! Watch..."

The last two dancers dropped as the crowd

surrounded them, raining blows down on them with sticks. There was no escaping their wrath. Bones cracked and gashes opened beneath the relentless assault until Tex and Maybelle lay still, their bodies broken on the floor. Neither drew a breath. They had danced their last two-step.

The wind whipped furious, relentless around the tent as Artemus and Adoline rushed out onto the midway.

That massive dark cloud Adoline had seen earlier was twice as large now—which meant it was twice as close... and moving toward them. Spectators standing at the edge of the tent stood transfixed, unsure whether to stay in a tent that had nearly collapsed earlier or venture out into *that*.

Their decision came too late, as a frenzied gust of wind uprooted the canvas from its moorings. The central pole teetered, then fell... just before the updraft abandoned the canvas, dropping it unceremoniously on the unfortunate souls who remained underneath.

Artemus grabbed Adoline's hand and pulled her away. "We'd better get out of here until all this dies down." He called out to Val and Morgaine, who were watching from a distance. "Go find that yellow-bellied sheriff and let him know it's time he shuts this mess down."

"You're just going to walk away?"

"It's not my mess to clean up. Look at it this way, Adoline. At least we don't have to give out that ridiculous $5,000 prize you advertised."

Adoline shook her head.

"But no," Artemus added, pointing at the dust cloud barreling toward them from the horizon. "I have no intention of walking away. My dear, I think it's time to *run*."

STEPHEN H. and SHARON MARIE PROVOST

THE CARNIVAL
OF INSANITY

The carnival exists in a world of liminality, at the crossroads of the real and the possible. The midway is a passage to another world, where children celebrate their youth and their parents can reclaim it—if only for a few short hours. The big top stands at the nexus of hope and incredulity, where light and darkness coalesce into a maelstrom of endless shadow. What lies beneath the makeup of a clown? What blind fury lurks in the heart of a caged beast? Presented for your consideration: a carnival housed in an asylum, where the broken are left for dead and living spectres walk the earth. Are the poor and the persecuted truly blessed? The answer awaits where joy meets sorrow, where hope and despair reflect one another... in a place called Carnivale Darke.

—Artemus Darke

1938

Looking back, the stop in Vermont was doomed from the start. Carnivale Darke should have just moved on to the next stop. Billing that weekend as the Carnival of Insanity was just that: pure madness.

The country was deep in the throes of the Depression, pushing Americans to the brink. Most of the traveling carnivals or circuses had long since closed down. The few still running, like Carnivale Darke, found it increasingly difficult to find an audience with money to spend, or a town even willing to let them in.

Artemus paced up and down the train car, eager to arrive. They'd been delayed trying to pick up supplies, which had become an ordeal. The government had severely rationed sugar, coffee, meat, eggs, and dairy products, forcing his food vendors to get more creative. Carnivalgoers were surprisingly pleased with the new menu of potato candy, water pie, Johnny cakes, peanut butter sandwiches, and—when they were lucky—Mulligan stew made from whatever cheap cut of beef and vegetables he could obtain. But procuring them frequently led to long stops to barter and haggle.

When the train finally came to a stop, Artemus jumped down onto the platform and was surprised to find the police chief and another man waiting for him. The chief held out his hand, palm outward, "Hold up there, folks. Nobody's getting off this train."

"What's the meaning of this, Chief..."

"Waters. Chief Waters."

"You denied us a permit to operate in town, so I made arrangements with the county board to set up my carnival at Hallsworth Manor."

"If you did, no one told me about it," the chief groused. "And Minister Mather here has lodged a complaint that you're operating too close to his church." He pointed to the other side of the meadow, and Artemus followed his finger.

"I don't see any church, offi-... uh, chief."

"It's several miles from here, through those woods, but that makes no difference. A complaint has been made and must be addressed. I've determined that you're too close."

"The evil one's scheming knows no bounds," the minister said gravely.

The chief nodded. "He's right. We're a poor community, and the people here have suffered enough without you bringing your devil worship here."

The way they were talking it was hard to tell which one was the minister—especially since they were both carrying copies of the Bible. The only thing to distinguish the pair was the chief's badge.

Artemus adopted his calmest demeanor and a silky-smooth tone. "Gentlemen, I must admit I am a bit perplexed. The owner, Mr. Kerber, has told me all about the history of Hallsworth Manor. It was, until just a year ago, a poor farm. If I'm not mistaken, some of its residents were not just destitute, but considered mentally ill, even criminally insane. Why didn't you think to object to its presence *then*? Surely it's a lot less dangerous now that it's no longer occupied."

Minister Mather stepped forward and thrust his Bible in Artemus' face. "Satan, get behind me!" he commanded.

Artemus just chuckled. "In the first place, my name is *not* Satan. In the second place, it would be a lot more difficult to hold a civil conversation with you if I were to stand behind you."

The minister looked flustered, but the chief held his composure. "You haven't been listening," he said, as if talking to a child. "This place poses a far greater danger now than it did when it was occupied. Then, it was staffed by men who knew how to keep its residents in check. It might have taken some whippings, and they also had the hole..."

"The hole? As in solitary confinement?"

"No, an actual hole in the ground sealed shut by a wooden door out in the graveyard across from the manor. Once someone came out of there, they never made much trouble again."

"*If* they came out of there," the minister added, a thin smile on his lips. "They forgot some of them until it was... too late, so they just filled in the hole and dug another."

"Word is," the chief added, "their spirits still haunt the manor and the surrounding woods. People have been disappearing quite regular up here, and we ain't never been able to find them. Or who took 'em."

The minster nodded solemnly. "We wrestle not against flesh and blood, but against principalities, against powers, against the rulers of the darkness of this world, against spiritual wickedness in high places." He pointed to the knoll in the distance, where the manor sat.

"Ephesians 6:12," the chief added.

"Come, come now, gentlemen. If you're trying to chase me off with some old ghost stories, it's simply not going to work. If I might suggest a sizeable donation to your church's treasury. I have a check right here." He pulled out his checkbook. To whom should I make it out?"

"Mr. Darke, if you're seeking to bribe me...," the chief began, but the minister put a hand on his forearm and gripped it firmly.

"How much?" Mather asked.

"How does $200 sound?"

"That'll do," said the minister with a sly smile. "If you would, please make the check out personally to Samuel Mather."

Artemus nodded and quickly scrawled the check out and offered it to the minister, who snatched it greedily from his hand. "Chief," Mather said, "I hereby withdraw my complaint."

"Just stay clear of the town limits," the chief warned. "If you don't, you'll have a world of trouble on your hands. I'll make sure of it."

The sky was the kind of overcast that didn't just hover over the green Vermont landscape; it actually seemed sprawled out like a festering corpse on the land, pressing down on the grass so that the wind couldn't disturb it. If there had been any wind, that is. The air was completely still, almost fetid.

Adoline had seen a pool of standing water near the road, but the air was just as oppressive here. Curiously, she hadn't noticed any mosquitoes in the water, but with autumn having supplanted the summer heat, perhaps that was understandable. What she couldn't understand was the absence of any insect life, as far as she had noticed, in the vicinity. Again, though, they'd been in the South not long ago, where the buzz of cicadas and the chirping of crickets was constant—and maddening.

The only life she noticed were the earthworms, burrowing up from the ground to writhe in the moist grass. She'd even seen what looked like a line of them crossing the road from the graveyard where the residents of the poor farm had been interred, as if on some holy pilgrimage to the manor.

Adoline stared up at the massive four-story brick building with a central gable, sitting by itself on the top of the small hill above her. It cast a dull shadow on the land in front of it despite the absence of direct sunlight. As she turned around, surveying the property, she took in the manor, the graveyard, and the trees that had shed their leaves uncommonly early in the fall. How could they ever create a happy, fun-filled carnival where people could go to escape their problems in this ominous, depressing setting? And what had the police chief meant by his warning? Silly superstitions and ghost stories? Or was there more to it?

"You look so serious standing there, Adoline. Speaking of that, *why* are you just standing here? The carnival isn't going to set itself up. We're going to be opening a day late as it is, and darkness is fast approaching."

"Does this really look like the place to set up Carnivale Darke to you? And aren't you concerned about what they said?"

"Where would you have me set up instead? We were booted from the town."

"But they said..."

"They were just trying to scare us away. I know money isn't a concern for you since I provide for your every need and desire. But I am a businessman. I already spent $200 paying off a moneygrubbing minister. Would you have me waste the money we already spent traveling here and just turn back around, our tail between our legs? I may be rich, but that's simply impractical."

"I understand, Artemus."

"Do you? We're nearing the end of the season. We don't have much time left to make some money before I have to provide for all of you back in Florida for the winter. Or should I leave you to take care of yourselves?"

"Fine, Artemus. I don't want to argue. Tell me your plan then."

"I was thinking we'd bill it as the Carnival of Insanity."

Adoline looked at him as if he'd lost *his* mind.

"Don't give me that look. I know it's a little early for Halloween, but it *is* September. The world is beginning to get that fall look. And then there's that," Artemus pointed up at Hallsworth Manor. "Who's to say we can't start celebrating a little early, make the place into a real haunted attraction? We could line the stairs with Jack O'Lanterns, bring in a few black cats, dress our vendors up in costume. The possibilities are endless."

"You can't! That's disrespectful."

"How? This place did house the criminally insane, did it not?"

"Well yes, but as a poor farm. Most of the residents weren't criminals at all, and most of them were perfectly sane. Many of them were indigent, mentally or physically infirm, alcoholics, and tuberculosis patients."

"What does it matter, Adoline? Do you think it's an accident that it's located out a mile from the city limits? Not a chance! It's a source of shame. Nobody cared about those people... any of them. It was simply a matter of out of sight, out of mind. I think it will draw people in all the more."

"You're sick, Artemus. This is a bad idea."

"That may be, but I guess we'll see who's right. You don't have to be a part of this. You could walk away from your position."

"Tell me where we're setting up everything."

"That's what I thought, Adoline. When push comes to shove, morality goes out the window. Oh, by the way, when are you marrying the love of your life, Thomas?"

"Go to hell, Artemus!"

Artemus chuckled as he turned and pointed up at the building. "We're setting up the midway games and the sideshow inside, on the first floor. There are so many rooms available, it will work perfectly and save us time from having to erect all the other tents. The big top will be across the street in that big open field, with the animals housed back behind.

"By the cemetery?" Adoline interjected.

Artemus continued as if he hadn't heard her. "The food vendors will be at the top of the hill on the lawn in front of the building. And the rides will be right here," he pointed at the other large flat area where they were standing, just down from the institution.

"And how are the townspeople getting out here?"

"Simple. Tonight, Mr. Kerber will take our posters into town and spread the word. We'll have our parade as usual, but it will start at the edge of town. Not many of them have cars, so we'll use our wagons to give people rides from that point. Mr. Kerber and his sons have graciously offered to take people back and forth in his two wagons as well. The kiddies will love a hayride."

"How will we control the flow of people to make sure they're all buying tickets?"

"Your ticket booth will be set up on the road where the wagons drop people off. I will station some of the roustabouts around the edges of the property to make sure no one tries to sneak in on foot."

"You've thought of everything it seems."

"Don't I always?"

"I could think of a time or two..."

"Don't start again, Adoline. Your concerns are duly noted."

"I have one question, Artemus. What happened to the residents of the poor farm when it closed down? Did Mr. Kerber say?"

"From what I understand, they were turned out. Poor farms are closing all over the country. It's not like they had anywhere else to send them. Some of them live in a hobo encampment down by the river. Others sought shelter in the woods. The lucky ones returned to the families that had abandoned them."

"But what about the mentally ill? Were the criminally insane still housed here when it closed?"

"I assume the dangerous ones were transferred to other asylums, but the rest were turned out with everyone else."

Adoline looked around nervously, scanning the treeline.

"Now who needs a lesson in sensitivity?"

Adoline stormed away up the hill. She didn't even want to think about how much work she had to do before the carnival opened.

Hallsworth Manor smelled even worse than the fetid water down by the road. As Adoline stepped through the front door, her nose was greeted by dank air with a stench that smelled like a mix of mold, urine, and decay. Exactly what had been decaying there was anyone's guess, but the mold was apparent enough, peeking out from behind peeling yellow-and-red-rose wallpaper and collecting up in the rafters, where some of the ceiling had fallen away.

The entire place had a greenish-gray tinge to it, and a faint buzzing reached Adoline's ears from somewhere, although she couldn't identify its source. The first thing she noticed upon entry was that the lights didn't work;

she chided herself for not having expected that in a building that had been abandoned for a year. She held herself responsible for noticing such things because she had to; Artemus, with his impatience and obsession for "the big picture," never did.

They had some battery-powered strands of lights they could use, along with some old-fashioned lanterns.

Adoline looked around, peering through the muted gray light from dusty sunbeams that crept in through the windows.

Anything of value had long been plundered, probably by the refugees, or their spirits, or whatever else lay in the shadows of those woods. Adoline had never believed in ghosts, but this place was making her rethink her long-held incredulity. The only decoration that remained was a dusty old lamp fixture high above the foyer that had once illuminated a portrait of Daniel Hallsworth, the original owner of the house back when it really *was* a manor.

The portrait still hung there, as no one had any use for it, so it had been abused with long-dried feces that had been smeared across his peacoat. Two holes in the canvas peered out from where his eyes had once been, giving the painting an eerie, hollow look.

Adoline bypassed the staircase and moved down the first-floor corridor, where she began inspecting the rooms that were to house the midway attractions. Many were littered with debris: an old mattress on a metal bedframe with springs sticking up through it; a wooden chair deprived of its back; a wheelchair thrown over on its side and missing one of its wheels. Shards of broken glass and china littered the floor of one room.

She heard a loud crack as she took a step and quickly raised her foot to reveal the broken skeleton of a long-dead rat.

What am I going to do *with all this?* she asked herself.

Just then, she heard a loud thump overhead, and her eyes shot to the ceiling. She thought she heard a faint voice of a man muttering to himself. Mr. Kerber had assured them that the manor was vacant and they'd have no trouble from any squatters.

Thoughts of ghosts returned unbidden to Adoline, and she had only just banished them when another voice spoke up from right beside her.

She jumped.

"Need some help?" Charlie Macon asked.

"Yes," Adoline said, brushing down her dress to compose herself. "These rooms are filthy. I need you to get Henry and clear them all out."

Charlie nodded.

"Carry any old furniture you find upstairs and leave it there; we won't be using the top two floors. But be careful. I heard noises up there." She pointed toward the ceiling. "So keep an eye out for anyone who might be squatting."

"Probably just bats," Charlie said. The tone of his voice indicated he wasn't worried. "Or ghosts." He chuckled, but stopped abruptly when he saw Adoline was not amused. "Don't you worry, ma'am," he said, winking. "Whatever's up there will be gone by the time we're done with the place."

Adoline awoke the next morning to the sounds of people hustling about. She made her usual rounds to ensure everything was ready to go, then went down to the ticket booth as the procession left for the parade starting line.

Artemus was disappointed to see only a few people waiting at the edge of town when they arrived. However, within a few moments, more came strolling down the road to greet them. Artemus, in the lead wagon, snapped the reins, cuing the team of large Belgians to move forward.

"Set one foot in this town, and I'll arrest the lot of you," Chief Waters bellowed as he ran onto the scene.

Artemus ignored him, turning the wagon a mere 3 inches from the town limit. "Step right up, folks. Come join Carnivale Darke at Hallsworth Manor for a once-in-a-lifetime experience, and explore The Carnival of Insanity... if you dare."

Clowns pulled a small cart with a calliope, which began to play and the parade began. The townspeople streamed forward, boarding the wagons that would take them to the carnival. It was not every day that they had an opportunity to *join* the parade when a carnival came to town.

Minister Mather cried out to his congregation, begging them to come back. "Don't be tempted by Satan," he shouted. "Stay on the path of righteousness. Matthew 6:13—'And lead us not into temptation, but deliver us from evil: For thine is the kingdom, and the power, and the glory, forever. Amen.'"

Artemus looked back with an evil grin. "You're welcome to join us, minister, free of charge. You too, Chief Waters." With a chuckle, he cracked the reins, and the wagon began to trundle away.

The two men stood there looking helpless.

Artemus dropped off the first wagonload of passengers at the ticket booth and then disembarked, passing the job to Charlie. Within minutes, the carnival was bustling as the carnies reported to their posts, and operations began. Artemus proceeded to his tent and finished making plans to finish out the season.

Fred peered out from the trees, watching all the hubbub at his old home. Until its recent closure, he'd lived there for 15 years, ever since he'd been committed for life for murdering his whole family with an axe.

No one could understand how cruel his family had been to him and that it had been his only means of escape. Just because he was a tall, strapping boy of 17 who stood 6-foot-4 with a broad chest, he'd been forced to do all the chores. They said his 4-year-old twin brother and sister were *too young* to chop wood, feed the livestock, or plow the fields. Father had whacked him with a belt when he busted Andrew Fisher's nose so he could steal his baseball. And Mother had slapped him *on the face* just because he knocked his sister down, breaking her arm, in his rush to get to dinner first. Somehow, *he* had been labeled the violent one.

But now he was free.

The money to run Hallsworth plum ran out, and they forgot all about what a danger I s'posedly represent to society. Funny how that works! But here's my chance. I always wanted to work for the circus as a clown. If I just show up all dressed for work and show 'em what I got, I know they'll hire me on the spot.

Fred returned to his campsite, tucked safely back in the woods where no one would disturb him. He rummaged through all the items he'd scavenged from the manor and found in trashcans around town, trying to figure out what he could use for his makeup and costume. Finally, inspiration came to him.

Weary Willie!

CARNIVALE DARKE

He'd seen news stories about some guy creating a clown character that looked like a Depression-era hobo. That was something he could pull off. Fred was still wearing his institution-issue uniform with a shirt made of a coarse light-blue fabric and jeans. It was filthy and stained, but it would pass muster. He put on the old suit jacket he'd found hanging on a clothesline in town.

He pulled out a tube of toothpaste and smeared that across his entire face, including his lips. Then he dabbed his fingers in the soot from the previous night's fire. He rubbed it around his eyes in large circles, then smeared the lower third of his face with it, leaving only a thin white line around his lips.

With nothing to rouge his nose, Fred returned to the rabbit carcass he'd thrown out after breakfast that morning. He smeared the bloody fur on his nose and then looked into a shard of broken mirror.

I look just like him. They'll be so impressed.

Fred walked out of the woods and headed toward the carnival, which was now in full swing. He noticed a man who seemed to be watching for trespassers, so Fred waited until he was distracted and slipped onto the property.

I'll just join up with the crowd and entertain the kiddies.

Later that afternoon, Artemus emerged to see how the carnival was running. As he rounded the back side of the building, he heard animated voices speaking in tones that didn't sound pleased.

"Get away! Leave my child alone. She doesn't want that dirty little dolly."

When Artemus turned the corner, he saw a woman using her handkerchief to wipe off her daughter's fingers. She kept looking over her back, angrily.

"Pardon me, ma'am. Is there a problem?" Artemus asked.

"Yes! Who are you?"

"I am Artemus Darke. I own this carnival."

"There was a clown over here that looked like a dirty bum—and smelled like it too. He was bothering my daughter. He tried to give her a soiled doll he must've gotten out of the trash." She pointed to the filthy, tattered ragdoll lying on the ground a few feet away. "I thought you ran a better operation than this. All your other clowns are clean with proper makeup. And they've been giving out balloons, not"—she crinkled her nose—"garbage."

"I assure you that you are not describing an employee of mine."

"Do you commonly let any old riffraff in then?"

"No, ma'am. Of course not. I will send my men to take care of this issue immediately. Did you see where he went?"

"That direction, toward the food stands."

Just then, Artemus saw Adoline walk by. "Adoline, please come over here for a moment. Would you see to this dear woman and her child? Make sure her daughter gets a proper toy to play with and anything else they require."

Adoline gave him a puzzled look, then squatted down next to the little girl. "What kind of toy do you like?" She stood up and gestured to the woman as she held the little girl's hand and led her over to the souvenir stand.

Artemus stalked over to Jimmy Swanson who was manning security near the entrance, pulling him aside. "We seem to have an issue with the homeless population. There's a grimy, malodorous man walking around here, dressed as a clown it seems, pestering my customers. Find and expel him immediately."

Jimmy rounded up several men from his crew and set off to find the hobo. However, he returned to Artemus' tent an hour later to report that the man hadn't been seen since.

"Make sure your men keep an eye out for him and anyone else trying to sneak in. Somebody slipped up, and I won't stand for that."

"Yes, sir. In our defense, we are trying to man a very large unfenced area."

"Then put more men on it!"

Jimmy turned with a quick nod and left.

Fred had seen the man talking to that woman who wouldn't let him play with her daughter. He couldn't take a chance that one angry woman would ruin his opportunity to become a clown, so he'd taken refuge inside the manor. Once inside, he'd gone up the hidden backstairs that the nurses had used and found his old room on the third floor.

He'd fallen asleep, curled up on the floor in a shaft of

light coming through the boarded-up window. When he awoke, he crept down the stairs and walked through the midway games, trying to entertain the masses.

"Get away from me. You stink!" The teenage girl pinched her nose and fanned her hand in front of her face. Her friends giggled at her reaction.

"It's Stinky the Clown. See? He's black and white, just like a skunk!" The tall brutish boy shoulder-checked Fred hard, bouncing him off the wall.

Fred fell to his knees when another boy used his foot to shove him hard in his lower back. The nail head sticking up from a loose floorboard ripped his jeans and tore a deep gash in his shin. "Boys, I think he lost his way. We need to take him back to the freak show where he belongs."

Two boys grabbed his arms and yanked him up, dragging him across the floor with the toes of his worn shoes bouncing across each slat.

The girls skipped behind them, chanting, "Stinky freak! Stinky freak! Everyone run from the stinky freak!"

When the boys reached the first of three rooms housing the freak show, they tossed him in. Fred landed face-first with a thud. He rolled over, moaning with blood pouring from his nose.

"No entry without a nickel, buddy," Alfred, who called himself "Slither," said from his perch in the back corner of the room. Born without arms and legs, his act was to move along on his stomach like a snake.

Fred looked over at him. "Don't have no money."

"Then you gotta go. How'd you get in here in the first place if you ain't got no money?" Thomas the Half-Man said as he scooted across the floor on his hands. "Wow,

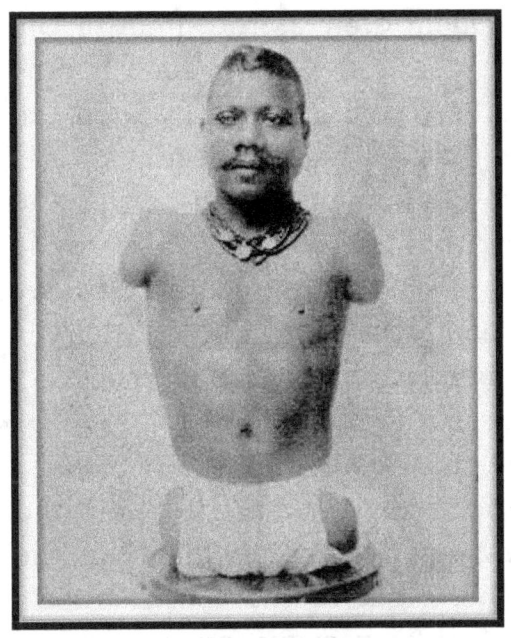

did you crawl out of the dump?" Thomas backed up and covered his nose with a handkerchief.

"Hey, he must be that guy they were looking for earlier," Slither said. "Hugo, go get Jimmy."

Hugo the Claw-Fingered Man left the room at a trot.

"I swear I'm not causing no trouble. I just wanna be a clown." Fred clambered to his feet and backed out of the room. He ran out through the side entrance and limped back across the field toward his campsite in the woods.

Just as he reached the treeline, Jimmy came running into the building. "Where is he?"

"He took off into the woods," Hugo replied. "I don't think we'll be hearing from him again. Those kids worked him over pretty hard."

"Not half as hard as I would have. Let me know if you see him again."

A tall figure in a baseball cap watched from the shadows and shivered. Those freaks didn't know who they were messing with, but if they weren't careful, they'd find out soon enough. They didn't know what a *real* freak was. At least *he* knew well enough to steer clear of Freaky Freddie Wallace.

Evening fell and excitement grew as the time for the big top show approached. The midway and food booths were filled to capacity as everyone eagerly awaited the talker's shout announcing that seating had begun.

Adoline cut through the manor to check on the midway games on her way from the cookhouse back to the ticket booth. She saw a man standing in the hallway outside one of the game rooms, eating a hot dog. His eyes were locked on the scene before him, and he seemed anxious, shifting from one foot to the other.

She didn't know why, but from the side he looked familiar. All the hairs on her arms stood at attention, and a creepy feeling ran up and down her spine. Just then, the man turned and looked her right in the eye. Adoline's stomach dropped to her feet as recognition dawned. It couldn't be him, but yet, she was sure that it was. Twenty years later, and here he was again.

She fought to control her emotions. She couldn't let him know that he'd been recognized. There were too many defenseless people around... women and young children. Thomas and the other freaks were just steps away. She'd be damned if she'd let anyone get hurt... or killed... again!

Adoline caught Hugo's eye and signaled him to join her. "I need to go find Artemus and Jimmy Swanson immediately. It's an emergency. Don't look over there till I tell you, but do you see that nervous guy in the hall outside the milk bottle game?" Adoline waited a moment and then nodded at Hugo.

Hugo looked over at the man and then met her eyes again.

"I need you to keep an eye on him. Don't let him out of your sight. If he heads toward the game, can you try to

distract him? But be careful! He's very dangerous!"

"Yes, ma'am. But hurry please." Hugo held up his lobster-like hands. "I'm not exactly fit for hand-to-hand combat."

Adoline gave him a quick peck on the forehead and ran out the side door.

To her delight, she found Jimmy coming up the stairs from the lower lawn where Artemus' tent was set up.

Adoline grabbed his arm. "Jimmy, go get your strongest men and meet me back here in two minutes. I have to get Artemus."

She flew down the stairs two at a time and ran at breakneck speed across the field, nearly pulling Artemus' tent down when she ran inside.

"Zeb Douglass is here!" she burst out in a shrill tone.

"Mind explaining who the Sam Hill that might be?" Artemus asked with a scowl.

"That boy with the baseball bat. The one who went on a rampage through the carnival 20 years ago in Boston!"

"How can that be?"

"We don't have time for questions. Jimmy's waiting for us." Adoline grabbed Artemus' arm and dragged him behind her.

"What's going on, Adoline?" Jimmy asked as she sprinted up the stairs.

"Zeb Douglass is here by the milk bottle game. I think if you enter from the back, you have the best chance of taking him by surprise."

"That psychopath dared show his face here again? This'll be the last time anyone sees him."

"You two take the side. Harry, go in from the front. Charlie and I will come from the back. Leave him to me, boys!" Jimmy ordered as they hurtled up the stairs toward the building.

Artemus and Adoline followed and waited outside for the all-clear.

Jimmy entered the building and ran up the center hallway toward the front. As he rounded the corner, he saw Hugo, eyes wide, talking to Zeb. He was skinnier than Jimmy remembered, with a patchy growth of beard, but he was still wearing that Red Sox cap from years ago. It was probably the only possession he had left.

Hugo backed away as Jimmy melted up behind Zeb and wrapped his arms around the other man's, locking them behind him.

The other four men surrounded them, blocking the exchange from view.

"You're coming with us, slugger!" Jimmy growled in Zeb's ear.

The two men shuffled down the hallway as one, the others following. The excitement for the show to come was so pervasive that the crowd never noticed what was happening. Charlie scooted around the two men and peeked out the back door to see if anyone was around. The coast was clear, so they took Zeb outside into the twilight.

Harry untied the bandana around his neck and used it to gag Zeb, who was then led down the back of the hill to the roustabouts' tent.

Jimmy shoved Zeb onto a wood chair. Charlie and Harry set about tying him up, while Jimmy untied the gag.

"How the hell did you get here, Zeb?" he demanded, hot breath in the other man's face.

"I live here, or at least I did."

"What are you talking about?"

"Hallsworth Manor. I was a resident."

"How's that possible? I followed the story in the papers. Court said you were criminally insane and sent you to Danvers Lunatic Asylum in Boston for life."

"Yes. But the place got overcrowded, and they transferred folks like me that didn't pose a threat to poor farms. We were supposed to live out our lives here."

"Yeah. Yeah. I get that. But that still doesn't explain why you're here right now. Hallsworth closed a year ago. They musta sent you somewhere else. Did you escape when they were transferrin' ya?"

"No. When it closed, we didn't get transferred nowhere. They just left us all here and walked away."

"Don't play me for a fool." Jimmy slapped Zeb hard across the face. "They mighta let the sick folks and the indigent walk out, but they wouldn'ta just let murderers go scot-free."

"That's what we thought, too, but seems like they just forgot about us."

"We? Us?"

"I wasn't the only one here for bein' a psycho killer."

"There's more of you?"

"Well only one now, but there were five of us originally."

"Where's this other guy?"

"I'm not sure. I saw him earlier. Some kids were pickin' on him. Not very smart if you ask me."

"Well, no one's asking you, asshole." Then Jimmy paused for a minute and seemed to be thinking. "Don't tell me he was dressed like a clown?"

Zeb nodded. He seemed calm, almost docile. Jimmy wondered what they'd done to him at Danvers. Electroshock therapy? A lobotomy? He didn't look that far gone, but he did look... broken.

"And what did this fucking clown do to get locked up?"

"Killed his whole family with an axe. He's got an awful temper. We both live out in the woods, but I try to avoid him. He run me off a couple o' nights ago, an' I've been sleepin' upstairs in the manor."

"If you're so scared of him, why didn't you just stay where you were. Why come down here to the carnival?"

"I just had to. I had to try that blasted game again. I haven't practiced in years, but I know I could take them damn bottles down—that's if you dirty rotten scoundrels aren't still riggin' the games!"

Zeb's previously calm demeanor flipped like a light switch. He struggled against his bonds, throwing himself forward to get at Jimmy. "That bottom jug was weighted. And the bat! A worthless forgery. It weren't no Louisville Slugger! The Babe ain't never touched that stick. You bastards!"

Jimmy walked around behind Zeb as he spoke, "Just as

I thought. A tiger doesn't change his stripes! You'll never hurt anyone here again at Carnivale Darke."

Anger and vengeance boiled in Jimmy's veins. He'd been waiting years for just this chance to pay back this sniveling boy—now a man—for what he'd done to his best friend, Oliver, that day.

He flexed his rippling arm muscles, built from years of pounding metal stakes into the ground to hold the tents in place. He picked up his heavy sledgehammer from under his cot and slammed it down on the back of Zeb's skull, caving it in.

Blood spattered the tent wall as he raised the sledgehammer again. It whistled through the air and plunged deep into Zeb's brain. Blood rained down Jimmy's face and stained his shirt.

Jimmy ripped off his shirt and used it to mop himself off. "Clean this mess up. When darkness falls and everyone's in the show, dump him in the river. Weigh him down with some rocks, so he won't be found till long after we've left town." Jimmy stomped out of the tent and jogged up the hill.

"He's been taken care of." Artemus and Adoline jumped at the sound of Jimmy's angry voice. "He'd been sleepin' upstairs the last couple of nights; said it had somethin' to do with bein' afraid of that fake clown the freaks dealt with earlier."

"Wha... what'd you do?" Adoline stammered. At least the mystery of the noises from upstairs was solved.

"It's no concern of yours."

"Did anyone see anything?" Artemus asked.

"Not a thing. And they'll be nothing to connect back to Carnivale Darke neither." Jimmy replied.

"Good." Artemus strode down the hill, heading back toward his tent. He called back over his shoulder. "Show's about to start. Get back to work, Adoline."

Jimmy returned to the tent below. "We need to keep a lookout for that other guy."

What Jimmy and the others didn't know was that Fred had snuck back into the building earlier and had been watching them from above.

Fred grabbed a chair and slammed it against the wall in fury. His breaths came out in ragged gasps. He picked up the knife on the floor and stabbed the old bedroll in the corner. "No more pain!" he roared as he picked up the axe he'd retrieved from his encampment.

"They're gonna pay. No one's gonna hurt me ever again."

Fred rushed down the stairs and out the back door. He ran down the hill, plunging into the roustabouts' tent, axe raised high above his head.

"What the..." Charlie spun around, his eyes widening in the second he had before the dirty clown reached him.

Charlie tried dodging to his left but was stopped dead when the axe plunged through his forehead. Blood dripped down his face, his left eye oozing clear fluid where it had been sliced open. Fred yanked his arm back sharply, pulling the axe out with one fluid motion.

Charlie slumped to the ground, motionless.

Hearing voices, Fred slipped over to the side, concealing himself from the tent opening. Several men were coming this way, with Jimmy the first to arrive. In a flash, Fred swung the butcher knife up and sank it into the underside of Jimmy's chin.

He fell to the floor, blood gurgling in his windpipe.

"You okay, Jimmy?" Harry poked his head in to see what had happened to his boss. Fred brought the blade of the axe down on the back of Harry's neck, nearly severing his head.

"Bastards!" Fred retrieved his weapons and walked to the back of the tent, where he'd seen the still-bloody sledgehammer underneath a cot as he'd rushed in.

This will suit me just fine. Now for the rest of them.

Fred trotted through the field abutting the hill and crossed the street toward the big top. It sounded like the show was just winding up.

They'll walk right out into me any moment now.

Fred stepped into the darkness under a large tree just a few feet from the tent's exit.

A freckle-faced youngster came running out, giggling with glee. Fred reached out and ran the blade across her sweet throat with the flick of his wrist. A crimson waterfall rushed over her yellow polka-dot dress. She put her hand to her throat and turned to find her parents, who walked out of the tent to see her stumble-step toward them. Her father rushed forward just in time to catch her as she fell into his arms.

"Oh my God! Jenny! Help!"

Fred swung the sledgehammer with brutal savagery, catching the father on the side of his head, then bringing it down on the back of the mother's neck, bones splintering.

Fred buried the knife up to the hilt in the chest of a man who rushed to the family's aid. He left the sledgehammer beside the slain family and pulled the axe out of his waistband, twirling it around in front of him.

It's party time!

Fred reached the tent flap as the flood of happy carnivalgoers headed out. He swung the axe around wildly, hitting whoever he could reach with deadly accuracy.

The people ran out of the tent in every direction, trampling those who had been knocked to the ground. They fled down the dirt road back toward town, screaming in panic.

The sound of a siren and a flashing red light came flying up the road, narrowly missing terrified townsfolk who scrambled to jump clear. The sheriff jumped out of his car, grabbing a panicked woman's arm. "What's happened?"

"There's a man killing people in the circus tent! He has an axe!" She pulled away and continued running.

The sheriff ran to the tent, pulling his Colt revolver before ducking inside.

It was just as the woman had said: There before him was a hobo dressed as a second-rate clown, swinging an axe wildly and cutting people down.

"Hands up, or I'll shoot!"

The man wheeled around: It was Fred Wallace, the young man he'd arrested back in '22. "Fred, stop this now. I don't want to kill you, but I will."

Fred raised the axe and hurled himself headlong at the sheriff, who shot him point-blank in the chest three times.

The sheriff checked Fred's pulse and felt none, so he left the tent to call for an ambulance to help the victims.

Artemus came forward, his hand extended. "Thank you so much, Officer..."

"Sheriff!"

"I apologize, *Sheriff*. We appreciate you coming out here. How did you know...?"

"You damn fool! Your pompous ass got people killed. Chief Waters warned you that it wasn't safe. Why didn't you listen? I just knew something bad was going to happen, so I was waiting out here."

"I didn't know."

"You didn't *care*, you mean. All that matters to you is money."

"How do we need to handle this, Sheriff?"

Artemus started to reach into his tailcoat for his wallet.

"Put your money away. You're going to have to clean up this mess and then settle up with the town. The chief told you this town has been through enough turmoil—struggling to survive and feed their families—without this mess here making it worse." The sheriff waved his hand around, pointing at all the injured and dead. "We've been searching for that man, trying to stop the senseless tragedies for a year, but he's been like a ghost. A body turns up, but he disappears into the wind."

"That's terrible. How can we help?" Adoline sobbed.

"You are going to bury all the dead in that old cemetery over there. Then this area will be sealed off from the public. As soon as you're done, pack up this abomination and leave. Don't ever return to my county again, or I'll make you disappear next. Got that?"

"Yes, sir." Artemus replied.

"And if I hear you've mentioned one word about what's happened here, I will hunt you down. Clear?"

"Crystal."

Carnivale Darke's employees worked together, under

Adoline's guidance, to respectfully inter all the town's murdered residents and their own employees in their final resting place. Then, before the carnival packed up and loaded everything on the train, Adoline took one last walk through the manor to make sure they had everything. She was almost done when she heard the same noises coming from upstairs that had reached her ears during set-up: another loud bang, then a second one this time, followed by more muttering. She told herself it was probably just Kerber, making the rounds himself, but there was no way to know for sure. She couldn't understand those muttered words, but she wasn't about to stick around to find out.

A chill swept over her body as she clutched her arms tightly to her chest and hurried out the front door, nearly tripping as she went down the stairs in front of the manor and hurried toward the wagon waiting to take her to the depot. Looking behind her once, she saw that suffocating mist descend upon the manor, finally swallowing it entirely.

Adoline boarded the train and went to Artemus' personal car. "We're going to Florida. The season's over *now*."

"It was a loss anyhow." Artemus replied and turned his back on her.

AFTER
HURTGENWALD

One thing separates humanity from the baser animals. Prideful men pretend it lies in our intellect, while the barons of industry see it reflected in their accomplishments. Yet it is only that: a reflection of something darker that we spend our lives denying. What sets us apart, in the final analysis, is our awareness of one stark reality: the inevitability of our own demise. These man of intelligence and accomplishment mask their cowardice behind false bravado. None are willing to look their most formidable foe square in the eye. In their folly, they tell themselves that death is something that happens to others. Always others. Never them. In denying themselves this awareness, they reduce themselves to the level of brute creatures. The brave stand tall in their awareness, announcing to the cowards: "Remember you must die, that you may truly live." And if they turn a blind eye to this truth, a reminder awaits them... in Carnivale Darke.

—Artemus Darke

1946

The night's pulse pounded in my ears, like my own forgotten heartbeat assailing me from without. The phantom bass drum setting the rhythm for a chorus of crickets and cicadas, chirping in a cacophonous frenzy, welcoming in the deepest dark of eventide.

Distant music called me forward, and others heard it as well. Their silent footfalls joined mine on the Old Toll Road, entranced by the sounds of life and merriment. The carnival hadn't been by this way since the second great war broke out; not that I would have known: I'd been dispatched overseas myself to fight in the European Theater, and had been twice decorated before a German bullet found me during our advance through *Hürtgenwald*. I received the purple heart for that one, and they'd sent me home just days before the three-month-long engagement finally ended, and only five months before the bastards finally surrendered.

But the battle itself had been a disaster. A strategic attempt to pin German reinforcements down before they could join their compatriots fighting to the north in Aachen, it had lasted longer than any other American engagement on European soil and ended in abject failure, leaving as many as 55,000 American soldiers dead or sorely wounded, of which I was one. My own experience there had been nightmarish. We traipsed across muddy trails in deep and narrow ravines, choked off all too frequently by prickly, gnarled underbrush. Tall pines rose above us, limiting our visibility, and the trails we followed became streambeds in the rain.

The rain.

It fell down on us for days, now in a deluge, now in dribs and drabs, relenting only long enough to subject us to the feeling of being soaked to the skin before renewing its assault. Blasts rocked the forests intermittently as the enemy's mines exploded with flashes of bright light that left yet another soldier's limbs rent from his torso or his bloody ribs poking out from his caved-in side.

That place left its mark on a man. It had been two years since that nightmare ended, but not a day went by that I didn't feel the sensation of a soaked uniform plastered against my skin, unyielding, as though it encased my body, somehow holding it together. Not a day passed that I didn't see the flash of an exploding mine or enemy fire in my mind's eye, which was more keenly sighted than my actual vision these days.

I never left that forest, which cast its shadows on the road before me and the memories that lay behind me, no matter whether it was night or day. The night, however, was by far the worst. The wind taunted me as it whistled through the evergreens I'd left behind in *Hürtgenwald*. I felt the pricks of briars stabbing at my ankles. Phantom howls reached my ears, like the distant wail of dismembered soldiers dying in the muck. Now, though, those wails arose from both sides of me, marching forward toward the carnival in the distance. The lights grew brighter, raising hope within me that they might disperse the shadows. But the shadows clung to me like a black veil, and enfolded the figures advancing with me, hiding their features behind a swirling black fog. The sounds of the carnival grew louder, but the wails beside me would not be silenced; I even heard myself wailing now, though I didn't remember opening my mouth or feeling any need to cry out.

Then I was back in *Hürtgenwald.*

I was in a daze. The field medic assigned to our unit said I'd been wounded grievously; I could expect bouts of delirium and even hallucinations—whether from extreme pain or from the morphine they would use to treat it... if they could get me to a hospital in time.

His voice was troubled, filled with doubt.

I drifted in and out of consciousness, always ending up back in *Hürtgenwald* in my fevered dreams before fighting my way back to the surface, a man drowning in remembered terrors.

The pain stopped eventually, and I felt a sensation that I told myself must be the morphine. It felt like a chill river in my veins and a fog in my head, a sensation that never left me after that. It remained my constant companion, burrowing deep inside me and dancing around me like mad dancers around a maypole.

I felt myself going mad; it had been happening for some time now. But there was nothing I could do about it.

The carnival gate was just ahead, but the clanging of the bells, the whir of the rides, and the voices of the talkers weren't growing any louder. If anything, they seemed fainter. As I looked out on the dancing lights in red and gold and amber, it was as though I were looking through a tunnel with black, fuzzy edges all around my line of sight. The effect was to make everything seem more distant, almost detached from my inner reality.

What was I doing here? And what of these others with me? Looking over my shoulder, I could see a line of them, perhaps as many as thirty, velvety black shimmers only visible because they moved against the even darker backdrop.

I turned my head toward the shrouded figure at my left. "Why are you here?" I asked in a whisper.

"I just am," it said in a monotone voice, distinguished only as belonging to a man by its deeper, though hoarse timbre.

"Were you at *Hürtgenwald*?" I don't know why I asked that question, but it somehow seemed important.

"No. Normandy," came the reply. I could see no lips move, and the man didn't seem interested enough in our conversation to slow down even a little bit.

I kept pace with him, not so much because I wanted to, but because I felt the need to. Why had I even asked about the war at all?

"Can I bum a cigarette?" I asked.

A shake of the head was his answer.

Fatigued already with our conversation, I turned toward the person at my right.

"Hey, Waldron," he said before I could open my mouth. He spoke in the same drone as the first one, his tone one of disinterest but with a spark of recognition.

"Mullins?" I said. But how...?"

Corporal Remus Mullins *had* been with me at

Hürtgenwald. Always the first to crack a joke or share a smoke, he'd always kept our spirits up through that long, dark nightmare. I recognized his voice right away, even cloaked as it was in that air of detachment. But that air of detachment was the odd thing about it... or it would have been odd if I hadn't heard the same lethargy in my own voice. How long had we been marching? I couldn't remember, but perhaps long enough to account for his—and my own—numbing sense of fatigue.

"Same as you," he said, neither surprised nor bothered that I didn't know the answer myself.

"When did they send you home?" I asked. He had still been there in that forest when they'd shipped me back to the States.

"Can't remember. Shell shock. Like it happened a hundred years ago."

"With me, it's like I'm still livin' it."

"That too."

His answer made no sense, but it was the same way I felt. He'd mentioned shell shock, or battle fatigue as they were calling it these days, and decided that was probably what I had too. It would explain the hazy memories; the feeling of still being stuck in *Hürtgenwald*, and the panic that came with it; and the sensation of living outside real time. The world seemed to be passing more slowly than it had in Germany.

Mullins turned away from me, directing his gaze forward without any further acknowledgment. He was still marching at the same, slow pace we all were, taking even steps and swinging his veiled arms in an unchanging arch, like a metronome keeping time to the music.

I realized now that there *was* music—and that it was

not coming from the carnival. It was all around me, timed to our marching and to that phantom bass drum that mimicked my heartbeat. Soon, other instruments joined in, and as we passed through the gate, I could hear distant murmurs of carnivalgoers taking note of our procession.

"Who's that?" said a barrel-chested man with long, golden locks. He was pointing at the gates—it seemed directly at me—with one of his muscled arms.

Beside him, standing on a hay bale, I could see a doll-sized but big-bosomed and perfectly proportioned Mae West lookalike. She was squinting into the darkness and shrugging her shoulders. Her voice was softer, but I could hear her even so: "Looks like a new act to me. It's Halloween. Artemus always brings in special entertainment to spook the kiddies."

"Hey," said the Muscle Man. "Listen to all that wailing and moaning, Molly Dolly. It's comin' through louder than anything else here in the carny, and they're still outside. That's enough to spook *me*. All that's missin' is the rattling of chains."

I saw Molly Dolly rub the Muscle Man's back reassuringly. "There, there, baby...," she cooed. "Just a show." But I saw her give a sudden start when the carnival lights flickered around them—not just the lights on one of the rides or attractions, but *all* the lights in the carnival, flashing and buzzing simultaneously, providing accompaniment for us as we entered. We weren't just marching now, but I saw the others had begun whirling and twirling, their misty shawls billowing out around them, and realized that I had—involuntarily—begun to do the same.

We stopped for a moment and began dancing in place,

all of us in the same moment, as if on cue.

We danced faster, throwing our hands in the air, which made us seem like tiny tornados or whirling dervishes.

It was as though the lights' malfunction had given all of us new energy. They kept flickering in a clear pattern, like a code, made to accompany the beat of my phantom drum.

But that mind-numbing cadence was no longer solitary. Around it, a growing chorus of sounds began to rise. I could see no orchestra, but I heard a collection of musical notes that mimicked the sounding of instruments, yet in a loud, persistent echo. Drums pounding like distant thunder. The thumping rhythm from a stand-up bass. A slow, seductive saxophone, alternating with the sound of a deep trombone. The drone of a snake charmer's instrument, blending into the buzz of bagpipes stuck on a single note.

I saw the Muscle Man shudder. "I don't like the sound of it," he breathed.

I became aware then that my sense of hearing was heightened, and I could filter out whatever sounds I didn't want to hear. I hadn't been able to do that in *Hürtgenwald*. I'd never wanted to hear the sound of enemy fire, the loud crack of a branch, or the metallic crash of an exploding mine followed by the sound of debris (and, often, body parts), *splatting* on the wet earth. I had heard them even so, and found myself wishing I'd had this new selective hearing back then.

The music still sounded like an echo, but I could hear the sound of human voices clear as a bell. So much for shell shock.

"It's probably gypsy music," I heard Molly Dolly say, not sounding entirely convinced. "I've heard sounds like that coming from the fortune-teller's tent. Thought it was a phonograph, but when I went in there, she didn't have one. You never know what Cassandra might be up to."

"Cassandra's an old witch," the Muscle Man said. "You're not doin' a very good job of reassurin' me, Moll."

"Hey, I ain't your mama. Ol' Artemus has just outdone himself this time. It's all just smoke and mirrors."

Artemus. I recognized that name, but I couldn't place it. The name was, in some way, connected to a circus... this circus. I looked up and saw a sign that read "Carnivale Darke," and it clicked that the man in question was none other than Artemus Darke, renowned circus owner and one of the world's richest men.

Just then, another woman arrived. She wore her red hair tied up neatly in a bun and covered with netting, and a formerly white apron covered in food stains. "Bite your tongue," she scolded. "No smoke and mirrors here. You *know* Artie don't put up with any shenanigans. If he hired this act—which he musta done—you better believe they're legit."

Molly burst out laughing. "That would mean they're actually dead."

"Well...," George stuttered, extending his hand toward us again.

"Of course, they ain't dead," Molly chimed in. "An act's an act, an' actors are actors. That doesn't make 'em phony. It just makes 'em professionals, an' they're damn good at it, too. Artemus only hires the best. Wouldn't expect any less of him."

"That's a very sensible thing to say." The three of

them turned around to see the imposing figure of an older woman standing behind them.

All three of them stood at attention, almost like soldiers, and Molly said in a very formal voice, "Hello, Adoline."

The woman didn't return her greeting, but instead continued with what she'd been saying. "Very sensible, indeed. But I assure you, Artemus didn't hire them, and neither did I. I have no idea who they are or where they came from."

Dead? What had she meant by that? I knew I wasn't dead, and I knew no one had hired me to do any kind of performance. I'd just found myself walking toward this carnival, or traveling circus, or whatever it was. What disturbed me was that I didn't remember waking up in the morning, starting out on the road, or anything else after *Hürtgenwald*.

How was that possible?

How could I be so bad off that I kept reliving that horror again and again, and that it had overwhelmed the memory of everything that came after it? I couldn't even remember *wanting* to go to the carnival, let alone setting out for one. My head was aching, and the pulsing drumbeat was growing louder, not inside my skull but like a hammer hitting it from the outside.

I felt sick to my stomach, but something wouldn't allow me to stop and retch. We had moved on, past the gates and down the center of the midway. The crowds parted as we approached, women gasping and young children crying out as though we were lepers or outcasts. What right did they have to treat us this way? We were war heroes! We had fought the Nazis. We had been through hell. We sacrificed or limbs, our sanity, and some their very lives to protect democracy and the American Way. And this was the thanks we got?

Ingrateful bastards.

Even the men were running away from us, taking refuge in the Ten-in-One tent, the big top, on the rides, or wherever they could find it. It occurred to me that this was good for business, and if Artemus Darke *had* planned it as a means of herding lot lice into his attractions, it would have been considered a stroke of genius.

Except that many of the carnivalgoers were just waiting for us to pass before running toward the exit.

I could feel the anger rising in me, and in the others around me as well. The music grew louder and more insistent. The lights flashed more brightly, like strobes, bathing the grounds in blinding light one moment, then leaving them shrouded in dark the next. It created an eerie effect as we danced: We appeared to be jumping directly from one place to another without covering the space in between.

We began to disperse now, each of us seeking to call them back—drag them back if necessary—to witness our dance. They *would* acknowledge us. They *would* respect us, no matter what it took.

As we danced deeper into the black heart of the carnival, some of us fanned out, each seeking a suitable station from which to grab their attention.

Mullins and some of the others latched onto the moving Ferris wheel and begin to climb. Shadows outlined by the carnival lights, they blinked in and out of view—one moment on the bottom—the next standing atop one of the cars. A young couple screamed when Mullins spun like a top on the edge right behind their heads, the black streamers of his death shroud brushing across their faces.

The girl screamed in alarm and terror as he reached down and pulled her up to dance with him.

"Joe, help me! I'm going to fall," she cried out to her boyfriend, who sat there, frozen, watching in horror.

Mullins pulled her along as he leapt from one car up to the next. She struggled and leaned back, trying to break his grip, but his gaunt hand was unyielding. When they reached the apex of the ride, Mullins flung himself into the open air and the girl plummeted downward, hitting the ground with a sickening splat.

The Ferris wheel operator abandoned his post and ran toward the gate.

He didn't get far.

One of the other phantoms grabbed the man and began pulling him along, kicking and screaming to the midway games. The shimmering black form stopped in front of the High Striker and forced him down on the platform as he struggled frantically to escape. Two more of my kind arrived to hold him down as the first grabbed hold of the hammer and raised it high above his head.

A few straggling lines of an ancient poem I'd learned in school floated through my memory.

> *Therefore, send not to know*
> *For whom the bell tolls,*
> *It tolls for thee.*

But the bell would not toll this day. Instead of striking the plate and sending the weight rocketing toward the top of the tower, the hammer came down with a sickening crack on the carny's head. It exploded like an overripe melon hitting the ground; splashing onto the pink dress of a little girl standing nearby. Fragments of bone and chunks of brain blew onto the wall of the midway tents surrounding the game.

The woman they had called Adoline screamed and ran toward the body of the young girl who'd been thrown from the Ferris wheel. The girl's face, flattened by the impact, was an oozing mask of torn flesh; her limbs, a jumbled pile of broken bones, were twisted into unnatural positions. The girl began to moan and twitch in time to the beat of the drums, their thumping growing louder until I could feel it in my bones.

The carnivalgoers could feel it too—their bodies began to move in time to the thrumming as they tried to flee, but were instead drawn inexorably into our dance. I twisted and turned, making my way over to the fallen girl. She lifted her head and held her hand out to me, the gossamer strands of her new black shroud floating to join mine. We linked hands, one crossed over the other, and began to spin in a circle, as children do, until we let go and flew apart to find others to join our mad dance.

I heard a yelp and turned to see another man teetering from the top of the Ferris wheel. He'd closed his eyes and refused to acknowledge our invitation to dance... or our existence. This was his punishment: Two of our number, one on each side of him, pulled him back and forth, swaying to the music. We couldn't let him ignore our sacrifice. We would not be forgotten.

With one final yelp, he was cast down from the top to forevermore be a part of our procession.

The calliope had begun to play, its strained notes long and drawn out, creating an eerie song. Our dance had slowed—our hands joined together as our serpentine path crossed the lot, looking for others to join our march. Black streamers flowed out from the broken man as he rose, leading the way to our next destination.

Adoline scampered back when the dead girl began to moan *and* move. Her head had been cracked open like a coconut, spilling brains across the dirt. Her shattered limbs had been twisted and contorted like a ball of twine, yet they began to straighten and she rose to her feet.

Adoline climbed to her feet and ran back over to Molly and George. She called out to Sam to join them.

"George, Sam, I need the two of you to find some other men and stop these people. Did you see what they did to that young girl?"

"Ye-Yes, I did. But I also saw that girl rise up and go dance with them! I... I am not getting involved," Sam backed up, hands raised in surrender. "You can fire me!"

"I don't think that will be necessary, Sam."

Sam nearly jumped out of his skin at the sound of the voice behind him. He spun around to find Artemus standing there with a smirk on his face, Cassandra at his side.

They all jumped when they heard the man from the Ferris wheel hit the ground with a thump.

"We've got to do something, Artemus. They're killing people! Who are they?" Adoline implored them.

"Just as they appear, GIs from the war... those who did not return," Cassandra said.

"That's not possible." Adoline's voice rose in anger.

"Anything is possible here at Carnivale Darke. You should know that better than anyone, Miss Darke." Cassandra's deep, scratchy voice betrayed a hint of humor.

Adoline was at a loss for words. She didn't know what to say because she'd seen the impossible happen over the past fifty years.

"What do we do then? What do they want?"

"There's nothing to be done. They simply want to be seen and heard. Remembered," Cassandra replied reverently. "The nation held grand celebrations for those who returned. Kissing and dancing in the streets. But what of these men? They came home in boxes, remembered only by those who experienced their loss."

Artemus pointed in the distance where a long procession was headed that way. "I don't know what to make of this," he said, "but we will stand here and watch their dance. Pay our respects."

I entered the big top with others behind me and found

it full of people, engrossed in the circus. They didn't care to see us. Our long black veils and solemn dance had been ignored.

We would make them see.

We walked amongst them, plucking people from their seats. We bowed our heads over their mouths and sucked the life out of them. Wrapping each soul in black cloth, we held them aloft as we bore them out of the tent and marched through a black fog, leading a procession of the dead through the grounds. They could no longer disregard our dance. The beat of the drums receded, no longer echoing through my brain. We were pallbearers for our own demise.

A jazz band that had been playing in another tent emerged to accompany us. A clarinet joined the slow, soulful notes of a muted trumpet, celebrating our life—and our sacrifice—while sending us off to our slumber.

Our number had grown, and we led them past the onlookers I'd seen when we arrived. A tall, stately elderly gentleman stood at the front, watching us as we passed. Somewhere in my memory it occurred to me that this was Artemus, the man who owned this carnival. He was dressed in a top hat and burgundy velvet tailcoat, like a ringmaster. He tipped his hat at us as we made our way out of the carnival, leaving no trace of our visit.

When it was done, I rejoined my companions, returning to our formation in a somber march back whence we had come. I realized for the first time that I was naked beneath my shroud and covered in dust. I should have been caked with sweat after such exertion, but I was not; I wasn't even out of breath. No blood stained my cloak, as it was not made from material to be stained.

As I stood there, the shroud itself dissolved into tendrils of fine mist, whisked away into the darkness on a light breeze.

I couldn't remember the way to my home, or even what it looked like. All I remembered was the *Hürtgenwald*, that dreadful place I could never escape. Had never escaped. I was walking back to that cursed forest, my energy waning with each step as I dragged myself down the road that led away from the carnival.

I could no longer see it behind me.

The gates had gone dark, and a small clearing, choked by trees, rose up before me.

As soon as it vanished, it fled my memory as well, just like everything else except *Hürtgenwald*. Always *Hürtgenwald,* taunting me from a past set in stone, ever-present and unyielding. That reality stood behind me, and with my demise upon that accursed soil, I had been certain that nothing lay before me in the future. But now, for the first time, a sense of what lay in store for me visited my spectral mind, warring with the shame of *Hürtgenwald* for supremacy in my dulled thoughts.

That sensation seemed to grow as I stood pondering it, beckoning me closer. Pulling me in. I felt myself drawn to a spot of ground underneath a willow tree. The others had deserted me now; I was alone, yet I felt at peace. That was the sensation that washed over me now: peace and acceptance of my fate. The ground beneath me seemed undisturbed, worn smooth by rains and covered in newborn grasses. But I knew where I was now.

I was home.

As I lay down, two more lines of that ancient poem echoed from some distant shore of forgetfulness. How wrong they were; oh, how wrong indeed...

No man is an island, entire of itself.

The words faded into nothing as I melted into the moist, forgiving ground. I *was* an island, entire of myself.

My journey was complete.

Tears streamed down Adoline's face as the last of the procession exited through the gate. She scanned the grounds, but she could see no signs that anything untoward had happened. The Ferris wheel was operating again, as usual. Children laughed and danced through the midway, greedily devouring circus peanuts and cotton candy. Floto the Clown scurried up to them, blowing up balloons and twisting them into giraffes, poodles, horses, and wiener dogs.

"What happened to those people who fell off the Ferris wheel and the ones they carried out above their heads? I don't see their bodies." Adoline looked stunned as she questioned Artemus.

"That is not for us to question. They have gone with *them*." He pointed toward the gate through which the phantoms had disappeared. "That's all we need know. We've had enough run-ins with the authorities over the years. Let's not invite another one."

Adoline glared at Artemus' back as he walked away. How could he be so calm?

Cassandra cupped Adoline's hand in her own, patting it comfortingly. "No worries, my dear. They have joined our fallen heroes in their eternal rest. Those souls will be at peace with them."

STEPHEN H. and SHARON MARIE PROVOST

THE LEGACY

s the 1950s have dawned, I realized it was time for me to start preparing for my retirement. Having entered my 90s, it had become apparent that I no longer had the energy required to oversee a traveling road show. And I was running out of time to see the next step in the evolution of Carnivale Darke reach fruition.

To keep "The Show to End All Shows" fresh and

enticing to the modern audience, I hired Julia Morgan, the architectural genius behind Hearst Castle, to help me realize my vision of creating a permanent home for Carnivale Darke. Julia was on the verge of retirement, but she consented—after I offered an enormous financial incentive—to design and engineer my crowning achievement, Darke World. Her only condition was that the park be built in her home state of California, which seemed the perfect choice.

Darke World would be the premiere amusement park on the planet, a true theme park, as I called it, that would set the standard for all others to follow. The centerpiece of Darke World would be a horseshoe-shaped park-within-a-park, modeled after the original Dreamland at Coney Island—which had burned down in 1911—complete with a replica of the large tower that had presided over it. I even brought Coney Island's original Loop the Loop roller ride from adjacent Luna Park.

But it would be far more than a West Coast version of Coney Island. Darke World would house a full-fledged circus, midway, and entertainment experience with a permanent big top and thrill rides that could be built from the ground up.

Most of the animal acts now had a permanent home in the Darke Gardens Zoo, where visitors could see them when they weren't performing.

I'd build the biggest rollercoaster in the world, the Atlas. The tallest shoot-the-chutes water ride on the planet would descend into a massive swimming pool surrounded by a "beach" with imported sand. A train that encircled the park would let attendees off at Santa's North Pole Village, The OK Corral, and an underground

attraction based on the Roman catacombs I called Descent Into Madness.

I had buildings dedicated to scientific exhibits and marvels, but the age of the Freak Show was passing, and society was no longer so accepting, so we had no choice but to let most of them go. We did our best to find jobs for some of them, but our options were limited: The same hypocrites who had always come to gawk at their unique attributes and talents would recoil in horror if they saw one of them taking tickets or serving ice cream.

This saddened me greatly, as I had always sought to celebrate the unique individuals as prodigies and nonpareils, but the economics of the situation left me with no other choice.

Some of our acts caught on with Zimmerman Jr.'s show, which had come upon hard times precisely because it was built around its freaks. There were rumors that he was thinking about selling his carnival, but I put no stock in those. "The Brain" was arrogant enough to believe he could think himself out of any predicament, and he needed to keep his freaks around him, not because he cared about them, but because he feared being shunned by society at large.

When it came time to choosing a location for Darke World, I chose the barren site in San Francisquito Canyon and greased the palms of some skeptical county planners to make it happen. The canyon had been the site of the state's worst flood in '28, only because the shabbily built St. Francis Dam had burst at the seams. The dam wasn't there anymore, but neither was anything else, so the land was just sitting there—still relatively cheap and ripe for the taking.

I signed a contract with Bob Clampett, the genius behind Looney Tunes mainstays like Porky Pig, to create a whole new cast of animated characters exclusive to Darke World. We'd have Crimson Cat, Randy Rabbit, Doodles the Poodle, and a loveable hillbilly family, the Ozark O'Darkes. Animated shorts featuring this band of Madcap Minions would be played on the grounds and in movie theaters, with information about Darke World at the end of each one. We even entered into discussions with the DuMont Network for a regular afterschool spot.

Unfortunately, by the time Darke World was completed, my health had deteriorated to the point that I could no longer take personal charge of the operations. Adoline had, sadly, passed on just the year before, and I didn't trust anyone else to run the show without me. On the other hand, though, I wasn't about to let Darke World become the most expensive white elephant in history.

I therefore began searching for a successor to keep the

Darke Universe faithful to my one and only non-negotiable standard. Everything *had to be* real. No trickery. No fraud. Some safeguards were already in place, created long ago thanks to my most trusted employees—a collaboration between Magnus and Cassandra. The carnival had always been my whole world, and Adoline's too. We never had any time for spouses and children, so there are no successors in the Darke line to take the reins.

I interviewed several prospects and, having eliminated most of them straightaway, began negotiations with Marcel Dubois, a young man who came from a long line of successful businessmen. Our agreement called for him to uphold my high standards of excellence and authenticity; to maintain Darke World in the condition at its time of purchase; not to close down any of the attractions; and only to add specific attractions I listed in the agreement, should advancements in technology make it feasible to build them.

In addition, he would have to retain all my employees for a minimum of ten years, or until such time as they left voluntarily. A board of fiduciaries accountable to my vision would monitor the park to ensure that all conditions were being met. Should any of them be broken, the buyer would be obliged to forfeit the property to a trust, pending its purchase by a new owner who would sign an identical contract.

"You'd better be serious about the contract you're about to sign," I told Dubois. "For your sake."

So ended the golden age of Carnivale Darke. Little did I know that, without me at the helm, it would never regain its former glory.

1984

The Brain read the front-page article in the *Los Angeles Times* with glee. The centerpiece photo on the cover showed a rundown amusement park in San Francisquito Canyon, its rides closed and broken, the parking lot covered with weeds. The old zoo stood deserted, and the midway abandoned. Vandals had broken in to scrawl graffiti on the walls and make off with souvenirs like rusted milk bottles and unclaimed prizes left in the midway booths. (The stuffed animals remained, sad and forlorn, having been soaked and soiled under the open sky where wooden roofs had once been.)

The headline on the front page, set against an aerial overview of the abandoned park, read "Darke Ages." The subhead elaborated: "The glorious rise and precipitous fall of the Southland's first great theme park."

The Brain devoured the article, which explained that Darke World's demise had begun with the coming of

Disneyland, several miles to the south in Anaheim, in 1955. Crimson Cat and Doodles the Poodle were no match for Mickey and Minnie, promoted as they were by ABC-TV's *Mickey Mouse Club* and *Walt Disney's Disneyland* (forerunner of *The Wonderful World of Disney*). Darke World's eponymous animated afternoon show, featuring Bob Clampett's creations, only lasted a few weeks... at which point the DuMont Network shut down for good.

Darke World, however, had its own brand and loyal followers, which allowed it to endure while Hopalong Cassidy's Hoppyland in Venice and Pacific Ocean Park in Santa Monica came and went. The death knell only came in the 1970s after Magic Mountain opened just a few miles away in Valencia. Known for its rollercoasters, the new park debuted its "Revolution," a giant version of the Loop the Loop that was billed as the first modern vertical loop coaster, to celebrate the Bicentennial. The wooden "Colossus," billed as the fastest, was added two years later.

Darke World simply couldn't keep up, thanks to shrinking profits and the constraints its founder had placed on new attractions being built.

The Brain read every word of the *Times* article to the last line, which announced that a foreclosure sale would be held at the county courthouse in downtown Los Angeles. He circled the time and date in red. No one would want a dilapidated park on a flood plain, so it was bound to be available for pennies on the dollar.

Most of his advisors thought he was crazy for using his savings to purchase Darke World. But over the years, they had told him he was crazy to hang on to Dr. Zim's Carnival of Oddities too, and, against all odds, he'd managed to keep that enterprise afloat. He was confident that his own superior intellect would show him a path to profitability for Darke World, which he planned to rechristen ZimLand, as well.

Finally, after all these years, he would get the best of his dear, departed nemesis, Artemus Darke.

The Brain arrived at the foreclosure auction and found no serious buyers... only a couple of busybodies curious to see what would happen to Darke World. Just as he suspected, he was able to purchase it for a mere $100,000—fortunate since the park was so dilapidated he'd need to spend at least three times that much to refurbish it.

Seeing as how he'd never set foot on the property, he spent the new few weeks investigating, looking for anything worth saving. The project was going to take more time than he'd expected, so The Brain realized it was time to fully turn over the reins of Dr. Zim's Carnival of Oddities to his son, whom The Brain referred to as Dr. Zim III.

The Brain had been reluctant to pass on the family business to his son before now. While his son's intelligence was above average, the boy didn't have the same "enhancements" as he himself did. In his forties, The Brain had finally found a (barely) suitable partner to bear his progeny, but she'd refused to let him make modifications to their child. By the time Harold Zimmerman III came of age, he wasn't interested in any upgrades himself.

The original Dr. Zim's carnival had always been built around oddities of every kind—mutated creatures and humans, strange practices, or the unexplained. With time, though, all the freaks at the carnival had been artificially transformed, and that distinction had allowed the carnival to survive and eke out an existence, even when all the others had gone by the wayside. People came to the park never knowing what new grotesquerie they might encounter. But still, times were hard for any amusement park trying to compete with the mega-dynasty of Disneyland.

Harold III had agreed to take on the persona of "Dr. Zim" due to his creative flair and knack for excellence in creating new oddities. Because of that, he'd been running the lab almost exclusively for the past five years. Ever since his takeover and the implementation of some new ideas he'd had, Dr. Zim's Carnival of Oddities had once again started to flourish.

This hopeful change of events gave The Brain the confidence he needed to devote every moment to what had become his obsession: seeking revenge on his father's old nemesis, even if he was dead. That cocky know-it-all, Artemus, had only truly cared about his legacy and that ridiculous authenticity requirement. Zimland would be just the thing to make that bastard roll over in his grave.

As the weeks went by, The Brain found that Darke World was even in worse shape than he could have imagined. He brought a builder with him one day and was shocked when the man gave him an estimate for all that was needed. His estimates for fixing the rides and midway area alone exceeded what The Brain could afford, so he decided, reluctantly, that it was time to raze the property and try to sell the land to offset his loss.

But he couldn't relinquish it before conducting one

last search on the property. He'd been over most of it with a fine-tooth comb, but he had yet to explore Artemus' storage area in the back of the park. There was always a chance he might find some hidden gem there—something that could make him some money and confound Artemus' ghost at the same time. Artemus' health had been in such a poor state that he'd never actually run the park when it was completed, but he'd supposedly had great plans that he'd intended to implement. Maybe there was something there worth saving.

The Brain entered the large, dusty storage area and was confronted by a sea of boxes containing everything from costumes to midway prizes to old notebooks for attraction ideas. He waded through the morass and, just as he was about to give up, he came upon a large container labeled "MasterView."

The Brain remembered getting into an argument with Artemus about his Virtuality Maker—based on the MasterView—and the massive 3D production he'd put on at the girls school and nunnery years ago. He had thought the technology was lost, but now here it was, staring him in the face. He didn't know how he'd put this to use yet, but he was sure it was exactly what he'd been looking for.

When Harold arrived at his father's secret technology workshop, he'd barely seen him over the past six months. His father had always been happiest at the Carnival of Oddities, surrounded by all his creations. But ever since The Brain had embarked on this obsession, he'd worked day and night—alone.

"Father... ahem, I mean, The Brain, I'm here. What did you want me to see?"

The Brain didn't respond.

"Hello? Are you here?"

Harold wandered around; the room was filled with an enormous computer that took up most of the space. He finally found The Brain typing in code; he was so engrossed in what he was doing that he hadn't heard his son.

"Oh, hello, Harold. I'm so glad you've come. I have the most exciting news for you. I've done it! It's complete! I was just about to test it, and I wanted you here to see my supreme triumph!" The Brain, a trim man in his seventies—who looked barely strong enough to hold up his oversized head—was beaming with pride, chest puffed out.

The younger man chuckled at The Brain's excitement: He had never been prone to such exuberance. He'd always behaved less like a giddy child and more like the evil scientist who twisted his moustache as he cackled deviously. Something like Professor Nutty Nut-Meg from those old Felix the Cat cartoons.

"Triumph over who or what?"

"Artemus Darke, of course!"

"I'm not sure I understand. He's been dead for nearly 30 years."

The Brain continued as if he hadn't even heard his son speak. He raised his finger high in the air to accentuate his words. "Plus, my superior intellect has allowed me to make a technological breakthrough of massive proportions!"

Harold wrinkled his brow, deep in thought.

"I present to you, the ImmersiView." The Brain held up a helmet with built-in earphones and what looked like a pair of large blacked-out goggles attached.

His son tried his best to look excited, but the contraption looked unwieldy, and he couldn't imagine what use it would be.

"What is it? A game?"

"This is no mere game. All those kids who hang out at the video arcade won't know what hit them. Pac-Man? Donkey Kong? They're nothing compared to what I have created. This is the wave of the future!"

"So what *is* it, then?"

The Brain rubbed his hands together in glee. "I have re-created Artemus' Darke World—with some key upgrades. Thanks to my magnificent genius, you can experience any ride, show, attraction, or game from the comfort of your own home. But even better! You can see what it's like to be The Strongman. Live life as one of his freaks. Feel the terror on the Loop the Loop—and other new rides that couldn't possibly exist. The player will then be shown what Darke World looks like now—a heap of rubble—before being taken to the superior attractions at Dr. Zim's Carnival of Oddities. They'll even receive a discounted admission."

"You didn't discuss that part with me."

"I don't have to. You may run *my* carnival, but it doesn't belong to you: not as long as I still draw breath. With my brain, I'm sure I'll find a way to outlive you, my boy. Keep that in mind!"

The younger Zim rolled his eyes. "Yes, *Father*." Harold knew how much his father hated it when anyone didn't refer to him as "The Brain."

"So why am I here?"

"To watch me, of course. I'm about to do my first trial

run. No doubt, my first and *only* trial. You'll be able to monitor it on that screen right there. Pity you won't be able to be immersed in it as I will—not only the sights, but the smells, sounds, and feelings."

"One question first."

The Brain nodded with a scowl, impatient to show off his invention.

"What about Artemus' rule that everything must be authentic? Anyone who bought his park had to agree to that."

"That was null and void the moment Darke World entered foreclosure and went up on the auction block. Besides, what's he going to do to me?"

"Whatever. But we can't afford a lawsuit from that board of fiduciaries."

"There's no way they're still around. I'm sure they were dissolved the moment Darke World went under."

"True. So, let's see this eighth wonder of the world." Harold pulled up a seat next to The Brain, surprising himself at how eager he was to see what his father had come up with.

The Brain pulled on the headset, tightening the band around the goggles to block out all outside light. He reached out and found the red button to start the ImmersiView. The screen showed a point-of-view rendering of the front gates at Darke World and four ticket lines filled with people waiting to get inside. Harold saw a hand reach out to push through the turnstile.

The back of the park was filled with rollercoasters with interconnected paths. The Loop the Loop had been built in such a way that another coaster shot right through the middle of it. The air was filled with the sounds of screaming, joyful people.

"I can smell hot dogs and buttered popcorn!" The Brain exclaimed.

How could that be? Harold wondered how The Brain had managed to design such a feature—or whether it was all just a product of vivid memories triggered by such an immersive experience.

The Brain went on one of his newly designed, impossible coasters and yelped when he felt the ground fall away beneath him as the car jumped over a missing piece of track. It jolted him when it landed a hundred feet away, zipping toward a corkscrew 360-degree loop. Harold was giddy watching what The Brain had created, and he couldn't even experience the full scope of his father's creation.

The Brain went over to the freaks tent and took on the body of Ella the Camel-Legged Girl, trotting around the tent like a show pony. Then he went to the Globe of Death, hopping on a motorcycle to join four other men in the metal cage as they drove tight, criss-crossing circles inside. From there, he went to the Wheel of Death, a large rotating apparatus with a round cage on either end. He entered one of the circles and began walking inside as it spun like a round treadmill beneath his feet. Then he grabbed onto the edges and climbed on the outside, walking around the circle to keep from falling as the entire apparatus spun, jumping at the apex of the revolution in order to keep up.

Harold could see his father was exhausted both mentally and physically by the exertion of his adventure— even if it was only virtual.

Having completed his trial, The Brain let out a contented sigh. The test had exceeded his wildest expectations.

"It's ready for prime time!" he exulted as he reached up, releasing the straps from the goggles, and trying to pull the helmet off his head.

It wouldn't budge.

He'd pressed the button to stop the ImmersiView simulation, but it didn't shut off.

Instead, the scene changed. As he fought to get the helmet to release, he felt himself walking into an old-fashioned circus tent.

The Brain stopped struggling and looked around.

His breath caught when he saw Artemus Darke in front of him, just as he'd looked back in the '20s and the '30s, at the height of Artemus and his father's rivalry. An old gypsy woman stood beside him alongside another man, who appeared to be a magician.

"Hello, Harold Jr." Artemus' eyes twinkled as he smiled at The Brain wickedly.

"Wh-what are you...? How are you...?" Even The Brain's hyper-intelligent mind couldn't keep up with what was happening.

"You didn't expect to see me?" Artemus replied. "I'm disappointed. You must not be nearly as smart as you claim. But that's really no surprise to me. Your father always had a penchant for playing the charlatan. Why should it be any different with you?"

The Brain slammed his hand down on the button repeatedly, frantic to end the simulation, but nothing happened.

"I'm afraid that won't work. You and your father thought my insistence on authenticity was short-sighted and ridiculous. But who's the one in control now? Me!"

Harold nearly jumped out of his skin. He'd heard that bellow coming from the headphones in the helmet. He jumped up and ran toward The Brain, trying to help him remove the device, but it was like it had become part of his body.

"Let me introduce you to Cassandra D. Vine. You'd call her a gypsy, but she was my *Romani* fortune teller. And this here is Magnus the Magnificent, my magician. They were both involved in the creation of my MasterView, the invention that you've chosen to corrupt with your sham recreation of Darke World."

"I can do whatever I want with it. I purchased it legally."

"True, you did buy my park and everything inside it, but you knew there was a caveat. No fakery! Nothing that you've created in this so-called experience is real. There were rules that had to be abided, but you did not. Now you will pay the price. There was magic linked to Carnival Darke, and this invention came with a curse should anyone seek to misuse it."

The Brain became aware that he was hearing a low hum, like a hive of bees. The noise and the vibration grew with each passing second. He could feel it reverberating through his body, then proceeding up to his head. Within a minute, the feeling had become painful. His blood felt like it had started to boil. The pressure in his head kept him from thinking—at one moment it felt like a vice crushing down—at the next, like a balloon being blown up, ready to explode at any second.

The Brain jumped out of his seat and began to slam his helmeted head on the table, trying to knock the apparatus loose. He let out a volley of screams that made his son's blood run cold. Harold grabbed The Brain and pulled on the helmet with all his might, falling to the ground when it suddenly came off in his hands.

"Let me out! Let me out! I don't want to do this anymore!" The Brain screamed, his eyes were vacant, like he was looking at another world.

The Brain turned toward Harold as he clutched his head, which was literally throbbing. The skin stretched taut, and the skull underneath cracked each time it pulsed outward. "Help me," he pleaded. "I can't get out of this simulation. He won't let me go."

Artemus' entire face filled the screen.

"I've been waiting to witness this moment for decades."

The Brain's head ballooned out several more times, to nearly twice its normal size, before exploding. Harold was covered in blood. Chunks of his father's mutated brain plopped to the ground and stuck to his skin.

Seconds later, the screen went black. The room-size computer started arcing and smoking as little explosions occurred inside it. Harold's hands started to burn as the helmet melted into a black goo as he held it.

As Harold ran from the room, he heard a disembodied voice call out, "Darke World has gone dark."

ABOUT THE AUTHORS

Stephen H. Provost is a former reporter and columnist with more than 30 years of experience at daily newspapers. Over the past 11 years, he has written or co-authored more than 60 books. In addition to six novels and three novellas, he has produced an extensive collection of nonfiction works on topics ranging from Nevada's pioneer days to the history of retail in the United States. He has written more than 20 books on U.S. history in the 20th century focusing on highways, towns, and culture. Stephen is the founder and publisher of Dragon Crown Books. He lives in Carson City.

Sharon Marie Provost is an award-winning author who specializes in horror, thrillers, and speculative fiction. Beginning her career in late 2023, she has published a novella, two short story collections, and two collaborative collections of short stories with her husband. Her first novel, *Dark Arts: Love Me Tinder*, was published in 2024. It has received acclaim for its detailed and chilling story of a serial killer who turns his victims into works of art. In 2025, her *Shadow's Gate* received the Imadjinn Award for Best Short Story Collection, and she published two collaborative novels with Stephen H. Provost: *Azrael's Assassin: Testament in Blood* and *Evermore: Dark Soulmates.* Sharon is the publisher of ScreamCatcher Books and chief operating officer of Dragon Crown Books. She has lived in Carson City since 1987.

DID YOU ENJOY THIS BOOK?

Recommend it to a friend. And please consider rating it and/or leaving a brief review at Amazon, Barnes & Noble, and Goodreads.

Also on
Dragon Crown Books
Sharon Marie Provost

Horror
> Dark Arts
> Shadow's Gate
> Shades of Love, Vol. 2

Paranormal
> The Last Train to Clarksville

Stephen H. Provost

Science Fiction
> Crimson Scourge
> Identity Break
> Identity Forge
> Meteor Ridge
> Starry Nightmares

Fantasy
> Academy of the Lost Labyrinth
>> The Talismans of Time
>> Pathfinder of Destiny
> The Only Dragon

Horror
> Nightmare's Eve
> Shades of Love, Vol. 1
> Need
> Death's Doorstep
> A Twisted Carol

STEPHEN H. and SHARON MARIE PROVOST

Children's
Madeline the Redheaded Witch
>The Reluctant Little Witch
>Madeline's Dragon Quest

The Adventures of Mark Twain in Nevada
Waffles the Poodle Dragon
Feathercap

History
Mark Twain's Nevada
The Comstock Chronicles
Virginia City Then & Now
America's Historic Highways series
>America's First Highways
>Yesterday's Highways
>Highways of the South

Highways of the West series
>America's Loneliest Road
>Victory Road
>Sierra Highway
>Bonanza Highway

Roadside Illustrated series
>Happy Motoring!
>Signpost Up Ahead: The West
>Signpost Up Ahead: The East

Fresno Growing Up, 2024
The Century Cities series
>Cambria Century, Carson City Century,
>Charleston Century, Danville Century,
>Fresno Century, Goldfield Century,
>Greensboro Century, Huntington Century,
>Roanoke Century, San Luis Obispo Century

Humor
Please Stop Saying That!

Sports
The Legend of Molly Bolin
A Whole Different League
50 Undefeated

Spirituality
The Phoenix Chronicles
> The Osiris Testament
> The Way of the Phoenix
> The Gospel of the Phoenix
The Phoenix Principle
> Forged in Ancient Fires
> Messiah in the Making

Sharon Marie Provost
and Stephen H. Provost

Horror
Carnivale Darke: The Show to End All Shows
Evermore: Dark Soulmates
Nevada Nightmare's Eve
Christmas Nightmare's Eve
All Hallows' Nightmare's Eve
BONE: Best of Nightmare's Eve

Cross-Genre
Azrael's Assassin

Lief Sorbye
and Stephen H. Provost

Biography
What I Tell My Friends, Vol. 1

Gary Kinst
and Stephen H. Provost

History
The Lincoln Highway in California

Mark Twain

Horror
Dark Twain

Ken Sutherland

Science Fiction
Balance

Detective
Heartbreaker
The Hollywood Diamond Murders

Anthologies

Horror
Nevada Nightmares, Vol. 1
Nevada Nightmares, Vol. 2

Northern Nevada Authors
The ACES Anthology 2023
The ACES Anthology 2024

From Stephen H. Provost on
Linden Publishing

Science Fiction
The Memortality Saga
Memortality
Paralucidity

History
California's Historic Highways series
Highway 99
Highway 101
The Great American Shopping Experience

Praise for Other Works

"The writing was superb, the attention to detail shows she knows what she's doing when it comes to police procedure, and the kill scenes are very detailed and disturbing... For fans of serial killer stories with plenty of graphic imagery. Highly recommended."
— Justin Boote, author of *Soul Searchers*,
on **Dark Arts** by **Sharon Marie Provost**

"One of the best books I have EVER read! Messed-up, cringy, tense, sickening, thrilling, exciting, disturbing and complete!"
— Kim Sloan, author of the *Billy Bob Adventures* series,
on **Dark Arts**

"Haunting and beautiful. This book is so good! All the stars!!!"
— Angel Van Atta, author of *In the Tall Trees*,
on **Dark Arts**

"I love this book. The different stories leaves you wanting more. Takes your imagination in places that leaves you just WOW. Sharon Provost is in my top 3 as now. If you haven't read this book yet, get it. You will not be disappointed. Hands down Amazing."
— Kristy Chandler, Amazon reader,
Shadow's Gate by **Sharon Marie Provost**

"I read this book in one sitting, something I rarely do. The story is fast paced and crisply written, the description of the crimes, though tough to read, are expertly and vividly written. There are plenty of believable twists and turns. The ending is fabulous."
— Catherine Riddick, former *Fresno Bee* assistant managing editor,
on **Dark Arts**

"Heartwarming, heart-wrenching. The romance broke my heart and then mended it."

— Carol Purroy, author of *Tiara*, on
The Last Train to Clarksville by **Sharon Marie Provost**

"A collection of so many good little short stories that pull you in and show us the ugly side of love, the dark, jealous side. How love can wind into every fiber of your life and grow into an obsession, not love. It shows how love can hurt, the pain of one-sided love that is a slow descent into madness. You'll see so many different stories... legends, grief horror, stalkers, slashers, paranormal, myths, revenge, and so much more."

— Micki-d, Amazon Canada reader, om
Shades of Love, Vol. 2 by **Sharon Marie Provost**

"Keeps you on your toes! Thrilling adventure from an eccentric mind! Twisty-tales to get your heart pumping and your mind wandering! Don't read in the middle of nowhere, alone, and in the dark."

— Steven J. Ponte, Amazon reader,
on **Shadow's Gate**

"I loved the story and the twist at the end. It's my kind of book! I had no idea and I love to be tricked and intrigued by an ending! Highly recommend it if you are a fan of everlasting love!"

— Sue C. Dugan, author of *A Slow Climb Up the Mountain*, on
The Last Train to Clarksville

"The genres in this volume span horror, fantasy, and science-fiction, and each is handled deftly. ... **Nightmare's Eve** should be on your reading list. The stories are at the intersection of nightmare and lucid dreaming, up ahead a signpost ... next stop, your reading pile. Keep the nightlight on."

— R.B. Payne, Cemetery Dance

STEPHEN H. and SHARON MARIE PROVOST

"Punchy and fast paced, **Memortality** reads like a graphic novel. ... (Stephen H. Provost's) style makes the trippy landscapes and mind-bending plot points more believable and adds a thrilling edge to this vivid crossover fantasy."

— Foreword Reviews

"Stephen has taken a subject that has been well-covered over the years—the famous Nevada silver mining town of Virginia City— and crafted something fresh and easy-to-digest. With his knack for clever wording and journalistic eye for detail (he is a former newspaper editor/reporter), Provost provides readers with an informative but not dry book about the one-time "Richest Place on Earth's" most colorful characters and important events.

— Richard Moreno, award-winning author, historian, and journalist on **The Comstock Chronicles**

"When I saw the title, I got excited—thinking it was another Mark Twain book. I'm a huge fan of Samuel Clemens! But what really surprised me was how easily I got pulled into the story. Stephen's writing is so engaging—it felt like I was right there with him, discovering things I hadn't read in other Twain books. His storytelling is vivid and full of detail, and it's clear he puts a lot of effort into his research. Living in Nevada, I recognized many of the places Twain visited, and now I want to go back and see them again with fresh eyes. Stephen has a gift for capturing the heart of a story and sharing pieces of history that others often miss."

— Jeadene Solberg, cofounder of Northern Nevada Ghost Hunters, on **Mark Twain's Nevada**

"The story feels so close, so intimate, we as readers experience the emotions, the events, and the conflicts, in what feels like real time. Gut-wrenchingly so."

— Stephen Mark Rainey, author of *Blue Devil Island*, on **Death's Doorstep**

This entertaining book is an easy read. Each Nevada town with which Samuel Clemens had interaction or visited is briefly described, along with historic photographs, some modern ones, and brief notes about its fate. Included are directions for those wishing to visit these towns, many now ghost towns or entirely vanished.

Jim Collett, Goodreads reader, on **Mark Twain's Nevada**

"Stephen and Sharon Provost did an incredible job preserving this piece of history. Thanks to their research and storytelling, this place won't be forgotten. A hundred years from now, people will still be able to read about it—and that's something special."

— Jeadene Solberg on **Chinese Camp**

"Sharon and Stephen will pull you into this page-turner from the very beginning. **Evermore** will take you down the dark side of soulmates and the desires that exist from one life to the next. Each time making them more mad, desperate to get it right or move on again to the next life to try it all over again. Will they finally find love and conquer it, or will they die trying? Read the book. You won't be disappointed.

— Maureen, Amazon reader

"The complex idea of mixing morality and mortality is a fresh twist on the human condition. ... **Memortality** is one of those books that will incite more questions than it answers. And for fandom, that's a good thing."

— Ricky L. Brown, Amazing Stories

"From time travel to karma earned, these short love stories range from thought-provoking to heartbreaking."

— Blue Bookwyrm Reviewer
on **Shades of Love, Vol. 1**

"Among the greatest what-ifs ever conceived—the power to bring back loved ones! This story defies genres by taking that question to its next level. You really can't put this book down.
— Ruth Goyne, former wire desk editor at *The Tennessean*
on **Memortality**

"**Memortality** is a terrific science fiction thriller that imprints on your mind like an unforgettable snapshot."
— John Palisano, award-winning author of *Nerves*
and past president of the Horror Writers Association

"**Memortality** takes a concept we've all dreamed of and turns it into our worst nightmare."
— Michael Knost, Bram Stoker award-winning author

"Provost sticks mostly to the classics: vampires, ghosts, aliens, and even dragons. But trekking familiar terrain allows the author to subvert readers' expectations. ... Provost's poetry skillfully displays the same somber themes as the stories. ... Worthy tales that prove external forces are no more terrifying than what's inside people's heads."
— Kirkus Reviews on **Nightmare's Eve**

"Stephen H. Provost has nightmares to sell. But be wary, this is no ordinary merchant of dark dreams. These are tales and poems of every sort from a writer to watch."
— Mark Onspaugh, author of *The Faceless One*
and *Deadeye Jack*, on **Nightmare's Eve**